HOW TO SURVIVE
Camping

THE MAN WITH NO SHADOW

HOW TO SURVIVE
Camping

THE MAN WITH NO SHADOW

BONNIE QUINN

SIMON & SCHUSTER

London · New York · Amsterdam/Antwerp · Sydney/Melbourne · Toronto · New Delhi

First published in the United States by Saga Press, an imprint of Simon & Schuster, LLC, 2025

First published in Great Britain by Simon & Schuster UK Ltd, 2025

Copyright © 2020, 2025 by Bonnie Quinn
Previously published in 2020 by Bonnie Quinn

The right of Bonnie Quinn to be identified as author of this work has been asserted in accordance with the Copyright, Designs and Patents Act, 1988

1 3 5 7 9 10 8 6 4 2

Simon & Schuster UK Ltd, 1st Floor
222 Gray's Inn Road, London WC1X 8HB

For more than 100 years, Simon & Schuster has championed authors and the stories they create. By respecting the copyright of an author's intellectual property, you enable Simon & Schuster and the author to continue publishing exceptional books for years to come. We thank you for supporting the author's copyright by purchasing an authorised edition of this book.

No amount of this book may be reproduced or stored in any format, nor may it be uploaded to any website, database, language-learning model, or other repository, retrieval, or artificial intelligence system without express permission. All rights reserved. Enquiries may be directed to Simon & Schuster, 222 Gray's Inn Road, London WC1X 8HB or RightsMailbox@simonandschuster.co.uk

Simon & Schuster Australia, Sydney
Simon & Schuster India, New Delhi

www.simonandschuster.co.uk
www.simonandschuster.com.au
www.simonandschuster.co.in

The authorised representative in the EEA is Simon & Schuster Netherlands BV, Herculesplein 96, 3584 AA Utrecht, Netherlands. info@simonandschuster.nl

Simon & Schuster strongly believes in freedom of expression and stands against censorship in all its forms. For more information, visit BooksBelong.com

A CIP catalogue record for this book is available from the British Library

Hardback ISBN: 978-1-3985-4293-8
Trade Paperback ISBN: 978-1-3985-4294-5
eBook ISBN: 978-1-3985-4295-2
Audio ISBN: 978-1-3985-4296-9

This book is a work of fiction. Names, characters, places and incidents are either a product of the author's imagination or are used fictitiously. Any resemblance to actual people living or dead, events or locales is entirely coincidental.

Interior design by Lewelin Polanco

Printed and Bound in the UK using 100% Renewable Electricity
at CPI Group (UK) Ltd

In memory of Aunt Kathy,
who believed in me.

RULES TO HELP YOU SURVIVE YOUR CAMPING EXPERIENCE

1. When planning your camp, allocate three extra feet per tent. This leaves room for ropes and stakes.
2. If you're camping on an incline, dig a 1" wide and 3" deep trench that will direct water around your tents and common area. This will minimize flooding.
3. Don't follow the lights. (I can't believe I even have to say this one.) *Don't follow the lights.*
4. Have a sturdy, waterproof container that holds a spare change of clothes and a blanket. This will ensure you have something warm and dry if your tent does flood.
5. You can buy ice from the children who approach your camp ONLY if they have a wagon. Those are the children of other campers trying to make some extra spending money. If a group of children approaches you *without* a wagon, do not buy ice from them. Act like they don't exist. The ice is not worth the consequences.
6. Place solar lights near your tent stakes. This will keep people from tripping over them or the ropes at night.
7. Keep track of what time the charge on the solar lights typically runs out. If the solars go out before then—if *all* the

lights go out—keep your eyes shut. Get back in your tent and do not leave until sunup. Whatever you do, do not look outside.

8. Pack some heavy blankets. It can get cold at night.
9. If you see a group of people dancing in a circle around a fire, you may join them. If they welcome you in, dance with them until the music ends. Do not look at the musicians. If they do not welcome you, but instead stop and stare, back away slowly and then leave. If they follow you, you can try to run, but it is likely already too late. Pray that death comes swiftly.
10. Be wary of a friendly man who may approach you in shaded areas. Try to convince him to move into the sunlight. If he casts a shadow, you can assume it's another camper. Otherwise, end the conversation immediately and leave as quickly as you can.

Welcome to Goat Valley

I'm Kate, and I'm a campground manager. My family has owned Goat Valley Campground for generations, ever since we came to this area, and I inherited it during my final year of college. It's about three hundred acres, most of that shaded by forest, and the rest is an open field. We occasionally host events, like dog clubs, music festivals, and weddings, but our primary focus is camping. The summer is our busy season, as camping is a cheap and pleasant vacation. Hammocks get erected in the trees. Grills get unloaded from the backs of trucks. There are some pretty elaborate setups. Some people come back year after year.

The return campers are smart. They know what they're doing. They unload efficiently, as a group. Tents start to spring up. Community areas and kitchens go in the same place every year, where they've found the land suits their layout best. Tent locations may move around, but every camper knows in advance exactly where their tent is going in their allotted land. It's a far cry from the disheveled masses that show up and simply expect everything to work out with no prior planning. By noon on setup day the experienced campers are sitting under their sunshades, sipping beer, while the newbies are relocating tents because they didn't leave enough room for walkways. And that's not the worst thing they can face here.

I try to help. I work with people organizing the big events. I have equipment to pull cars out of ditches, and the camp store carries essentials that people don't know they need. I even put together this guidebook. Everyone receives it in the mail once I have their registration info and payment. I wish people would take it more seriously. It's built off all the knowledge my family has passed down, along with a decade of my own experience running the campground.

This is old land, after all.

A parcel of land obtains a sort of significance when it's been passed down from heir to heir. It becomes an old place in the world, not yet an ancient place—which has its own set of issues—but old enough to have attracted the attention of certain... *things*. Things that see humans as food.

I try to minimize the risk to my campers. I train my staff in recognizing and containing the inhuman, and we set out traps for creatures stupid enough to fall into them, so that they can be dispatched. I do as much as I can, even if that puts me in considerable danger.

It never feels like enough, though. So I wrote up easy-to-remember rules and began to distribute them.

This is the part that the new campers don't take seriously. They think my rules are a prank, some little joke of the reclusive camp manager who perhaps doesn't spend much time around other people. The experienced campers try to tell them otherwise, but they don't always listen. Unfortunately, telling people what they need to do isn't an effective technique for changing behavior.

You know what does help people change their behaviors? Storytelling. It's one of the best techniques, far better than just having a list of rules. Instead of telling someone "do this," you tell the person a story that demonstrates the behavior you want. Preferably true, as that carries more weight. And the more personal it is, the more the individual will relate and subsequently accept what you are trying to instruct them to do.

So I'm telling you my story.

I don't have a list of rules because I'm trying to ruin your fun. I have a list because I'm trying to keep you from coming back to camp and finding your tent collapsed and full of rainwater and having no dry clothes or place to sleep. I'm trying to keep you from spending half of your precious vacation setting up tents because you didn't plan where everything would go in advance. And I'm trying to keep you from doing small, simple things that could result in a horrific and most assuredly agonizing demise.

But I can't do everything. I can't save people from themselves.

PART 1

Late Summer

In late August and early September, lots of sunshine and moderate temperatures make for great camping, but don't forget to pack sunscreen. Nighttime temperatures will fluctuate, and may be an indication of inhuman activity, so stay alert after dark. Make reservations in advance; Goat Valley is popular at this time of the year.

Leave Foraging
to the Professionals

Every morning, I circle the camp on a four-wheeler. I'm looking for any new developments on the land, such as a tree that needs to be pulled down or signs that something more alarming has happened in the dangerous hours of the night. I leave directly after I finish my breakfast and a cup of coffee. My house is on the campground, so it's easy for me to take the early shift.

The whole thing began one morning last August. There's never usually many people awake during my first patrol, so it was especially noticeable when I saw him approaching, walking down the middle of the road. A man in his thirties, bald, bare-faced, his face and ears covered in piercings, and with rings on every finger. His clothing was ordinary, a black hoodie and jeans. He walked slowly and deliberately, his head bowed so that it was difficult to see his expression, and—as always—he carried before him in both hands a cup made from a human skull. I pulled the four-wheeler over and waited, my stomach twisting with apprehension.

I have drunk from his cup before.

Years ago, he stopped me on the road. I thought he was a camper needing assistance, until he handed me the skull cup and bade me drink. I did, as I had already learned that when a being of power asks something of you, it is better to comply.

He lifted the cup to my lips and I drank. One swallow. Another. He kept the cup there; his thin fingers brushed my hair back when it slipped past my ear, and I drank almost half of the cup's contents. The liquid inside tasted bitter and salty with a vegetal undertone. My stomach burned, and I swallowed hard, struggling to keep it down.

"Thank you for the drink," I said when I was done, trying to sound sincere.

He knew I'd lied, for he smiled briefly, his dark eyes flashing with cool amusement.

"It was wise to not refuse," he replied.

He told me what he would have done had I not drunk, and my insides crawled with horror as he spoke, and I wanted him to stop, but to interrupt would have been a dire insult. His words were etched into my memories, and for days after I shivered whenever I thought of the fate I had so narrowly avoided. I still feel cold and small when I think about what he told me.

That evening, I threw up my dinner. I threw up the crackers I'd eaten. I even threw up water. Finally, I stopped eating and drinking altogether and waited a full day to try again. I was weak and miserable, but I survived.

Now, seeing him approaching on the road, I mentally cursed

my misfortune. This was our busy time of year. I couldn't afford to be sick for a day.

He stopped just before he reached me. Raised a hand and beckoned for me to come closer, flashing that thin, dry smile at the look of dread on my face.

"Are you not thirsty?" he asked mockingly.

"Not particularly, but if you wish to offer me a drink, I will not be so rude as to refuse."

My heart hammered in my chest.

"Be at ease—I did not come to offer you a drink. I came to give you a warning: your campground is stirring. They seek the unwary... and one of your charges has conducted business with the children."

I stood there, staring blankly at him. He sighed, almost imperceptibly, and even though his expression did not change, I felt the weight of his disapproval when he spoke next. These ancient beings do not enjoy having to explain themselves.

"The Children with No Wagon," he said, speaking slowly, as if that would help me understand. "Someone bought ice from them."

"Oh," I said dumbly. "Oh no."

> **RULE #5:** You can buy ice from the children who approach your camp ONLY if they have a wagon. Those are the children of other campers trying to make some extra spending money. If a group of children approaches you *without* a wagon, do not buy ice from them. Act like they don't exist. The ice is not worth the consequences.

It wasn't until the Man with the Skull Cup was almost out of sight that I realized I didn't have any idea which campsite had purchased the ice, and there were a lot of people here right now. I did the dumb thing. I jumped on the four-wheeler, turned it around, and went after him. I pulled up along the side of the road, a respectful distance away, and called out to him.

"Hey, what campsite was it?"

He paused almost imperceptibly.

"Are you thirsty after all?" Even though his words were mild, I understood them for the threat they were.

"Nope, I'm good, sorry for bothering you."

I drove away before he changed his mind on granting me mercy. This was not good. The Children with No Wagon had been on the campground for generations, according to my family records, but they were a wild card. Just like human children, their behavior could be unpredictable. And dangerous.

There was, however, someone I could ask for help.

I went to see my longest-running camp. They're a group of friends who have been coming here for over two decades and are willing to work with me. As a result, I've given them the best campsite. It's up on a hill, nestled in a clear spot among the trees so that their camp has shade most of the day and there's spots to hang hammocks. A gas line runs up the hill, so I have to keep part of it free of trees, which funnels the breeze straight into their camp. It's noticeably cooler there than the rest of the site.

It's also the most dangerous.

I heard their shouting before I arrived. I slowed, cutting the noise of the engine down enough that I could make out words. I needn't have bothered. It was nothing but cursing. I couldn't tell if it was an intra-camp dispute (doubtful, they kept the drama to a minimum) or if they were angry at another group (plausible, they had a couple of feuds going on with the younger camps) or if it was something else. Bracing myself, I hopped off the vehicle and walked in past the line of tents that marked their boundary.

There were five people in the common area, clustered around the beer kegs. They had a cooler that was outfitted with four taps, and they ran lines up through a steel plate that was packed with ice, providing access to chilled beer from the tap at any time. Right now, they had all four taps open, and dark liquid was spilling out onto the ground. There was an odd smell in the air that turned my stomach.

Like a butcher's shop, I thought.

"Is that... blood?" I ventured, walking closer.

"YES." Erin, the woman who brewed their beer, kicked one of the kegs. "All of them are blood. Is this an omen? Do we need to pack up and leave early?"

I lifted the cooler lid and found a maze of tubing enmeshed in a pile of ice. Ice that was no doubt bought from ordinary, human children, but that didn't matter anymore. No one was safe.

"It's more like a threat," I said grimly. "I'm going to deal with it, though. I just need to talk to the Thing in the Dark."

"Sure." She jerked her head at the back of their camp, where the trees crowded in close enough that their shadows overlapped, and the forest floor was noticeably darker under the lattice of their branches. "We haven't seen the solars go out all week, though, so maybe it's not home."

> **RULE #7:** Keep track of what time the charge on the solar lights typically runs out. If the solars go out before then—if *all* the lights go out—keep your eyes shut. Get back in your tent and do not leave until sunup. Whatever you do, do not look outside.

Some of the creatures on my campground are less malevolent than others. So long as they are respected, they won't kill you or even seriously harm you. My father had spoken to the Thing in the Dark once, asking it what it wanted. It didn't want anyone to look at it. That was all. And I'd visited the Thing too, back when I needed to put the senior camp near its lair. I asked if their proximity would disturb it. It replied that it would not, but nor would it hesitate to take any of the campers, should they break our agreement.

The creature's lair is nothing more than a mound of broken branches, easily mistaken for a pile of stacked debris. The creature itself rarely leaves, but when it does, well, people vanish.

I crept into the forest, wincing at the branches that cracked under my feet. The air grew colder as I approached. Sound fell away, encasing me in silence so heavy that the only thing I heard was my own heartbeat. As I drew nearer, it felt like the darkness in between the piled branches was reaching out, gathering up all the light, and dragging it to its doom. I shut my eyes.

"Excuse me," I whispered, my voice cracking. I coughed and tried again. "Sorry to bother you, but I have a question."

A long silence. Then it spoke. Its words were rough, like stones rolling against each other. I winced in pain, for it felt like my head was between those stones and my skull would crack under their weight. It asked me what I wished to know.

I told it about the children. That someone had bought ice from them.

"The children are displeased by their lack of prey," it finally replied. I pressed my fingers against the bones near my ear, as if that could help relieve the pressure. "They rejoice at finally being given an opportunity."

"To do what?"

The pile of branches moved. The earth shifted and I stumbled. Its shrug had nearly thrown me to the ground.

"This is just the start," it sighed. "More will suffer. All will suffer."

I felt cold inside. All of my campers were at risk. Goat Valley itself could be at risk.

"What can I do?"

"Eliminate the one that started it." The ground bucked violently, and I was thrown to my hands and knees. "Either they bear the consequences alone . . . or everyone else will in their stead."

I stumbled to my feet, gibbering my apologies to the Thing in the Dark for disturbing it and my gratitude for its advice. Then I fled, fighting the urge to look back the entire time.

I called over the radio for my available staff to convene at the barn. If we were going to find out who bought the ice, we'd need to go from campsite to campsite talking to people, and I try to leave the whole socializing part of this job to employees with actual social skills. It's important to know your weaknesses when you're in a leadership position.

Bryan was the first to arrive. He brought his dogs, because Bryan *always* brings his dogs. The massive black hounds are a fixture on the campground, part of the package when I hired Bryan shortly after I took over. His family is from Ireland. They came over during the potato famine and have retained that Irish heritage fairly strongly in their bloodline. Most of the family are redheads, except for Bryan and his dad, who have jet-black hair.

Bryan is my most reliable employee; he always shows up on time and doesn't start drama—mostly because he prefers the company of his dogs over that of the rest of the staff. He entered the barn, almost swallowed up in the sea of charcoal fur around him.

I've had more than a few panicked phone calls from campers who have mistaken the dogs for wolves.

Two more of my employees trailed in shortly after. The campground is divided into sectors, and I gave the three of them each a couple to check, along with instructions on what to ask the campers, and then sent them on their way. Then I waited. I waited a bit more. Then I finally got on the radio and asked where the hell Jessie was.

"I haven't seen her for the past two hours," Bryan replied. "Want me to go look for her?"

"No, I'll handle section N myself," I sighed. "She probably forgot to charge her radio again."

Normally an absent staff member was cause for concern, but Jessie was . . . well. Jessie was a problem. She didn't want to be here. She didn't like the manual-labor parts of the job. And her dislike of the campground had extended to the staff who *did* like working here, which soured those working relationships pretty quickly. I tried to assign her tasks she could do by herself, like cleaning the bathrooms. The only reason she was still around was because she didn't have better job options in town, and the only reason I hadn't fired her was because her dad was the town's dentist. I had a strong interest in not making an enemy of the person poking around inside my mouth. I admit part of me hoped that a monster would get her and save me the hassle of managing her, though.

Eliminate the one that started it. Those words rattled around in my head as I went from campsite to campsite in section N, asking if they'd bought ice from the Children with No Wagon today. I received quizzical looks from the newer campers, but the older ones answered solemnly, understanding the gravity of my question. They knew the rules.

But apparently no one knew who had bought the ice. Clearly someone was lying, but, eventually, I gave up and radioed Bryan and the rest of the staff to tell them to go home.

I spent the evening digging through my books of camp

management and folklore, trying to find some sort of ritual or appeasement I could try. There wasn't much to go on. The children had shown up on the campground during my great-aunt Pearl's tenure, and while she'd given the family strict instructions to not "play along with their games," the details of what would happen had been lost along the way. My family's philosophy has always been that if a creature isn't an active threat, leave it alone. Don't interact; don't attempt to drive it off; just be glad it's not trying to eat the campers. As a result, the children had never been a big concern of mine. Sure, when they started selling ice a few years back, that was a bit alarming, but they didn't seem to be trying very hard. But now they'd succeeded. I stared at the notes arrayed before me until my eyes ached and the words swam meaningless in front of me. This was unprecedented. And I don't like unprecedented. At Goat Valley, unprecedented is dangerous.

Night fell, and I reluctantly abandoned my efforts until the morning. I slept fitfully and awoke an hour before dawn.

It was still dark when I threw on some clothing and headed to the garage for my four-wheeler. I even skipped making coffee. I needed to see what had happened overnight.

The Man with the Skull Cup stood on the road, staring off into the trees and calmly sipping the liquid inside his cup like he was taking his morning tea and not something that had made me vomit for twenty-four hours straight. I pulled up close by and killed the engine so we could talk.

"Skipped your coffee, did you?" he asked. "Want a drink?"

"I am quite satisfied, but I will gladly accept if you wish to share," I replied with gritted teeth.

That thin smile again. Now he was just messing with me.

I looked in the direction he was staring. In the distance was a line of people—twelve in all—dangling in midair. For one brief, horrifying moment I could only think of the last time I'd found someone who hadn't heeded the rules, their gutted body dangling uncomfortably close to my house, like it was a warning. The bloody remains that I'd had to clean up, alone.

"Oh no no no no," I gasped, abandoning the four-wheeler to run toward them.

They were alive. I almost wept with relief. Each person hung from the branches by their ankles, their bodies covered with bruises and scratches. It seemed they had been violently dragged across the ground before being strung up. But at least they were alive.

"Next time it'll be their flayed skins hoisted in the branches," the Man with the Skull Cup said from behind me. "You should end this quickly."

"I'm surprised by your concern."

I didn't take my eyes off the campers, calculating how I was going to safely get them down.

"I need people to share a drink with," he murmured. "I can't do that if everyone dies. Speak with camp H34."

"Wow, thanks, you could have told me that yesterday," I muttered through clenched teeth.

I called Bryan to help get the terrified campers down. They didn't fight much while we were doing this, just hung there limply, crying or whimpering softly. It made the job a lot easier. Deadweight is predictable, and we could pull them toward the ladder, get a good hold on them, and then cut the ropes and pass them down to the ground.

Eliminate the one that started it.

As the abducted campers were taken off to the local hospital for treatment, I delegated the police paperwork to Bryan and jumped on my four-wheeler. Camp H34. People don't usually recognize me as the camp manager, and so they don't realize that when I show up in person to ask questions, it means that something has gone horribly wrong. The campers in H34 were helpful, and it only took a few questions to identify the man who had bought the ice.

"Did they have a wagon?" I demanded. "Did you *read* the rules? It was number five. You don't buy ice unless they have a wagon."

"Oh," he said bleakly. "That one. Well, there are a lot of rules."

I took a breath. Held it a moment. Reminded myself that the majority of people are good-intentioned and don't do things simply to cause trouble. That it is my responsibility as both camp manager and a decent human being to be understanding and help people, because we have a common goal. I want them to have a safe and fun camping experience that they survive, and they probably also want to stay alive. This man didn't ignore my rule simply out of spite. It was an accident. An unfortunate accident. That's what I told myself. I really didn't want to do what the Thing in the Dark said I had to do.

I asked him why he'd glossed over that rule. My tone was polite and friendly without a hint of judgment. That's the important bit—people respond in kind. So long as I didn't accuse, he wouldn't become defensive, and we could have a productive conversation.

I've done a lot of reading on conflict resolution and behavioral change.

He hadn't taken them seriously, he admitted. He'd certainly read them. Intently, in fact, because he'd thought it was a joke, but it was a clever joke and he'd enjoyed it. But real? Nah. He pointed to his tent, showing how it had three feet of clearance between the other tents and that they'd brought a watertight container in case of flooding. The will was there. My system was flawed.

I swallowed some profanity. I thanked him for talking to me and walked away. Then I went into the woods and gathered some mushrooms.

They're called destroying angel. *Amanita virosa.*

I crushed the mushrooms and took the resulting juice (careful not to touch it with my bare hands) back to his camp. While the campers were out having lunch in the town, I snuck in and poured the juice into the man's reusable water bottle, swirled it around to coat the sides, and then left it to dry.

At first it seemed like mere food poisoning, but by the time his campmates took him to the ER, he was suffering from liver and kidney failure. They did their best, but I had put a generous dose in that bottle, and his body simply could not keep up, not even with medical intervention. He was dead within thirty-six hours.

And that was the end of it. When I saw the Children with No Wagon next, they were dourly hauling their bags of ice from campsite to campsite, their faces sullen with frustration. I waved at them as I drove past on my four-wheeler. They'd been so close to getting what they wanted. And I'd ruined it. The campground was safe again.

Or so I thought.

Dance till You're Dead

There are some benefits to being an early riser. Solitude. Seeing the sun rise. Finding the human torso lying in the middle of the road before anyone else.

Yes. The torso. Just the torso.

I sighed. It was shaping up to be one of those weeks. I pulled out my camera and took photos from all the important angles that the police would be interested in. Then I grabbed the large black trash bags I keep in the back of the four-wheeler and edged the body into one. I tied it shut, put another bag around it, and tied it again. Then I hoisted it onto the back of the vehicle and strapped it down. The blood was fresh enough that I could wash it off into the dirt with the couple of gallons of water I carried around for this specific purpose.

Now, I understand you may be astonished that I would clean up the scene of a violent death without first contacting the police. However, my family has an understanding with local law enforcement. The campground is very important around here. It brings a lot of people in, and during the peak of summer we double the county's population. They spend a lot of money on local businesses. A *lot* of money.

The police don't mind if we take certain liberties to ensure the normal operation of the campground isn't disrupted. It would be upsetting to campers if they came across a dismembered body or an active police scene. The police just request that we go through the sheriff for everything. Avoid traumatizing the boys in blue too much. That was a tradition that had started with the Old Sheriff, who'd worked closely with my parents.

I called the Old Sheriff as soon as I was back at the house, and then I started calling around for help. I'd only found the torso, after all. That meant there were two legs, two arms, and a head yet to be found, and I had no idea how many pieces those parts were in.

I like to think of my staff as family... because most of them actually are. While it's just me and my two brothers left in my immediate family, my extended family is pretty large. Very few people have moved away, except for my younger brother Tyler, and the family tree just keeps growing. It's useful to have lots of relatives to call upon when we need extra help around here, even if they are only distantly connected to you. I have a handful that I can count on, mostly great- and great-great-aunts and uncles who I've called aunt and uncle since childhood, and I'm certainly not going to stop now. To be honest, I don't keep close track of the family tree. My great-aunt Lorna does, and I ask her whenever I need clarification.

A handful live on the campground, in small houses scattered across the property with fences to keep the campers out.

My father's younger brother, Uncle Tobias, and his wife, Aunt Aleda, moved into one when they got married. The rest of the buildings are used by whatever cousin needs a place to stay at the time. They're the people I call upon when I need immediate, discreet help.

Around here, it's important to keep land in the hands of family. It might not matter to us, but the creatures in the woods care about such things.

I got ahold of Aunt Aleda, who took over rounding up my uncle, my older brother Chris, a second cousin from my mom's side, and my cousin April, who was living on the campground. While my family scoured the woods for the remaining body parts, I could deal with the police. The Old Sheriff responded alone, fortunately. I wasn't fond of his deputy, who was starting to take over some of the Old Sheriff's duties.

The Old Sheriff had been helping with our campsite difficulties since before I was born. I remember watching him as a child, talking gruffly with my parents in low voices. He'd always stop to say hello to me before he left and let me wear his sheriff hat. After my parents died and I took control of the campground, he'd show up even when there wasn't a body to deal with. Just to make sure I was okay.

We sat in my office and looked through the photos I'd taken on my computer, then he requested to see the body out in the backyard.

I pulled it off the four-wheeler and cut the plastic open. Mercifully, the body was still fresh enough that it hadn't started to smell of decay, just the sour, meaty smell of early death. The

Old Sheriff inspected the severed sockets, picking at the edges of flesh and muscle delicately with his fingers before sitting back on his haunches and stripping off his stained latex gloves.

"This is different than the other cases I've looked at," he finally said.

I blinked, taken aback. I knew that this could happen someday, that I'd be the one to deal with something new moving in, but it was a distant sort of knowledge, the sort that you decide to handle some other time and live in blissful ignorance of until it comes. Like writing a will.

"I should get Chris," I sighed. "He might know if our parents ever mentioned something like this."

The Old Sheriff looked at me oddly for a moment before reminding me that he'd worked with my parents on every death that had happened on the campground. He'd know if they'd seen this before. He went on to explain that the limbs were severed methodically. When we were dealing with a wild animal—whether natural or otherwise—the bodies would be haphazardly torn apart. There'd be additional injuries from teeth or claw marks. But the torso was untouched. There wasn't even bruising. This indicated that the victim hadn't even been restrained—at least not by a method that left marks . . . or not on the only part of his body we had found.

The police might not be able to tell us what we were dealing with, but they could help narrow the possibilities.

They could also help with the cover story.

The Old Sheriff had brought the police van, so we carefully wrapped the body up and put it in the back for transport to the morgue. He asked that we bring the other body parts by, once we found them, and they'd start trying to identify the victim. Meanwhile, I planned to check in with the campers to figure out if someone was missing and try to find out any information about what they'd done or where they'd gone. Then the Old Sheriff would come back with some paperwork about a wild animal attack, and that'd be it.

We found all the body parts by midday. They'd been left deliberately, placed so that someone actively searching for them could find them, but the casual passerby was unlikely to notice.

My cousin April found the head. She called for me on the walkie-talkie, asking that I come look, and she sounded deeply shaken. April was from my mom's side, so she hadn't had much exposure to the campground yet. We weren't close growing up, as she was almost a decade younger than me, but she was easy to get along with and, most importantly, reliable.

The head was placed on a stake in the center of a narrow clearing. The air felt close, suffocating with invisible tension. The ground was spongy, as it sat in a depression that collected water every time it rained. Four more stakes were stabbed into the earth in a circle around it. I pulled out my compass and checked their orientation. They sat askew from the cardinal directions. I frowned. This was a deliberate perversion.

"Look," April whispered, pointing at the head on the stake. And I suddenly realized why she sounded even more upset than usual. "He's still alive."

I edged closer. My skin crawled, and I felt goose bumps break out on my arms as I crossed the perimeter of the circle. A middle-aged man, perhaps in his forties. His jaw was missing, leaving behind the upper row of teeth, and his eyes were wide with silent suffering.

He blinked.

I swore and stumbled backward. Rounded on April and told her to leave, to go take a break and recover her composure. As long a break as she needed. I'd take care of it from here.

Perhaps watching my parents die, a silent observer in a dream that felt like reality, had prepared me to withstand this sort of horror. I confess that it angers me, to see someone die in a manner that no one should have to endure, but I've long since accepted that this is life. My world no longer has room for the blissful illusion that humanity has no predators.

I told the head that it would be okay, that I could put an end to this and he'd finally, mercifully, die. A couple of tears ran down his cheeks, and I saw relief in his eyes. Then I went to the stakes and pulled them free from the ground. After I wrenched the last one from the earth, I stood and watched the man's face. His eyes remained open, long past when he should have blinked, and I was satisfied that whatever ritual had bound him here had been disrupted. The air felt different as well. Lighter.

I left the remaining detective work of identifying the victim to the police and Bryan, because of course Jessie was conveniently absent again. No doubt she'd drag herself over once everything was wrapping up, which was particularly aggravating as she actually had a few years of experience on the campground and knew how to handle these situations. She was better at this than Bryan, in fact, because Bryan doesn't like talking to the Old Sheriff or the police. He doesn't like talking to anyone except his dogs.

Then I locked myself in my office. It'd taken almost the full decade after inheriting the campground for it to finally feel like my own. The marks of my parents were strewn everywhere, and I had moved in slowly, replacing their presence with my own. Their books on folklore and camp management were still on the bookshelves, worn, the bindings broken, the pages crumpled and smudged. I wondered how many times my father and mother had leafed through these, searching for answers.

Folklore is not a tidy thing. Monsters and creatures of power don't fall neatly into categories. It is not so different from the natural world in this regard. We can look at a bird and know it is a bird, but what kind is it? Bird of prey or waterbird or woodpecker or pigeon or any of the other many types?

Similarly, was I now dealing with a spirit or a demon or a fairy or a god or something that fell into that gray area in between? And even if I could narrow it down, there were still variations within a category. If we were dealing with an incubus, was it one in the classical sense, or was it the kind with chicken legs from the knee down?

Yes, chicken-footed incubi exist.

I decided to try a couple of things. The use of ritual made me suspect fairies, but the perversion of it also made me think spirits. I gathered up some deterrents from the shed: iron stakes, hawthorn branches, stones with holes in them, and other assorted folk charms. Then I went about the campground and left them in strategic areas, mostly at crossroads and along the edge of the designated camping areas.

I erred. When something new moved into the campground, it was usually a brute creature that could be driven off, captured, or killed. Beasts that could be outsmarted.

Certainly not ones that would retaliate.

That night, I was woken by the sound of a voice outside my bedroom window. I didn't catch the words, for I came to awareness at the end of the conversation. Someone was talking to the little girl who cries outside my window every night.

That made me sit up straight in my bed. Who—or what—would talk to the little girl?

"Don't worry," an amused voice said to her. "I promise we won't kill her."

Her weeping stopped. There was the soft sound of her feet running in the grass—away from the house. Someone—or something—had sent the girl away. My heart began to hammer in my chest, and I quietly slipped out of bed, thinking of the shotgun I keep in the closet, wondering if it'd do anything at all.

Then my house shook as something slammed against the front and back doors in unison. A pause. Another impact that rattled the doors in their frames. A third, final impact and the crack and crash of both doors being torn off their hinges.

I stumbled to the closet, blind with fear, thinking of how my father had died, how he'd clawed with his bare hands at the beast's face as if he could fight it off even as its teeth severed his body in two. My hands closed over the shotgun's stock as footsteps echoed down the hallway. I stood, turned—and there was a hand against the shotgun's barrel, pushing it up and away, and then another palm against my cheek.

"That's enough," a female voice said. I couldn't see her face in the darkness of my bedroom. "How about you go for a walk with us?"

I don't remember much after that. I left the house with them. I'm not sure how many others there were. Only the woman spoke to me. We walked into the forest, and I'm not certain of the route we took, for it comes and goes as if I were slipping in and out of sleep.

When my awareness returned, I found myself standing beside a lit campfire, in among a ring of people. The ground around me was packed earth. The woman moved from person to person, a ceramic pitcher in her arms. She slipped a cupped hand inside and came up with a handful of water, which she dribbled on the brow of the person before her. Something felt wrong about this ritual. Unsettling. I tried to move or speak, but I found my body was slow to respond to my desires.

Finally, she stopped in front of me.

"Why don't you join us?" she murmured, pouring the water on my brow. It ran down my face and neck and into the neckline of my nightgown. It felt gritty, and I tasted salt when a drop touched the edge of my lip.

The people began to dance, and I was compelled to join them. My body was not under my control. Step. Turn. Stretch our hands to the night sky, spines arched. Twist and bend. Touch the ground. Then up, a hop, and then the music quickened. And I saw, as we spun, that the music came from a hunched group at the edge of the light. A violin. A hand drum. Something that reminded me of a flute.

We continued dancing. My legs began to ache. My breathing grew labored. Bright pain stabbed through my feet and ankles, and I thought, madly, that I felt blood against my bare feet with every step. Still the Dancers went on, their movements growing more aggressive, more frenzied, and I wept and pleaded in broken, panicked fragments for them to release me.

They did not.

Eventually, after what felt like hours, the woman's hand snapped up. She grabbed me by the neck, raising her arm, her fingers digging into my tendons.

"What were you trying to do, Kate?" she hissed. "All those things you left in the woods—that was for us, wasn't it?"

I stood on tiptoes, trying to ease the pressure on my throat.

"Trying to . . . make you leave?"

I added "please" as an afterthought.

She examined me for a moment and then let go of my neck. I stumbled backward, coughing. She laughed, a high delicate sound like the chime of a bell. The fire was to her back, and I could only see her chin and lips in the flickering light.

"The little girl and the beast have laid claim to your life," she said, and she grinned savagely, her white teeth shining in the darkness. "None of us will contest their right. However, there is still *so* much we can do to you before you succumb."

She was toying with me. But I hadn't got this far along in my camp manager career by being intimidated.

"Did you kill that man?" I gritted my teeth. "Why?"

Her eyes went wide, and she stared at me incredulously.

"You take advantage of your immunity from death," she said in amusement. "I like your boldness. I will tell you. It's not like you can keep anyone from the temptation of joining in our dance."

She glanced around the clearing, and even in my exhaustion and with the erratic light of the bonfire, I recognized where we were. Campsite N21. Flat, open, and prone to flooding when it rained. Great location for large parties.

"And we *will* be staying," she continued. "This is an . . . interesting place. Exciting things are happening on this land. I want to see where it ends."

My campers had to be welcomed in, she explained. Permitted to join their dance. She refused to elaborate on what sort of person they would welcome and who they would reject. There wasn't any sort of criteria, she said with a shrug. They just knew who they liked and didn't like.

And then there were some they hated. Nothing they did would matter. It would be too late, far too late from the instant they laid eyes on them.

Like the dismembered camper we'd found.

She leaned in close, and I felt her breath against my ear. Her body smelled of earth and plants.

"Don't try to drive us off again," she whispered.

Then she directed me to look at the musicians.

I did.

They raised their heads and looked back at me.

My next memory is of being on my knees, my fingernails stained with blood, the skin around my eyes and down my cheeks burning from where I'd clawed it raw. My chest heaved in gasps, racking my entire body with convulsions as it instinctively tried to bring in more oxygen to my battered lungs. Pain shot up my legs with every beat of my heart, and my feet burned. I lay there, writhing in the dirt, whimpering and openly weeping.

The Dancers were gone, and mercifully, they'd taken the musicians as well.

I'm not sure how long I lay there shuddering on the ground. It was Bryan who found me. I heard his footsteps approaching at a run, and then he hit the ground next to me, turning me over onto my back. A flashlight shone in my face, and I squeezed my eyes shut tight.

"Oh thank god," he breathed. "You're alive."

He took me home and deposited me on the sofa in my living room, asking me what had happened. "The Dancers," I said weakly. "The Dancers found me." His attention focused on that, and he asked a few questions—very specific questions.

"Weird," he finally said, convinced we'd encountered the same people. "I danced with them a few weeks ago. I don't think I've ever felt so happy in my life."

"You did *what*?"

"Well, the dogs didn't seem bothered by them," he replied defensively.

Even in my exhausted state, his words triggered a memory of something I'd read. Dancing is sometimes used as a cure for supernatural afflictions. The sick individual is sat down in the middle of a circle, and the Dancers move around them, thereby banishing their illness. Yet something felt wrong about their ritual, from the off-center placement of the stakes to the mockery of anointment. Were they a group of Dancers who had been cursed? Were they demons enacting their own, abhorrent, version of the very same ritual that was supposed to heal people?

Did it really matter? They were dangerous, and I wasn't going to try to drive them off again. They might not be so polite about not killing me next time. Sometimes I take risks, and sometimes I suffer for them, but I don't want to die in the process.

I had to warn people. They intended to entice my campers to join them, and if I couldn't drive them off, then I was going to thwart them by other means.

> **RULE #9:** If you see a group of people dancing in a circle around a fire, you may join them. If they welcome you in, dance with them until the music ends. Do not look at the musicians. If they do not welcome you, but instead stop and stare, back away slowly and then leave. If they follow you, you can try to run, but it is likely already too late. Pray that death comes swiftly.

I thought it was simple. I'd killed the one who'd bought the ice. Yet here I was with a dead camper, my cousin April was probably traumatized, and I was writing a new rule for the first time in years. The Thing in the Dark had tried to warn me, but I'd assumed it was talking *only* about the children. Yet here I was, bloodied and suffering. All *will suffer,* it had said.

Something bigger was coming. I could feel it.

Some Local History

If the truth be told, my side of the family was never meant to inherit the campground. Back then it wasn't a campground yet. The land belonged to my great-aunt Pearl, and she intended to pass it down to her children. But about sixty years ago there was a terrible scandal, and the town council was looking for any reason to take it away from her.

It started when Great-Aunt Pearl showed up with a baby. She tried to keep it quiet, but word got out and rumors started churning, as rumors always do in a small town. Having a child out of wedlock was one, of course, but there was another, more dangerous rumor that began to spread. They said the child was a changeling. The town was a little nervous at that time, after Bryan's great-grandfather had come home with a wife who wasn't as human as she appeared.

But my great-aunt was smart. She decided to turn her enemies into her allies. She went around to the most prominent families with the child and let them inspect the baby. Let them see how normal she was. But she always refused to reveal the identity of the father.

Great-Aunt Pearl took that secret to the grave.

I don't think there was anything unnatural about the baby's father. I think she refused to say who it was because of local politics. Someone influential. Possibly an affair. My great-aunt must have liked him quite a bit to not drag him down with her.

That soured relationships with the town, though. And Pearl couldn't weather both that and the council learning that our land was old.

There have always been strange things in this world, and our town was not without its troubles. But some enterprising soul started keeping track of the creatures attacking the locals and realized they were coming from our land. That it had been in our family for too long, and now it had a history, lore, and thus could shelter the inhuman. We were the light that drew in the moths . . . assuming the moths had a penchant for human flesh, that is.

The town demanded we break up our property and sell it. Destroy the accumulated history and scatter the monsters. It wasn't a *real* solution. The creatures would just go into the fields and farmland of Goat Valley, to prey on the people living there. It would only *look* better on paper, like a layoff to boost the stock price.

So my grandfather made a proposal. He'd take the land from his sister Pearl, and since it wasn't being handed down to a direct descendent, that'd stop it from being old land and give us a few more generations before we had to worry about monsters again.

The plan settled most of the grumbling. Great-Aunt Pearl stepped out of the public eye to raise her confirmed not-a-changeling baby in peace. Grandpa turned our land into a campground, believing that would be easier to make money off of than farming. And the transfer let people believe that now that the land had changed hands, the monsters wouldn't keep showing up.

We had bought ourselves some time to recover from the scandal.

Then something started robbing the graveyard.

Uncle Tobias, my father's younger brother, liked to tell this story. He was twelve years old at the time. My father was fourteen. Dad didn't like to talk about it because he didn't like killing anything. He had a soft heart. Even though it was sometimes necessary, he didn't like to kill things simply because they were acting on their nature. In this, at least, I take after my mother.

The first few disturbed graves were discovered by the groundskeeper, and he buried them again, telling their relatives nothing. Not about the holes, the askew headstones, and certainly nothing about the shattered coffins and the missing bodies. He understood that these things happened around here, and it was best to not upset people unnecessarily.

The first grave robbery that was discovered by the town was when a local family made their routine Sunday trip to the cemetery to leave flowers on a relative's grave. The man had died unexpectedly, possibly from a heart attack. On approaching the gravesite, the dead man's wife thought that something was strange, because there was loose dirt strewn all around the cemetery. She believed at first that maybe the groundskeeper was doing some maintenance but told the children to stay back. She had a bad feeling, she said.

The grave had been partially exhumed. There was a hole that exposed half the coffin, dug in a slope like a dog digs, kicking the loose soil all across the ground around the grave. The coffin itself was smashed, the wood splintered and snapped apart, exposing the dark, empty hollow inside.

Then one of the children shrieked, coming across a human skull, and the mother ran to them and told them they were leaving. The skull was fake, she said. It was just someone's idea of a bad prank.

In her heart, she knew the truth, but this little lie at least distracted the children until they were old enough to handle the reality that something had dug up their father's grave and devoured all of his body but the skull.

Perhaps it would have ended there, if, a few nights later, the oldest of the boys hadn't climbed out the window when he heard his father's voice calling from outside. That boy, too, was devoured.

The mother blamed our campground. We aren't that far from the cemetery. She also needed someone to blame, I suspect, and we were an easy target. A town meeting was held. The issue of whether our land should be split up and sold was on the agenda once more. My entire family went to the meeting, led by my grandfather. They stood in the back, silent and watching, and perhaps this was deliberate. To remind the town of just how long my family had been around and how many of us there actually were. To remind them of the hardness of our eyes, the grim set of our stares, the strength of our will.

Grandpa told the council that our family would take care of this creature, regardless of whether it came from our land or not. We weren't the only ones whose land harbored strange things, he said. They all knew someone who suffered dead livestock, strange claw marks on doors, apparitions and visions without explanation. We were, however, the only ones who had the resolve to deal with those things. And let them come to Goat Valley Campground he continued. We—none of them—could keep the monsters out. We would protect them from all this, and more, if they at least had the courtesy to treat us with respect.

Then he walked out without even giving them a chance to respond.

My grandmother set to the work of expanding the campground. The more campers we brought in, they reasoned, the more money they'd spend in the town, and the more amenable the locals would be. Certain goods wouldn't be available onsite. Food, for instance. The general store's supplies were kept deliberately lean, and maps of local shopping facilities were printed for the main office. My grandfather dealt with the more immediate problem of the monster stalking the cemetery.

It was a simple plan for a simple creature. He and his sons, all carrying a rifle, stood watch in the graveyard each night, waiting for the beast to return for another body. Uncle Tobias was scared. He'd never hunted anything more dangerous than rabbits and could only think about how the boy who had been eaten was just a few years younger than him. Fear tightened around his neck like a noose, and the shadows took on life, hunkered under the thin moonlight like malevolent beings, waiting for him to turn his back. It was an effort to keep his gaze poised on the side of the graveyard he'd been assigned to watch. Grandpa and my father were at his back, watching the darkness beyond the edge of the faint bubble of light their lantern permitted, and he ran this through his head as a mantra.

His father and brother were there. He'd be safe.

On the third night, Uncle Tobias fired on something that was moving around the edge of the graveyard. The gunshot echoed through the night, followed by the rustle of grass as something fled. Grandpa scolded him for firing. It was too small, he said. Probably a groundhog. Don't shoot until you're certain of what you're shooting at. Didn't he remember that from when he went hunting for rabbits?

And Uncle Tobias, embarrassed, swore he wouldn't make that mistake again.

It almost got my grandfather killed. But no one held that against my uncle. He was only twelve, being asked to do something that the grown men of the town wouldn't do.

The following night, Tobias saw it, in the corner of his vision. A subtle streak of movement, like water flowing along the ground. Pale, dead flesh. A trick of the light. The latter is what he told himself it was, as he forced his fingers to relax their grip on the gun. They ached from hours of strain in the cold night air.

THE MAN WITH NO SHADOW

It came up just at the edge of his vision, sliding between the tombstones, in a blind spot where no one could see it clearly. It moved like a dog, belly to the ground, the yellowed flesh draped loosely on its bones. Uncle Tobias, so determined to not shoot at shadows again, kept his gaze fixed on the darkness at the edge of the graveyard, searching for something real, and missed the faint impression of movement at the edge of his eyesight.

Missed it, until it was almost upon him.

Luckily, Grandpa saw the ghoul before it could lunge at my uncle. He stepped between them, raising his shotgun, but the creature was in mid-leap, and it hit him squarely in the chest. My grandfather fell to the ground hard, the air knocked out of him in a rush, and the creature landed on his chest. It clawed at his shoulders and his neck until Grandpa got the barrel of the shotgun interposed between them. The ghoul threw its full weight against the gun, stretching out broken fingernails toward Grandpa's eyes.

My dad was standing by in agony, unable to find an opening in which to shoot the creature. He didn't trust his aim, not with the two twisting and thrashing on the ground. The ghoul bobbed like a bird, kicking and clawing, trying to land its teeth in something vital enough to put an end to my grandfather's resistance. Then, in a flash of inspiration, my father ran around to the side of the combatants and stuck the rifle down and angled the barrel back up into the rib cage of the monster. It froze for a second, but it was too late, and my father pulled the trigger.

The bullet ripped through the ghoul's chest and exited up and out. The force of the gunshot threw it off my grandpa, and it landed just a few feet away, directly at my uncle's feet. Tobias stood frozen, clutching his rifle to his chest. It seemed pathetic, rolling on the torn grass in front of him, its skin rippling as it convulsed in pain from its injuries. Its cries were like that of a cat, whimpering and mewling.

The thing raised its head and stared up at my uncle. Its lips were peeled back from a row of perfect white teeth, its eyes were bright, and its face was familiar. He'd met this man before, in the grocery store when my grandma took him on her errands. While he was still alive, before he died of a heart attack and was buried, and before the ghoul dug him up and ate what scraps of flesh remained on his bones.

Uncle Tobias couldn't move. He couldn't think; he couldn't breathe. The human face staring up at him with mindless hate in its eyes robbed him of all reason.

Then Grandpa got to his feet and limped over. He caved its skull in with the stock of the gun. He didn't stop until its head was a mess of battered tissue, a gelatinous heap the consistency of cold oatmeal.

Uncle Tobias said that he didn't hesitate after that. These things were monsters, he realized, regardless of whose face they wore.

After the ghoul was dispatched, my grandfather went back to the town hall and told them the problem was dealt with. If we had the cooperation of the town, he said, and especially the sheriff, then we could continue to handle these things. He'd renovate the campground. Fund some roads being built along the wooded sides and put in a fence around the fields.

Establish a border, because boundaries are significant to the inhuman. Once a creature had entrenched themselves into the campground, they could no longer escape it.

He'd turn the land into a prison for the monsters, and everyone else would be safe.

This is the arrangement we have with the town, thirty-five years later. We keep the inhuman trapped on the campground, and they look the other way. But if we fail at this, if something slips our borders and the town suffers as a result . . . then as they did with Great-Aunt Pearl, the town will start asking if it's time to find a new campground manager.

Staff Benefits Include Hazard Pay

Our world is a dangerous place. The books in my office are filled with sticky notes marking the pages for everything from invasive beetles to the causes and cures for werewolves. Even simple things can be dangerous . . . such as the rain.

A week after the Dancers, just as my wounds were starting to heal, Bryan showed up at the office with a rather shaken camper in tow. It had rained overnight. The hot, dry days of summer were done with, and autumn was just over the horizon. Bryan told me that he'd been clearing out some of the underbrush when he'd heard some shrieking. He'd gone to investigate and found this young man on the ground, pinned by a woman.

A naked young woman with green hair.

They're called rusalki (singular "rusalka"). I've also heard them referred to as water spirits or mermaids, but with legs instead of a tail. They originated in Russia. They don't need the ocean to appear; any body of water will do—even something as small as a puddle left behind after a rainstorm.

The rusalka was in the process of tickling him to death.

If you laughed just now, stop and think about it for a moment. Imagine what it's really like being tickled to the point where you feel you can hardly breathe and your stomach and chest ache with exhaustion. Now imagine that doesn't stop, it keeps going and the pain just gets worse and worse until your lungs seize up and you pray that darkness sweeps you away just so it'll stop.

Imagine how long it would take to die in such a way.

If you're not ticklish, the rusalka merely finds a convenient puddle of muddy water and shoves your face in it until you drown.

Unless it's one of the northern variants. Those smother their victims with their breasts.

If you're thinking *That's a great way to die!* I should add that their breasts are iron, and I suspect it's less smothering and more "crushing their victim's face and skull into a pulpy mass of flesh," but hey, I only know what the books told me. I haven't actually seen a northern variant kill someone.

All of our four-wheelers are outfitted with useful supplies, both mundane and occult. Bryan grabbed the branch of hawthorn before charging at the rusalka. She snapped her head up, her beauty vanishing as her face contorted into a grimace, her eyes nearly swallowed up in the puffy folds of flesh. Bryan averted his gaze and "flailed a bit with the branch" (his words, not mine), and she fled. Then he helped the victim up onto the back of the four-wheeler and brought him to my office.

Bryan asked if there was anything else he could do, and I told him no. Dealing with the rusalka would be my job.

Well, that's not entirely true. It would be Jessie's.

I didn't have a lot of options. I hire from the local community, but most of my staff are seasonal help or people who work for a few months and then quit because it's too much to handle. Jessie had actually stuck it out. Her disappearances seemed to be more about avoiding work than not wanting to deal with the monsters, which wasn't much, but I'd take it. Aunt Aleda and Uncle Tobias weren't an option, as while both of them were quite used to dealing with monsters, they were past their "sprinting through the forest" years. April wasn't available, as she was taking some time off while coming to terms with the whole "finding the severed head the Dancers left behind" incident. Seemed unfair, it's not like I was the one who left it there. And neither of my brothers could help, because I needed a maiden. Not just any maiden, but a beautiful maiden. It was time for a banishment ritual.

Jessie grumbled, but the next day she showed up to work in some nice clothes instead of the campground uniform of a dark blue polo and khakis. The ritual required a maiden to be dressed up. It is the symbolism that matters. Clothing that is reserved for special occasions would signify that this is a matter of elevated importance, thereby conveying ritual status to what we were going to try.

Jessie also made sure to wear layers, because as a last resort, she could throw them at the rusalka.

Generally, when a boss tells a female employee that they should be ready to throw their clothing at a murderous mermaid in case things go horribly wrong, that's going to merit a sexual harassment lawsuit. However, this is an old land, and things are a little different here. The locals understand. Mostly.

As with any supernatural creature, there are multiple ways to banish a rusalka. We were going to try a fairly simple ritual, in which a young lady is dressed up and sent out into the woods. She is the avatar of the rusalka, and her symbolic "banishment" from the village (in this case, the employee lodge) would transfer onto the rusalka and banish her from my campground. If something went wrong, Jessie could buy herself time to escape by throwing her clothes at the rusalka. They're obsessed with clothing. They desire it more than anything and will stop to pick up and put on any article of clothing thrown their way.

I showed her the route to take on a map. She'd start at the lodge. All of the staff would be present to see her off. She'd walk through the woods, all the way to the opposite property line, about a half mile away. I'd be waiting there with the four-wheeler to take her back.

"And if something bad happens?" she asked miserably.

"Just be ready to throw your clothing behind you to slow her down," I said. "I don't recommend throwing your shoes. The road turns to dirt at the base of the hill and there's a lot of rocks. You'll want your shoes."

She nodded and plucked at her mint dress with a lace overlay. A neat white cardigan and running shoes completed the outfit. At least she'd prepared intelligently. I left her with the rest of the staff, reassuring her that this would be fine, that I'd be there waiting for her at the edge of camp. Then I got on my vehicle and headed out.

My older brother Ian relayed what was happening via radio. Ian told me that Jessie had left the lodge and he'd seen her off. That the rusalka had been lying in a ditch near the edge of the field (wallowing in the remaining rainwater, perhaps?) and snapped to attention as Jessie walked by. She had then slipped off into the woods after her.

"Well, that's not good," I said.

"She's got a cardigan," Ian offered hopefully.

There wasn't much I could do except wait. I kept track of the time. I had a rough idea of how long it would take someone to walk this far, and then I added another five minutes as a buffer. After Jessie failed to appear, it became apparent that something had gone horribly wrong and she wasn't making the rendezvous. I started the engine on my four-wheeler and began driving slowly down the dirt road, listening intently for the frantic laugh of someone being tickled to death.

Instead, I heard a birdcall. Okay, it wasn't a birdcall. It was a human voice yelling "kaw kaw!" at me in an attempt to subtly get my attention.

It wasn't really that subtle.

"Jessie?" I asked hesitantly.

"Yes," she hissed back. She was hiding behind a sizable tree. I watched as she poked her head out from behind it. "I don't think it worked. The rusalka started chasing me. I did what you said and threw my clothes at her."

"Are you at least wearing—"

"NO. I had to throw ALL my clothing away before she stopped."

With that question answered, I grabbed something from my four-wheeler. While not ideal, it would at least let me get her back to the employee locker room.

It's not in the rules, but I'm thinking of adding it: Always carry a spare tarp. They come in handy if the rain does something unexpected, your tent fails in some way, or you need an emergency cover-up for a naked employee.

I dropped Jessie off at the employee lodge, and once she was dressed, we reconvened in my office to discuss what had gone wrong. The rusalka had come at her as soon as she'd entered the woods, Jessie related. There'd been a gleeful, almost childlike expression on her face, but Jessie wasn't going to take chances. She'd thrown her cardigan, and the mermaid had stopped to pick it up and put it on. Jessie had increased her pace for a bit, trying to put distance between them, but she was quickly out of breath and had to slow down again. From behind her she heard someone humming, growing closer, and when she turned, the rusalka was only a few yards behind. There was an unnerving intensity to her gaze. Jessie kept walking, unzipping the back of her dress as she did, and then she stripped that up over her head and tossed it back to the rusalka.

Inside out, which probably bought her a handful more precious minutes as the mermaid struggled to turn it right side out again. Monsters can be particular about the strangest things.

And so it went. Jessie would gain some ground, the rusalka would catch up—humming the entire time—and my employee would discard another item of her dwindling wardrobe.

"I should have worn more layers," Jessie sighed. "It was like the worst game of strip poker, where the loser dies at the end."

Finally, the rusalka had seemed content with the clothing she'd put on—or perhaps she'd got bored or distracted—for the humming had ceased, and when Jessie had turned around that last time, she'd discovered she was alone. Then she had found a tree to hide behind and waited until I had come looking for her.

I wasn't certain why the banishment had failed. Perhaps because it's used to remove a rusalka from around a settlement and my campground includes forest, which is where rusalki are traditionally banished to. Regardless, I needed to make another attempt.

"There's something else we can try," I said.

I explained what we'd do. There's another ritual to banish a rusalka. An effigy is created to resemble the rusalka, dressed in clothing it covets, and then burned.

"Do you think you could scrounge up more of your clothes?" I asked. "Since the rusalka seems so fond of them."

"Are you going to pay me back?" Jessie whined.

I reminded her that yes, I would, and she would also get a hazard bonus for her participation in the first ritual. Did she even read the handbook?

I took care of building the effigy while Jessie returned home to raid her wardrobe. Aunt Aleda helped me.

"You need more hands around here," she said as she wove green thread into strands of hair. "I don't know if you're going to get April back, and you can't rely on Jessie."

"I've got my brother, he's been a huge help."
"But Tyler lives almost an hour away."
"No, Ian. He's back on the campground now."

She paused for a moment before murmuring that yes, that was right. I did have Ian. But she added that I should still think hard on it, as a new entity on the campground meant more work. I frowned. We could banish the rusalka, but the Dancers would still be around. I did have a staffing problem.

Everyone gathered for the burning, because as most rituals do, this one required an audience. They'd brought with them the camp's fire extinguishers. We use fire quite a bit around here, since it's one of the most effective weapons against the inhuman, but it's always a bit of a risk considering this is a campground with trees and dry leaves and lots of other fire hazards. I noticed that Aunt Aleda was standing close to Jessie, who had elected to sulk at the back of the small crowd. I dismissed her from my mind, focusing on getting the effigy evenly coated with gasoline without getting any on myself. Then I said a few words, because even though there's no documentation about any particular incantation, it just seemed like the right thing to do. Thanks for coming to this ceremonial burning, blah blah blah, please don't let any of the nearby trees catch fire.

Then I tossed a match onto the base.

There was a beautiful moment when the effigy went up in a glorious fireball, and all I could hear was the crackle of the flames, and everything seemed to be going right.

Then from behind me, Jessie started screaming.

I spun around just in time to get a brief glimpse of her,

standing there with the ends of her hair ablaze, the flames rapidly spreading up toward her scalp.

Then Jessie vanished from my sight because Aunt Aleda pounced on her. She tackled her to the ground, and then my uncle was right there, throwing a fire blanket over her head and smothering the flames. It all happened so fast that no one else really had time to react. I walked over, and my staff scurried out of my way. Jessie was sitting on the ground, sobbing, and the smell of charred hair hung heavy around her. The skin on the back of her neck was reddened as if with a sunburn, but she didn't seem to have suffered any serious injury.

I forced myself to snap out of my shock. Luckily, I had heard the sound of a second scream, coming from somewhere off in the woods. An echo of Jessie's, that same helpless, desperate cry.

The rusalka. Not dead, but banished.

But now I had another problem. I needed to get control of the situation. I was already having staffing issues; I couldn't lose more by them getting scared off.

"Well, that hasn't happened in a *while*," I said with a fake laugh, clapping my hands together. "Ancient rituals, so unreliable, am I right?"

No one else laughed.

"This is why we keep the fire blankets around. Bryan, can you and Uncle Tobias keep an eye on the bonfire until it burns out? Everyone else—I think we're done here."

Aunt Aleda was staring at me over the top of Jessie's smoldering head, her lips set in a thin line. This wasn't normal. This had never happened before. We'd done the ritual exactly the same as we had in the past; I was sure of it. We hadn't made any mistakes.

Jessie. It was something with Jessie. She was the only thing different this time.

"That's IT!" Jessie screeched, throwing my aunt's arm off her. "I'm *LEAVING*!"

She shot to her feet and stormed away. The staff who hadn't quite finished dispersing yet watched her go, no doubt relieved to hear her still yelling about how she wasn't going to come back, either. She wasn't exactly popular.

"Going to start the termination paperwork?" Uncle Tobias asked as we watched the spectacle.

"Nope," I replied. "She'll be back once she gets that hazard pay in her next paycheck."

"You could just fire her."

"I guess technically we did just fire her, with the hair and all..."

"Kate."

Uncle Tobias studied me for a moment.

"You're worried about something," he said. I hesitated. I hadn't realized it was that obvious. But I could use any help I could get.

"Something is going on around here. We had the Children with No Wagon; then something *new* shows up—and it's been ages since that happened—and now a rusalka appears? The timing is alarming."

"And the ritual burned Jessie as well."

I nodded.

"Has anything like this happened before? Like, before I took over?" I asked.

Tobias stared thoughtfully off into the distance, no doubt wishing as I did that my dad was here to teach me these things.

"We can get periods where the campground is unusually active," he said. "There's usually one creature in particular that's the problem. Stirs the rest of them up."

The bad years. They were rare, and while I'd heard of them from my parents, I'd been lucky enough to not experience one yet during my time as manager.

"I don't think it's the children or the Dancers," I replied. "I resolved the problem with the children, so it's not them, and the Dancers are newcomers. They won't have built any influence with the other inhabitants so quickly."

It was something else. Something that was keeping itself hidden, something devious, which in and of itself was a hint to our culprit. The campground creatures might have been reclusive until they were ready to hunt, but they were hardly subtle when they struck.

Except for one.

The Man with No Shadow

The rules of the campground were figured out across generations of my family. There is a system to these creatures, rules that must be followed, and consequences for breaking them. You didn't follow the lights into the woods, you didn't refuse the Man with the Skull Cup, and if you were of my family line, you didn't leave any doors or windows open at night as an invitation to the little girl. There was one creature on the campground that did not function so overtly, however. I knew to avoid talking to the Man with No Shadow, but little else. But I couldn't shake the feeling that our recent problems had something to do with him, as his plans had been in motion for a long time, ever since I was a child.

My ordinary childhood ended with him. Before then, I'd felt like a normal kid. I was eight. I attended school, and while I wasn't popular, I certainly wasn't bullied, and my classmates treated me with respect. No doubt there were conversations around the dinner table about how my family was the reason their parents had livelihoods and they were to not hassle my brother Tyler and me. Just in case.

I like to believe my parents wouldn't have retaliated if I had been bullied, but I've told you of the time I killed a camper, and he was by no means the first. I learned that from someone.

Perhaps I was a bit conceited as a kid, and I certainly enjoyed the attention of my peers, but I wasn't overtly cruel. I was mean in subtle ways, in how I made those around me feel lesser simply by how I put myself above them, and then I made them love me by deigning to grant them my notice. It netted me a number of loyal friends at school, girls who responded to this sort of manipulation.

There was only one who I considered my equal. Arrogant and intelligent, canny and sharp like a whip, a skinny girl with wild hair and coiled energy nestled inside like a snake ready to strike. Her name was Laura, and she became my best friend.

We loved the woods. We'd sneak into the tree line at the edge of the playground at recess and climb the rocks and branches until the teachers saw us and yelled for us to come out; then we'd go right back in once their backs were turned. We made our own elaborate games of make-believe, and Laura and I were both queens of our own lands, and the rest of our friends were our subjects. We'd wage war with sticks and array our armies against each other, until the teachers yelled at us again.

The campground was a much better playground for all of us. There were no teachers to yell. Just my parents and the staff, and during daylight hours, in the well-trafficked parts, there was little danger. We were told not to bother the people here to camp and definitely not to talk to anyone in the woods.

If you're taken aback at the idea of a bunch of young children playing in the woods of my campground, I should remind you that we see a lot of people pass through every year, and most of them return home safely. It's only the unwary or the exceedingly unlucky who come to harm. Your perception of my campground is perhaps a little skewed because I've told you the worst of it, because that is what is interesting and useful for the purpose of this guide. No one wants to hear about how someone spent two weeks reading in a hammock and taking naps.

It's apparent why the Man with No Shadow targeted Laura. She was always the leader of one team, and I the leader of the other. I'm not sure how he separated her from the rest—or perhaps he didn't; perhaps they forgot my parents' warnings as well—but at some point during our friendship, he approached her and they talked and then she belonged to him.

It doesn't take long for the Man with No Shadow to claim a new servant. One conversation, maybe two, depending on how strong the victim's will is.

He waited until my ninth birthday to use Laura against my family. I wanted a sleepover, and since my birthday is close to Christmas, my parents tried to ensure it felt special by letting me do whatever I liked. We were put in the living room with sleeping bags and snacks, and my brother was allowed to hide in his room and play video games all night while we watched movies and shrieked and laughed. At some point I fell asleep, along with a handful of my friends. Laura woke them up, careful not to disturb me. She told them to go with her. None of them remembered quite what lie she told them, but it was Laura asking, and they obeyed her as easily as they obeyed me.

I continued to sleep until the cold air creeping in from the front door woke me. I was disoriented and then frightened, realizing that my friends were gone and the front door hung open. I ran to it, terrified that my parents would find out, because they had told us over and over and over that we were to never leave a window or door open overnight.

The little girl sat cross-legged just on the other side of the doorway. I hesitated, reluctant to be so rude as to shut the door in her face. I asked why she hadn't come inside. She told me she couldn't, that only the proper residents of the house could invite her inside by leaving a point of entry open. Then she said that the Man with No Shadow wanted to see me. He was waiting at the edge of the woods.

I asked her if it was safe. She shrugged and rose, smoothing her white skirt with her palms.

"Nothing is safe," she replied. "You just try to pretend otherwise."

It was only one a.m. There was still time to find my friends and get back to the house before the beast showed up. This is what I told myself. I thought that if I woke my parents, they'd be so angry—at my friends, but especially at me for not keeping them safe. I didn't want any of us to get in trouble, and so I resolved to fix this before morning. I left, shutting the front door behind me.

I found the Man with No Shadow out by the trees, just as the little girl had said. He changes his appearance periodically.

At that time, he was dark-haired, tanned, tall, and muscular. He crouched as I approached, so that I didn't have to stare up at him so much.

"Hello, Kate," he said. "I can take you to your friends."

"My parents said I can't talk to you," I replied.

"Then I won't talk."

This seemed like an acceptable compromise, and when he stood and walked away, I followed. I was afraid, but not nearly as afraid as I should have been. Not enough to turn back.

The things in the woods treat children differently. Some are mindless beasts that make no distinction and view all humans as mere meat. But the ones that do understand? There are conditions that have to be met first before they will harm a child. A trial. A rite of passage. A failure to grow.

The Man with No Shadow was my trial, but not at this time. Not until much later. When I was nine, I was merely the tool that he wielded against my parents.

He took me to the grove with the stones. Giant, moss-covered boulders dug up by glaciers hunkered in the middle of a small clearing. This was where the Man with No Shadow could be typically found.

He stepped aside and let me enter the clearing. My eyes had adjusted to the dim moonlight by that point, and I could just about see the outline of bodies, seven girls, sitting with their backs against a boulder and their chins drooping to their chests. I went up to Maria and put a hand against her chest to feel that she was still breathing.

"Now run and tell your mother what you've seen," the Man

with No Shadow murmured from behind me. "Tell her that if she wants these children back, then I must have something in exchange."

I stood there, trying to think of something I could say that would undo all of this. My parents would be so angry. But the Man with No Shadow snapped that I should go before *he* got angry, and the harshness of his tone told me that there was no way out. I needed my parents.

I turned and ran from that clearing. The silent, still forms of my friends haunted my mind, and I thought if I'd been smarter or more careful or maybe if I didn't have friends at all... then this wouldn't have happened.

I was incoherent when I woke my mother. She quickly hushed my sobs and extricated herself from the bed, careful to not wake my father as well. Then, in the kitchen, I sat and gasped hysterically, getting my words out one at a time until my mother was able to put the pieces together.

The Man with No Shadow had my friends.

She told me to stay in the house. She put on shoes and a jacket and went to deal with him. And when she came back, my friends were with her, pale and shaking. Laura, however, was serene and she smiled at me, and this didn't escape my mother's notice, for she took Laura aside and questioned her separately. Then she immediately drove her home.

My parents sat me down the next day and told me I couldn't be friends with Laura anymore. They knew that would be hard because I was close to her, but she belonged to the Man with No Shadow now, and she wasn't safe.

At school the following Monday, I found that Laura was the only one who would speak to me, and I refused to acknowledge her, just as I'd been instructed. When I went to sit with my other friends at lunch, they all got up and left, leaving me sitting alone at the table. That's how it was after that. I think their parents had told them to stay away from me, just as I had been told to stay away from Laura. I was desperately lonely from that point on and spent my recesses in the library, where the librarian took pity on me and gave me her favorite books to read and talked to me when no one else would.

I didn't really interact with Laura again until after our high school graduation, many years later.

My family held a party for me, even though I'd said I didn't want one, because I knew none of my peers would attend. It was just aunts and uncles and so many cousins . . . and all the campground staff, which was kind of them. Some of them even brought gifts. At one point during the party, I stepped outside to get away from the crowd. Someone was walking down the path leading from the campground entrance, a person in robes and wearing a cap. For a brief moment I was elated, thinking that perhaps one of my classmates had actually come to my party. I hurried to meet them, then slowed and stopped as I realized who it was.

Laura. Laura was here.

"You still don't trust me?" she asked sadly, as she saw my apprehension. "It's been a long time."

"The Man with No Shadow never lets go of people," I replied.

"No," a voice said from somewhere just behind me. "I do not."

And he said something else, and I don't recall the exact words, for Laura lunged at me, fingers outstretched, reaching for my throat. Her lips were peeled back in a soundless snarl and her eyes were wide, and I thought I saw desperation buried inside them. Then there was no time left for contemplation, for we were falling, hitting the packed dirt of the road, and her fingers were around my neck.

I was the stronger one, physically. I spent my evenings and my summers working on the campground. I seized her and threw her aside, and then I was on top of her, and it was my hands around her throat.

I held her down while she thrashed beneath me, fingernails clawing at my face, froth speckling her lips, and her feet kicking helplessly at the ground. I hated her in that moment, because she'd betrayed me, because she was the reason I'd been so lonely all these years. Perhaps that isn't fair, but that hatred was strong enough to give me the will to keep pressing down on her windpipe even as her chest convulsed in a desperate attempt to bring in air, even as her struggles subsided and she went still, even as a bluish cast settled into the skin around her mouth and eyes, and I held on long after she stopped moving until she was well and truly dead.

Through all of this, the Man with No Shadow watched impassively with a slight smile on his face. I can still see it when I close my eyes, and my heart churns with rage at the memory.

He smiled the whole time I was killing my best friend with my bare hands.

"Now you are of age," he said, and he walked away.

I said earlier that the creatures of the forest will not harm children unless they fail their test. This was mine. The day I graduated high school is the day I first killed someone. It's when I realized that my childhood was officially over and nothing was left to protect me from the dangers of this world.

After Laura, my parents implemented a new policy. We evicted anyone we caught conversing with the Man with No Shadow. They were banned from the campground forever. We couldn't take that risk.

My family had been keeping an eye on Jessie since the rusalka incident, and it had paid off. She had been spotted conversing with the same person over the course of a few weeks. Which explained a bit why she'd been slacking off. And since we have inhumans on the campground and being able to recognize them matters, my family also made sure to tell me what he looked like. A tall and lanky man with messy red hair.

Uncle Tobias was the last person to see them together, and he was particularly concerned—he had a good sense for these things, having grown up on the land and all, and he was worried by the fact it was the same person. We didn't have campers staying for that long at that time. I knew. I checked the registrations.

I thought it could have been something that already lived here. Or it could have been just a random, ordinary person who had overstayed to flirt with the locals. I didn't know, but Jessie knew she was supposed to tell me about these things just in case it was something bad.

I asked my older brother if he knew anyone with red hair who was hanging around Jessie, and he said he did not. But that's not surprising, as he had spent the past few years on a deep-sea oil rig and was isolated from everything happening at the campground. He thought this wasn't something to be concerned about anyway, just some guy flirting with Jessie. But I wasn't so sure . . . I trusted my uncle's instincts.

Firing her wouldn't resolve the problem. She'd still be a threat. She'd be in town, always waiting in the shadows, until she was sent back to the campground.

Just like Laura.

Don't Follow the Lights. *Really.*

I have a love-hate relationship with the camp emergency line. I hate that it gives the campers direct access to bother me—especially in the middle of the night—for things that are often not actually an emergency. I'm not going to get out of bed at four in the morning to save the cell phone someone accidentally dropped down a porta-potty. The phone is gone forever. Deal with it. However, I love that it lets me respond quickly to dangerous situations happening on the campground, instead of simply finding a corpse the next morning.

Unfortunately, most of the time they call me once things are well past the point of being an emergency, and saving them is now extra difficult.

I was woken shortly before midnight by the emergency phone ringing. It was instinct at this point to grab it and answer, rolling out of bed as I did so. I'd found it was best to get away from the window so no one overheard the little girl crying in the background.

"Hey, we're *so sorry* to call," a female voice said, "but we're super lost."

"Any landmarks?" I asked.

The adrenaline shooting through my veins was working better than any coffee. Being lost in the woods was a little risky in any situation, but especially dangerous here.

"Uh, there's a road, but we haven't found any street signs yet. It's kind of a long road."

All the roads surrounding my campground are long. There isn't a lot else nearby, and the intersections are very few and far between. I struggled to pull on some jeans one-handed. Just because they weren't on the campground didn't mean they weren't in danger. The inhuman things around here might congregate on my land, but there could still be something out there, waiting in the darkness.

"Did you go through the woods before you reached the road?" I asked, trying to narrow down which road it might be.

"Yeah, we were ... following something."

I froze. There were too many "somethings" that could be.

"Was it the voice of someone you know?" I asked tightly. "Are you missing anyone from your party?"

"No ... it was like ... a floating ball of light."

At least she had the decency to sound embarrassed. I took a deep breath in an effort to remain calm. Ah yes.

> **RULE #3:** Don't follow the lights. I can't believe I even have to say this one. Don't follow the lights.

"Someone told us they were safe," she continued nervously. "He told us we could take photos of them if we got close enough."

I asked what he looked like. Red hair, she said. The person who my staff had seen Jessie talking to. Unease was gnawing at my belly.

"I'm going to come get you," I said. "Stay where you are and don't leave the road."

I'd make a lap around the campground and pick them up, and hopefully that would be all. I told them what my car looked like and the license plate and sternly added that under no circumstances should they accept rides from anyone else.

Then I put on a coat and my shoes and got my car keys. Dawn was a long way off, so I estimated that I'd be able to find them and return them to their campsite and still have time to get back to the house before the beast arrived. The little girl skipped alongside the car as I eased it out of the garage and down the driveway, but she was also still sobbing while skipping, so it was a bit unnerving.

It started raining as I was pulling through the gate and onto the road that led out of the campground. Inwardly, I groaned. The forecast had said only a 40 percent chance, but it seemed we'd gotten unlucky, for the rain quickly escalated into a downpour, covering my windshield in a sheet of water as I turned onto the road that wound along the west side of the campsite.

I was almost to the south road when the lost campers called me back. They were taking shelter on the front porch of a house, they said. There weren't any lights on inside, and no one answered when they'd knocked on the door, so they were just going to stay there until they saw my car. I drove slowly, across the south side and then up the east, and then I was at the northern border. They were still on the phone with me, and they said they hadn't seen my headlights when I asked.

I thought about it a moment, trying to place where they were. I asked if they could see anything like a fence or a pond, so I could figure out which of my neighbors they were bothering. No, they said. Nothing. Just the house. Then it occurred to me. The campground borders a major road to the south and some fields and houses to the east and west. The north is just empty land. They'd come out the north. They were on the ass-end of nowhere, and there shouldn't be any houses out there.

I didn't know whose front porch they were standing on.

I opened my mouth to say that I had a bad feeling about this and I'd like them to stay beside the road, please, when the phone call abruptly disconnected.

I called the Old Sheriff for backup. He'd want to be involved if this was an entity outside my campground borders. Then I turned onto the north road and drove slowly, peering through the dark and the rain, straining to see a house among the trees. I drove past it twice, and finally, on the third pass, I saw it.

A small, wood building was nestled not far from the road, at the base of a slight slope. I had never seen it before. The porch covered half the front of the house, and the windows were vacant and dark. No one stood outside. No flashlight beams illuminated the interior. I pulled halfway off the road, as far as I could. I waited in my car until the sheriff arrived, and I was deeply relieved to see his headlights appear in my rearview mirror. Waiting in the dark and the rain like that, with the house hunched ominously in the corner of my vision... it was a little stressful, to say the least. At one point a dead branch had fallen from a tree, and it felt like my heart was still hammering in my chest, even as I got out of the car to go greet the sheriff.

"That house shouldn't be here," he said as I approached, holding his umbrella out so I could duck under it.

"Yeah, no shit," I snapped, which he took with good humor. He was used to my temper when things were going wrong. "Two of my campers followed the lights. They dumped them off around here, and their phone disconnected after they took shelter on that porch."

The Old Sheriff said that he'd called for backup already. We'd wait until they got here, and then we'd go in as a group. Too bad about the rain, he said dourly, otherwise we could set the house on fire and destroy it that way.

Neither of us thought the campers were still alive. The lights led people to their deaths.

This is why I liked the Old Sheriff. He took care of things. While I relied on rituals and appeasements, he believed in assault rifles and gasoline. And sure, gunfire isn't going to kill everything—or most things, if we're being honest—but nothing, human or otherwise, likes being shot. It'd knock a lot of things down, and after that, well, that's what the gasoline is for.

Fire is far more effective than bullets.

We'd try lighting it up from inside, he continued. Once the bodies were out so they could be returned to their families. They could douse the interior and light it from the doorway and see if the fire took out the support beams and collapsed the roof. He sounded confident it would. I was only half listening at this point.

Something was moving inside the house.

I tapped the sheriff on the elbow and pointed. He fell silent and then pressed the handle of the umbrella into my palms. He moved toward the house, walking slowly, his hand falling to unclip his pistol in the holster. I followed just behind him, glancing back and forth to watch our flanks. Not that it would have done a lot of good. I'm used to the darkness, but out here, in the rain, it's like the world ends outside the narrow beam of a flashlight.

The sheriff paused just short of the porch. He shone the flashlight into the window, and the house swallowed up the glow, presenting us with an inky void and nothing more.

A body slammed against the window. I screamed and fell backward, slipping on the mud and landing hard on my ass in a puddle. The umbrella bounced away and the cold rain shocked the panic out of me, and I stared up at the house in naked horror as a young man stared back at me. His eyes were wide, the whites vivid in the light of the sheriff's flashlight, his skin pale where his palms pressed against the glass. His mouth was open. He was screaming something, desperately yelling at us, but I couldn't hear anything except for the roar of the rain.

Something jerked him backward. He flew away from us, hands outstretched toward the window, his mouth open in a shriek, his eyes still fixed on me in mindless desperation. The darkness inside devoured him, like he'd vanished behind a cloud, and the interior was an empty void once more.

The Old Sheriff didn't hesitate. He stripped off his rain jacket, wrapped it around his fist a couple of times, and then punched the fucking window in. He knocked the glass away and fumbled with the window frame, unlocking it and sliding it up. I scrambled to my feet, yelling at him to stop, to wait, that the backup hadn't arrived yet. He glanced back at me, one hand on the gun at his waist.

"They're not going to get here in time," he said calmly. "It never works out that way. We're always too late."

Then he put a leg through and eased the rest of his body into that house, and the darkness swallowed him whole.

I fretted. There was no way in hell I was following the sheriff inside. I can't even claim that I was doing the sensible thing and waiting to tell the backup what the situation was, because I knew in my heart that the sheriff was right. These entities—all of them, the things on our campground and the things that hunt elsewhere—never let numbers get the better of them. They slip away well before help arrives, and yes, this was a house we're talking about, but it had somehow gotten here where there had been no house before, and I did not doubt that whatever was inside would whisk its lair away before it could be stormed by angry people with guns and cans of gasoline.

These things only yielded up the dead and only on their terms.

So if I'm being honest, I didn't go after the sheriff because I was afraid. I contend with monsters and demons, but I don't think that's made me particularly brave. I think I'm only violent and decisive when it's easy, when my anger can take control and I just follow where it leads. The rest of the time . . . I'm afraid. I'm so very afraid. I'm still that scared young woman crying in my dorm room on the night my parents died, knowing I wasn't ready for this, knowing I was the only one who could take over the campground.

This next part is hard to talk about.

The front door was flung open. I saw the sheriff and he seemed larger, his eyes shone like an animal's in the light of my flashlight, and his frame filled the doorway. I think this is just my imagination, remembering him as something powerful, something indomitable. I wish it were so. He was just a man caught in the teeth of something terrible. Yet despite the odds, he had the young man with him. One fist was gripped tight on the back of the man's jacket, and he was hauling him along, the poor boy almost too terrified to move. Then he shoved him forward; the man stumbled on the steps of the porch and he fell into the mud, and I moved to help him.

And the sheriff went back inside. For the woman.

I dragged the man away from the house. He was babbling incoherently, something about the darkness and how it never ended, it just kept going and going. I told him to shut up and twisted on his jacket, pulling him along behind me until I reached my car and threw him in the back seat. I regretted my lack of towels as water began to soak into my upholstery.

"Stay put," I said sternly, which I'm quite good at and which is especially effective on the newly traumatized.

He nodded at me, pale and shivering, and I shut the door

on him and returned to stand vigil at the house, waiting for the sheriff's return. He'd gotten one of them out, and because of this, I allowed myself a faint glimmer of hope.

The door swung slowly back and forth in the wind. I peered into the darkness that my flashlight could not breach, waiting. And the sheriff emerged for a second time, both hands around a woman. She was screaming hysterically and fighting, thrashing and kicking at her rescuer. He had her in a bear hug and was literally carrying her from the building. I stepped forward, to the very edge of the porch, and reached out a hand to grab her from him . . .

The darkness boiled out of the house. It was like watching a pot overflow, thick bubbles of inky blackness churned through doorframe and around the sheriff, enveloping him in an instant. I saw his arms outstretched, shoving the woman to where I stood waiting. My hand closed over her wrist, and I pulled, but the darkness surged forward, thick pustules rolling over her as well, and there was a moment of pressure as it pulled back toward the house, and I dug my heels into the mud, felt myself slipping—

I considered letting go lest I be pulled in too—

And then it released her. I fell backward, stumbling wildly, and I hit the ground for a second time that night and stayed there, sitting in a puddle and staring at the wrist still clutched in my fingers. A wrist, an elbow, a shoulder, and part of a rib cage, and nothing more.

The house was gone, and with it the sheriff and the rest of the woman.

We claimed that the woman had had an accident in the rain, fallen and broken her neck and died in the woods. There's wild animals about, and that was why we could only recover part of the body. That's the excuse we gave.

The young man we said was separated from her and we recovered him, a little hypothermic but no serious injuries. I lost track of what happened to him after he was released from the hospital. The Old Sheriff's deputy firmly and not so politely told me that my involvement was no longer needed.

I kept going, as I always did. There was a campground to manage. But in the days that followed, I couldn't sleep. I didn't *want* to sleep; I didn't want to close my eyes and see the house and the woman's arm in my hands; I didn't want to remember how my mom was dead and my dad was dead and now so was the Old Sheriff. So one night, when it all became too much, I got drunk and destroyed my office. I threw books onto the floor. I kicked filing boxes over. And when it was done and everything was on the floor and there were holes in the walls, I sat down in the middle of all of it and tried to cry, but the sound just came out as dry, shuddering sobs that stuck deep in my chest. Then I started putting everything back where it belonged.

I lingered on my mother's journal when I came to it. I thumbed through the pages, not searching for anything in particular, as there was no organization to it. No index, no sections—it wasn't even chronological. I paused on the page that included a map of the campground, though, perhaps remembering something in the back of my mind, because I'd read through this journal many many times before.

There were small dots, done in red ink, all along the northern part of the campground.

Frantic, I reread the pages it had been inserted between. Names and dates and a few brief phrases. The names were all locals, no doubt contacting my mother with this information that, until now, had made no sense to me.

Wooden house. Black windows. Door open.

Over and over.

My mother had been tracking the vanishing house.

Then she died. And the campground and all the things she'd left undone were now mine.

Cognitive Dissonance
Is a Hell of a Drug

The tough part about my job is that most of the time, the monsters are insurmountable, and all I can do is clean up the pieces they leave behind. Except now the house had taken the Old Sheriff and it hurt, it hurt like when my parents died, and then it *vanished* and left me with nothing to hate.

So I picked something else to be angry at.

A few days later I stormed into the dentist's office. I took a good look around before I sat down, giving Jessie's father a moment to compose himself. Dr. Henry's office had too many mementos from Jessie's childhood for my liking. I hastily looked away.

This town has an unofficial motto. "We don't make bargains with evil things." But that's not really true. This town is no more upright than the rest of the world. It's got plenty of selfish and stupid people in it, and depending on how bad a week I've had, I might argue it is nothing but selfish and stupid people. There's plenty of folks around here who think they're clever enough to bargain with the devil and get away with it, or perhaps their greed overrides their fear. The motto, then, is more of a warning.

We don't tolerate bargaining with evil things . . . and if you do, we're going to do something about it.

"Did Jessie tell you about her hair catching on fire?" I asked as soon as the door shut behind me.

He startled, almost standing up. So that was a no, he hadn't been told. Interesting.

"She's a grown adult; I don't keep track of her—"

"Maybe you should. I'm starting to think her slacking off is cause for concern. She's been seen conversing with an entity, and now she was affected by a banishing ritual, of all things."

"Jessie wouldn't get mixed up with anything evil," Henry immediately said.

I explained that yes, of course she wouldn't be so foolish, but it was possible that entity had played a part in the Old Sheriff's disappearance into the house. I had concerns. Did he notice any changes in her personality? Was there anything that stood out to him?

"Bullshit. You're here asking if you can murder my daughter."

Wow. Rude. Fine then. I was tired of making the effort to plaster a fake smile on my face and adopt my nice managerial voice, anyway. Besides, Jessie knew the dangers when she took this job. I explain them very clearly during orientation, complete with a presentation and photos of what happens to people who don't follow the rules, just to drive the point home that it could be them lying in multiple pieces on the forest floor if they're not careful. If she'd done something beyond repair, then she only had herself to blame.

"I'm here as a courtesy," I snapped. "Because if I'm right, and if she is associating with or under the influence of something on my campground, then I'm going to handle it. If it's what I think it is, then there's no fixing it in a nice, civil way. This creature doesn't let go of his pawns. And when I'm done, you can get up in front of the town and scream and cry all you want, but you know they're all going to look the other way. There won't be a damn thing you can do about it."

He hunched his shoulders and refused to look at me. He refused to speak as well, so I told him I'd take that as a *Yes, Kate, you make a very good point, and I understand*, and I saw myself out.

The townsfolk don't like what we do. They don't like us. But they keep us around because we do the things that have to be done, the things they don't want to do themselves.

Let me tell you a story. I don't think it'll make any of you more sympathetic toward them . . . but maybe you'll understand my situation better. I'll tell you about the bridge and how my parents got to know each other.

The town has seen its share of troubles over the years. My campground is hardly the only danger that we've dealt with around here, and the locals have their own share of the blame. You'd think they'd learn, but these are not stories they tell to their children, and so each generation has to start over and make the same mistakes. Do you know the Bible verse about how the children will be punished for the sins of their parents, down to the third and fourth generation? I think this is what it means. They condemn us to repeat their mistakes through our ignorance.

Perhaps the town is ashamed. There are bones in the surrounding fields. Unmarked graves that they have tried to forget about. Oh, there was justification for everything they did. It's hard to keep your hands clean when you're dealing with monsters. But it doesn't change the fact that horrible things *were* done and blood was spilled, all in the name of keeping the town safe.

My family knows everything that's happened. My parents told me some of the local legends when I was a child and thought they were nothing more than ghost stories. Then one day, when the stories were starting to feel real, I went to the landmarks. There are a handful. The bridge is one of them.

It is a mere overpass. The road is narrow with barely any shoulder. The bridge is for trains. Small plants grow on the metal crossbeams underneath the tracks. It is wholly unremarkable save for it being the closest bridge to the nursing home.

The bloodstains have long since worn away—or perhaps they merely faded to the same color as the rust—and the asphalt has been repaved. Sometimes our mistakes hide themselves.

The story goes like this. I'll tell you like my mother told me.

Something ancient came to our town. It happens on occasion. Old gods and goddesses, devils of some variety, eternal beings whose names have been repeated across generations. Perhaps they are drawn to my campground, or perhaps they pass through all of our towns more often than we realize, and the locals here just know how to recognize the signs while the rest of the world remains ignorant. I think it is the latter, personally. Normal people might laugh off the primal terror that a sudden strong wind invokes, but my town looks at the sky, looks to the birds, and looks for the other signs that might mark the arrival of something new.

This is important. Whenever there is a strange storm or an unexpected shift to the weather, be wary of strangers. Someone in your town or city may be approached by an ancient being and not recognize it for what it is. It could be you that it comes to.

For my mother, the first sign that an ancient was present was the deer stuck in the fence around the nursing home. She volunteered there in high school. She started doing it because her friend asked her, and then when her friend lost interest, she continued on, merely because she believed in finishing what she started. But one day after school she drove to the nursing home and found two of the staff out by the fence. It is not a proper fence. Decorative. The deer can jump over it. This one, however, had somehow managed to catch its back legs on the top rung and then wrapped its body through and around. Like it'd been tied in a knot. It's stomach had split open from the pressure, and its intestines lay in a pile on the ground.

They mistook it for a doe. My mother, however, was willing to look closer at the mess and saw the bloody holes in its skull where antlers had been torn free.

She finished her volunteer shift without saying a word to anyone about the deer. Then once she was home, she called my grandfather. She didn't know my father at that time, except by reputation as the next person in line to inherit the notorious campground. That was the first time they talked, when he picked up the campground's office phone, and the only thing she said to him was that she would like to speak to his father, please, because he would know what to do.

My father says he was a little offended by the implication that he didn't know what to do, at the time.

Grandpa wasn't much help. He was mean even back then and told my mother it was nothing unusual and hung up on her. Then he went into the woods and hung wards all around the border to stave off whatever had arrived in our town. He only cared about protecting the campground; he didn't really give a shit about the town. My father, however, had listened in on the conversation. He found my mother the next day and told her what she should watch for.

Not dangerous on its own, he said. It would pass by peacefully, so long as no one invited it indoors.

There are many ancient beings like this. They're less of a threat these days because we as a society no longer practice hospitality. A stranger in the evening can simply find a hotel like everyone else and does not need to even have the door opened for them, much less be invited inside.

I would not be telling you this story if the ancient had simply passed through the town. But someone knew the stranger at their door wasn't human and invited them in regardless.

He wanted something. A bargain was made.

The residents of the nursing home began to die. This was not unexpected. It was a nursing home, after all. However, my mother was watching for more signs—as my father had warned her to do—and she found them. A resident complained about hearing a bird hitting the window, and so she went to check and found that it had not hit the window after all. It had been sitting peacefully on the windowsill when the open window fell down in its frame and crushed it. Fortunately, the occupant of the room was elsewhere at the time, and my mother could remove its broken body without alarming anyone. The next day, however, the resident was gone. Died in his sleep, the staff told her when she asked.

A month passed. Things felt off around town. Small things. Little accidents, a fall that twisted an ankle or a shelf in a store collapsing and destroying everything that was on it. People were uneasy and could not explain why. Some would cry for no reason and be bewildered for days at their outburst.

We know when an ancient thing is nearby. Somehow we know, even if we cannot admit it to ourselves.

The next time it was a cat. It got inside and then expired on the end of the bed in a resident's room. She woke that morning to find a dead cat on her legs and was inconsolable for the better part of the day. It was a stray, the staff told my mother. Probably already dying when it found a way to crawl inside and was looking for a warm place to lie down one last time. They pitied it. And they pitied the elderly woman when she died the next night as well.

Another month and another death, forewarned by the demise of a small animal close by. My mother spent as much time as she could at the nursing home, watching to see if anyone was acting suspiciously. She was named "volunteer of the month," but she said that she just threw the certificate on her desk when she got home and then lost it the next time she cleaned her bedroom. The only thing that mattered to her was figuring out who was marking the residents for death and how they were accomplishing it.

It was clear what was happening. Someone had made a deal with the ancient, and the price was paid with lives. The nursing home was an easy target because, well, people die there. Losing a resident every month? At one of the few nursing homes that served all the surrounding towns? Hardly remarkable. The only reason my mother noticed was because she was looking.

The deaths all occurred on the same day of the month, so two days before, she had a friend drop her off at the nursing home so her car wouldn't be in the parking lot. After she finished playing board games with the residents, she said goodbye to the staff, but instead of leaving, she hid in the closet of an unused room. She waited until the home shut down for the evening, and then, with only the night staff present, she lurked by the door and watched. Whenever she heard footsteps in the hallway, she peeked out through the cracked door to see who it was. For the most part, it was staff. Then, around two a.m., it wasn't.

It was one of the residents. A man whose son had been one of her teachers in middle school. At first she was going to dismiss him as just an old man wandering the halls at night, but then he crouched beside a closed door not far from where she knelt. There was a scratching sound, like wood on wood, and then he stood and walked away. In his hand was the antler of a young deer. At the bottom of the doorframe was a tiny mark, almost indistinguishable in the darkness.

My mother scratched it out with her house key before she slipped out a back door and called a friend to pick her up nearby. It didn't matter. The signal had been given, and the next morning the staff found that a rat had slipped into the resident's room, gotten tangled in the cord for the blinds, and hanged itself. And the following night, the resident also died.

My mother was a lot more impulsive when she was younger. Furious, she confronted the old man. Told him that she knew he'd made a bargain with an ancient being, and if he didn't tell her how to reverse it, she would go to the sheriff. He swore that he'd done no such thing, and my mother stormed off. A few hours later, once she was home, she got a call from the volunteer coordinator. They didn't want her to come back. One of the residents had complained that she was in the habit of using "foul language," and they expected better behavior out of their volunteers.

My mother didn't swear at the nursing home, but she sure used plenty of profanity after that call ended, she said. And that was what convinced her to resolve the situation herself—if the nursing home would so easily turn against her on one complaint, then what hope did she have of convincing the sheriff?

At the time, she only knew the Old Sheriff as the person

who gave her speeding tickets while scolding her about making good decisions and not doing things she'd regret when she was older. This felt like one of those things he'd lecture her about.

So she turned to my father for help—by then she knew to ask him in the hallways at school rather than calling the campground. He didn't want to get involved, not at first. My mother could be quite persuasive, however. She waited until the hallway had cleared out a bit and then slammed him into the lockers and threatened to smash the windshield of his car. And she did, when he still refused. That's when he gave in. He figured if she was determined enough to take a baseball bat to his car while it was in the school parking lot, then maybe she was a match for an ancient being.

He told her what to do.

That night my mother snuck out of her house. She went to a nearby farm and stole one of their chickens out of the coop. She had to run with it clutched under one arm, her hand clamped around its beak to stop it from screeching. The owners were slow to react to the commotion. She was in her car and fleeing by the time they got to the yard to confront the intruder. Then she drove to one of the empty fields that border the nursing home, killed the chicken, and removed its heart. She only had a pair of scissors, and they weren't strong enough to cut bone, so she had to snap the rib cage open with her bare hands, and by then she was covered in blood up to her wrists and figured it was just as well to pull the heart out with her fingers.

That's when the ancient being arrived. Some are evil. Most of them are neutral, indifferent fragments of gods who pay little attention to the affairs of humans. Some, like the saints, are benevolent. Some swing between the two extremes, helping one person, harming another. This was one of the evil ones. A passive evil, however, one that was fueled by human initiative and merely reacted to our world instead of trying to shape it.

My mother never turned around. She only felt its presence behind her, a weight, a smell she was never able to place. She felt its malice—but it was restrained. It was there not just because she'd called, but also because it was curious.

She asked why it was here. The ancient being laughed, and it sounded like branches breaking under the weight of winter ice. It'd been invited in, it said. It would not leave this town, and the misfortune would only deepen so long as it was here. Not just the nursing home, but the entire town would suffer from the pall it cast over every inhabitant. It sounded delighted at the prospect of the misery to come.

My mother asked what it would take to satisfy it. Not banish—that's a dangerous question. She sought appeasement. The ancient considered and then, still amused, told her what it wanted her to do. She would deliver the life of the middle school teacher before the night was over, or her own would be forfeit and it would stay. Killing the son of the man who had made the deal would be a delicious enough betrayal to sate its desire for misery, and it would move on to find another town foolish enough to let it in.

The sins of our parents indeed.

Perhaps the ancient hoped that my mother would fail, given such a short time frame. It misjudged her determination.

My mother said she wasn't even sure why she was doing any of this. At some point, while she was driving her car with her hands sticky with drying chicken blood, she realized how insane all of it was. But the terms of the agreement had been given, and there was no sense of what was fair or right; there was only the memory of that being's overwhelming malice, suffocating her with its weight, and the desperation that comes with being marked for death. It was like she'd thrown herself down a cliff, and she couldn't stop falling until she hit the bottom.

She drove to the teacher's house and broke in through a window. She had no plan. She was acting on impulse and adrenaline. She picked up a lamp on her way to the bedroom, and when the man came stumbling out, she smashed it on his head and he dropped. Then she tied him up with some rope she found in the garage and loaded him—and a bunch of other supplies from the garage—into the back of her car.

She took him to the bridge. The ancient had been specific in how it wanted its offering presented. And the teacher, conscious now, begged her to spare his life as she hoisted him up by his ankles from the bridge's beams, and then he could only scream as she drove nails into his eyes and cut out his tongue.

The ancient came to claim what was left of him after that. My mother didn't see any of it. She was off to the side of the road, vomiting. She was not raised with violence, as I was. She made it her own.

Perhaps this explains a little of why I am . . . as some have said . . . a borderline psychopath.

Yes, it is very uncomfortable to write that word out.

They found the teacher's body the next day and cut it down from the bridge. The skin around his neck was blackened in places and flaked like ash to reveal cooked meat underneath. It almost looked like the mark of hands, like something had wrapped its fingers around his throat.

If you're thinking—what about the broken window from my mother's hurried kidnapping? Surely there was an investigation. How did she not get caught by the police? Well . . . while my mother's prints were all over the house, the police didn't have them on record to match them to. There were also no connections between my mother and her former teacher. She hadn't interacted with him since middle school, after all. A seemingly random break-in and ritualistic murder committed by someone with no record whatsoever is quite hard to track down. Honestly, she might have gotten away with it if not for the stolen chicken. She hadn't quite been quick enough getting back to her car, and the owners had reported her license plate to the police. A stolen chicken is enough to connect someone to a bizarre death around here, especially when the events occur on the same night.

My mother had a reputation for being a troublemaker, but murder? The police were astonished and stalled on arresting her, and then my father got word of it, because the police gossip with my family, and he went to the station. He lied about being there on behalf of his father and told them it was campground business. Someone had made a deal with an ancient being, and my mother had elected to deal with it personally, in order to convince his family that she was capable. They were dating, you see, but of course his father didn't approve of it, because he didn't approve of anything.

The Old Sheriff had already recognized the signs that an ancient being was lingering in town. He stopped the investigation right there and let it remain unsolved. A handful of deaths at the nursing home and the loss of one person in town is actually a pretty good outcome when dealing with ancient things.

But then my parents had to actually go out on dates for a while to make the lie believable, and that's how they eventually got together.

And the old man who'd struck the bargain? He was dragged screaming through the center of town by his rib cage late one night as the ancient departed. The people living nearby heard his shrieks, and some of them looked and saw a huge figure, indistinguishable in the darkness, dragging one long arm behind it with a single claw hooked through the chest of a writhing man. He left behind a long, thin trail of blood that ended abruptly at the first field at the edge of town.

There is often collateral damage with these creatures. Never forget that. The purity of your intentions or your love will not save you or those around you. The only things that can are your strength and your will to fight.

Or, you know, just not making bargains with ancient creatures to begin with.

Cognitive dissonance is an unpleasant state to be in. It happens when something you believe (we don't make bargains with evil things) is inconsistent with reality (Jessie's hair caught on fire during a banishment ritual). It can be resolved by abandoning the erroneous beliefs ... or by getting everyone around you to *also* believe them, thereby making you *feel* like you're right.

And for Jessie to be innocent, someone else needed to be the villain.

Me.

A rumor was starting in town. They whispered that Kate was losing control of her campground. They blamed me for the Old Sheriff's disappearance. I couldn't just get rid of Jessie without good reason.

If I was to do anything about Jessie, I needed to be very certain of what I was dealing with. She needed to have a proverbial knife to my neck that I could point to and say *See? See how right I am?* Only then would they look the other way like they do for all my campers, and then ...

I'd kill her.

PART 2

Fall

In October, beautiful foliage creates a scenic environment to camp in. Temperatures can drop below freezing at night, so pack an appropriately rated sleeping bag and extra blankets. As Halloween approaches, be extra vigilant of our inhuman inhabitants. Make sure to pack s'more fixings for the kids.

A New Sheriff in Town

I hadn't thought much of it when the New Sheriff had first begun running for the sheriff's office. He was never going to win. The Old Sheriff was respected and had too much experience dealing with the spillover from my campground. However, because he had been the *only* person to try running in the last couple of decades, the Old Sheriff had made him a deputy. He'd figured he could probably use a successor, given the danger of the job. He'd been right. And now the Old Sheriff was gone, and one special election later we had a New Sheriff in town.

And he didn't like me. At all.

Sometimes I wonder if I shoved his face in his lunch during grade school. Seems like something I would have done.

About a week after he was formally elected, just as the leaves were beginning to turn, the New Sheriff finally deigned to show up at the campground. There was no particular reason other than he felt obligated to introduce himself, again, but this time as the sheriff and not the sheriff's deputy. I was in the dining room, in the middle of dinner, when his truck rolled into my driveway. I hastily went out to greet him. The only reasons I could think of for him to show up this late into the evening were all bad ones.

"Is everything okay in town?" I hollered at him from the front porch as he got out of the truck.

I hadn't gotten news about anything bad happening on the campground, after all. He slammed the car door, hard, and I winced at the noise.

"Oh everything is just *fine*," he snapped. "Couldn't be better, what with the Old Sheriff being dead and all."

"He might not be dead," I replied quietly.

I had to keep a cool head. The Old Sheriff had always said I needed to be able to get along with his successor. It was critical to have a good working relationship, for my campground and for the town. I took a deep, slow breath and tried out a friendly smile.

"Good as dead, because we both know you're not going to do a damn thing to get him out of that house."

To hell with good relationships.

"Why don't you go, then?" I snapped. "I'm sure your little gun will work just fine against whatever that thing is that can *tear a person in half.*"

His jaw tightened, flexed, and then released.

"I want to review our procedures for the campground," he said.

"It's almost sunset!"

"The Old Sheriff said you can have guests enter and exit through the front door without the little girl doing anything, right?"

"Well yeah, but—"

He strode up the path and brushed past me, inviting himself in. I noticed then that he carried a folder under one arm.

"Oh goody," I said, reluctantly following him in. "Paperwork."

I quickly realized that the New Sheriff wasn't reviewing the paperwork to "establish expectations," as he claimed. He was doing it to piss me off. That was the only plausible reason for why he'd shown up this late and insisted on reading every document line by line. Minutia about how we need to contact the police department if an injury requires transport but not if it's treatable on-site, *unless* an inhuman creature is involved, etc., etc. On and on. I was surprised to find out that some of these policies even existed. The Old Sheriff never brought them up with me.

"Does this really matter?" I finally sighed. "Look, I have most of a business degree, I like documentation as much as the next business bro, but this is ridiculous. We can just figure this stuff out like we always have, all right? Or maybe we can just have this meeting tomorrow."

Or never. My phone buzzed on the table between us. I politely ignored it. I'd given up on getting along with the New Sheriff in my heart, but I was at least trying to maintain appearances.

"Some of us don't have the benefit of extended training," the New Sheriff said with just a faint hint of disdain. "It's not like I grew up following mommy and daddy around the campground."

I dug my nails into my arms underneath the table. He knew what happened to them. The whole damn town knew. And he'd waltzed into my house and threw *that* in my face. I could take him, I thought. He was bigger but I was meaner, and I could tackle him from across the table and start hitting him in the face and not stop—

"I didn't get to pick when I took over the campground," I said, struggling to form each word through my anger. "I *wasn't ready*, and I actually have to deal with those things every single day, unlike you—"

My phone was still vibrating. I snatched it from the table, eager for a distraction. Manners be damned, the phone was the only thing keeping the New Sheriff's face intact at that moment.

"Have you talked to Sorcha yet?" the New Sheriff asked.

The Old Sheriff's wife. She kept to herself, and the town knew better than to go hunting for gossip about her.

"No. Have you?"

"Briefly. She's very calm about the whole situation. I don't think she's upset. It's more like she's . . . waiting. What do you know about her?"

"No more than anyone else." I wasn't paying close attention to the conversation. The phone was buzzing in my hand.

"All I know is that she showed up shortly after his first wife died, and they got married soon after."

"Weren't you invited to the wedding?"

"Yeah, it was small; no one from her family was there—"

Three missed calls. All from April. I swore and unlocked my phone, hastily calling her back. Behind me, the New Sheriff was saying something, but I was no longer listening. I walked down the hallway to get away from him as April picked up.

"I need help," she said breathlessly. "I'm being followed."

I went straight to my bedroom to get the shotgun.

When I came back out, the New Sheriff was standing in the living room, about to say something, but the words stuck in his throat as soon as he saw the gun. He went very still, his eyes wide, no doubt wondering if I hated paperwork just enough to shoot at him.

I breezed past him, heading for the garage, focusing on April's voice. She was telling me that someone had come to her house and was calling her name, but they refused to stand where she could see them in the porch light. Then she'd started to feel . . . strange . . . and she panicked and fled the house through a back window.

"Hey, Sheriff," I said, taking the phone away from my ear for a half second. "Get the fuck out of my house."

He looked livid, but at least he had the decency to do what I asked. I waited just long enough to lock the door behind him, and then I was in the garage, starting the engine on my four-wheeler, and I floored it out of there. The little girl watched me leave from the corner of the house, tears streaming down her cheeks.

April's house was near the edge of the campground in an area where I didn't put campers because it was too far for most people to walk. It was a small house, meant to help out family members who were working on the campground by giving them a rent-free place to live. Unfortunately, April was panicking and had gone farther into the campground rather than away from it and toward the road. The vanishing house, she'd said. She was scared it was waiting for her and would take her like it took the Old Sheriff. But if she could make it to my house, then she'd be safe from everything.

People don't make logical decisions when they're scared. The imagined fear in your head can feel far worse than the very real danger right in front of you.

I drove fast, bouncing along the dirt road. I could barely see anything past the beam of the headlights. Then a figure emerged from the darkness, running toward me in the stumbling gait of someone worn almost to the point of collapse. Her breath came out in puffs of vapor in the cold night air. I slowed but didn't stop, not until I swerved around April, and then I slammed on the brakes, putting the four-wheeler and myself between her and whatever was pursuing her. I snapped the shotgun up and aimed down the road.

"Flashlight," I said tersely. "On my belt. Shine it back there."

April at least had the presence of mind to follow orders.

THE MAN WITH NO SHADOW

She snatched the flashlight and fumbled for a moment before finally finding the button. A beam swept back and forth across the grass and the trees.

"There!" I snapped. "Back to the left!"

The figure slowed to a stop as the light fell upon him. I slid off the four-wheeler and began to advance, holding the shotgun ready. Could just be one of my campers. Wouldn't be the first time we got someone creepy on-site. The New Sheriff didn't like me, but I felt he'd be willing to throw someone in jail for a few nights for me. Might even be nice enough to overlook it if they came in with a black eye or two.

"Stay in the light," I ordered. "What were you doing at my cousin's house?"

"Oh, I think you know," he replied smoothly.

> **RULE #10:** Be wary of a friendly man who may approach you in shaded areas. Try to convince him to move into the sunlight. If he casts a shadow, you can assume it's another camper and proceed accordingly. Otherwise, end the conversation immediately and leave as quickly as you can.

I froze. He'd been talking to her, April said. Trying to have a *conversation*. I glanced down at his legs, trying to see past them, trying to see if there was a shadow falling directly behind him.

He took a step backward, his head snapping up and staring at some distant point behind me. His smug expression vanished, replaced by a tight alarm.

Then the flashlight went out.

"April?!" I called, not daring to lower the shotgun.

I listened intently, because my night vision was gone and I couldn't see *anything*. I listened for the sound of him running at me, ready to shoot, but I couldn't hear anything over April's panicked whisper saying that the light wasn't working, none of the lights were working—

And the stars were dimming, the distant glow of April's porch lights was gone, and the darkness was consuming even the shadows.

I dropped to the ground, placing the shotgun on the road. I squeezed my eyes shut and covered my face with both hands for good measure. I yelled at April to close her eyes.

The Thing in the Dark had left its lair.

I felt its presence now, rolling toward us like the edge of a storm. The trees groaned and creaked underneath the pressure, shuddering in the still air. I felt it against my back, pressing me into the dirt and fallen leaves, flattening my lungs and squeezing the breath from them. And I heard April, struggling to yell, calling my name in desperation. Blind, fearful desperation, because something was stalking her, she'd been hunted, and now there was *this*.

Like I said, people do stupid things when they're panicking.

She looked at it. She kept her eyes open, because she was scared that the Man with No Shadow was still coming for her, and I wasn't able to stop her. I wasn't right there next to her to grab her and hold her down, face into the dirt, until it had passed us by. She was mere feet away but alone, so very alone and so afraid.

Wind swirled around me like an anguished cry, high, keening, and small pieces of wood and leaves cut across my arms and the back of my neck. A stone struck my ankle. I cowered, trying to press myself into the dirt, covering my head with my arms. I heard April's scream—the roar of the wind swallowed it up—and then it was gone. Debris showered onto my back, falling from the sky as the creature's presence abruptly vanished.

I waited until I heard crickets chirping again. Only then did I open my eyes. Behind me shone the headlights of the four-wheeler. Beside it lay a flashlight, the beam pointing off into the woods.

April was gone.

My Brother Is Not My Brother

There were always things that had to be done on the campground. Even more so in October, as we had to prepare for Halloween. The campground was extra busy around the holiday, on account of the events we put on—hay-wagon rides, pumpkin carving, etc.—and while that might seem dangerous, our challenges with the inhuman on Halloween were more about *containment*.

The rules of how the world functions shift on Halloween. People disguise themselves as monsters. Monsters disguise themselves as humans. And boundaries grow weak as all the world becomes old land.

The whole town takes precautions for Halloween to keep the monsters out. My campground has to work to keep them *in*.

At least it was better than sitting in my empty house, alone with my thoughts and the memory of April screaming in terror as the Thing in the Dark swallowed her up. I told myself that I hadn't been that close to her, that she'd moved into the house on the campground only a few years ago, and that was why I felt strangely numb about it all.

I asked Tyler to handle talking to her family, because he was closer to them than I was, and he was just better at these things. Not because I didn't want to admit I'd failed to keep her safe. Just like the Old Sheriff. I was getting so tired of losing good people.

There was one additional problem I had to deal with this year. I needed someone trustworthy to watch over Jessie, and it couldn't be Bryan anymore. I guess a person can only take being peed on by a dog so many times before they storm into their manager's office and demand a change in working environment. Bryan claims they were "just happy to see her," and while I don't believe that was true, it was more hassle than I was willing to deal with. Not when I had other options.

My older brother Jeff was the obvious choice. He'd been pestering me a bit lately about being given more responsibility on the campground. He'd spent too long cooped up inside, working long hours as a paralegal at a high-powered law firm, and he wanted to be out in the trees. But he also wanted to do important things. He was ready to deal with the inhuman creatures, he said.

But I had most of a business degree, and that meant I believed in doing things the right way. It was time for some peer feedback before making a big decision like that.

I went to Bryan, as the person who had previously been monitoring Jessie. I found him out in the field, filling in a ditch that had only been a pothole until someone with a poor understanding of traction got their car stuck.

"So what do you think about Jeff being tasked with monitoring a potential inhuman issue?" I asked.

"Jeff?" Bryan replied. "Who the fuck is Jeff?"

And like that, something in my mind snapped into clarity, and the story it had been inventing to fill in the gaps crumbled. The person I'd been talking to for months was not who I believed he was.

Let me make this absolutely clear. I do not have an older brother. I'm the elder, and I have only one brother and his name is Tyler. He's two years younger than me.

I immediately called for an emergency staff meeting. I try to not hold many emergency staff meetings. Reserving them for actual crises ensures that everyone attends. For lesser matters I utilize the whiteboard in the staff break room. I did the trendy thing and bought whiteboard paint and painted an entire wall. It's popular for leaving notes like *I brought in cupcakes, they have pink frosting, don't eat the ones with green frosting I don't know* what *left them* or *the Lady with Extra Eyes says she's out of chamomile*, or *can anyone cover my shift this Friday???* Sometimes there are pictures or a game of hangman. I reserve the upper right corner for my announcements, and that's how I convey nonurgent information to my staff. That way, when I call an impromptu meeting, they know it's something important.

Then I called up Tyler and asked him to drive the hour to the campground and to pick up the family tree from Great-Aunt Lorna on his way in. He complained a bit about not just being able to take off like that, but I pulled out my big-sister voice and he reluctantly agreed.

The employee lodge is a barnlike structure with a corrugated steel roof and thin metal walls. There's the break room with a fridge, sink, stove, and countertop space. A couple of general-purpose rooms, including two at the entrance that we open up during our larger events for volunteer usage, and the meeting room.

The cupcakes with the green frosting were on the conference table when I entered. Subtle. Real subtle. I took them outside and left them on the ground. Hopefully, whatever left them would get bored and take them back. My staff trickled in, nervous at there being an emergency meeting and disgruntled at being interrupted in their Halloween preparations. The timing of this was less than ideal. Everyone was already on edge from it being October.

And this year, I was losing the most useful staff member I currently had, because they might not actually be human.

"Everyone knows my elder brother," I said. "He got back from hiking the Appalachian Trail and started working on the campground in August, right?"

The words flowed from my mouth so easily that for a moment I forgot why I was having this meeting. Everything was fine. There was no emergency. Then I glanced down at the framed picture sitting on the table before me, and the illusion my brain was cooking up quickly fell apart once more. I looked up to see my staff all staring back at me, smiling happily and nodding. Of course they knew him as Steven, who spent the past year by the ocean finishing his novel, or James, who had come back from California where he was a firefighter, or whatever else their minds were plugging the gaps with.

If you've found all these different stories about my older brother confusing, you can imagine how I felt.

I held up the picture.

"See this?" I told them. "Since this is old land, we take our family history very seriously. This is our family tree. I borrowed it from my great-aunt Lorna—the one that plays piano for church on Sunday. You know her, right?"

Vague nodding from the staff. They seemed confused as to where I was going with this. I pointed to the bottom of the left-hand side of the family tree.

"Does anyone notice anything strange about the last entry?" I asked.

No Ian. Or Jeff. No Steven or James or Eric. No elder brother at all.

"I only have one brother," I continued. "Tyler. He's sitting right there, and he's younger than me. I'm not sure what this 'older brother' is, but he's not my brother."

They all sat in stunned silence while I told them that I didn't have answers but that I was going to work at finding them. While this was certainly unsettling to hear—that the boss doesn't know what's going on—I believe in being honest with my staff. In the meantime, I wanted them to act like nothing was wrong but to take extra caution around this interloper. Don't go anywhere with him alone. Work in pairs. This was the standard procedure for October anyway, but it especially needed repeating now. And I told them all to get out their cell phones and set a reminder for every fifteen minutes that I only have one brother, a younger one. If we couldn't trust our brains to not lie to us, then we'd use technology to keep us straight. And I got out my phone as well, and we all sat there quietly for a few minutes while people tapped on their screens.

Then I asked Uncle Tobias to come with me. We were going to go on a visit.

We took one of the four-wheelers down through the camp road to the eastern edge. I haven't done much development to the eastern side of my land. It is still thick forest that drops into a depression along the southern side. It floods every year, and the groups that camp in this area have developed a multitude of ingenious methods for dealing with the mud. I didn't build this area out because I didn't have to—these campers roll in, unload, and do all the construction themselves. It's frankly impressive.

The lack of human structures also means that it's easy to hide things among the trees. The forest crowds in around things that don't want to be found. I shut my vehicle down and took my grocery bag and told Uncle Tobias to wait for me at the road. To come find me if I wasn't back in two hours. Then I started off into the woods, hoping that the person I was looking for was in the mood to receive visitors.

The Lady with Extra Eyes has been around for as long as the land has been old. She was regarded as "the witch in the woods" by the earliest generations of my family and shunned appropriately. That didn't last long. As the land grew wilder and more dangerous, my ancestors realized they needed all the help they could get—even if it was from something inhuman. Unfortunately, a lot of what the previous generations knew of her was lost when the relationship soured. My grandfather had been a cruel man, and she'd vanished for years, refusing to associate with him. He'd despised her in turn. She had reappeared once Grandpa died, and I have a lot of childhood memories of heading into the woods to play in the little yard around her house.

Mostly she just lets people talk and drink her tea. She recently got my employee Lewis through a nasty divorce. She didn't fix their relationship—honestly, I don't think anyone can; he's kind of a jerk, and I don't blame his wife for leaving—but he at least seems grudgingly at peace with it. He's still a jerk. He's the person I send with the tractor to pull people's vehicles out of ditches when I feel a camper needs to be terrorized about how traffic is supposed to work on the campground. One. Way. Roads.

Today, I was in luck. The lady was receiving visitors. I found her cottage shortly after entering the deep woods. It's small. Just a single room with stone walls and a thatch roof. Smoke curled up from the chimney. The door creaked open at my touch. Inside, the woman was busy with a teakettle hanging over the stove.

"I brought you chamomile," I said, holding up the grocery bag.

"Lovely, lovely. Put it on the shelf."

The floor of her cabin is packed dirt. The interior is merely a round dining table and another rectangular one against the wall for food preparation. I'm not sure where she sleeps. I'm not sure if she sleeps.

The lady herself is rather plain, appearing in her early thirties with long dark-brown hair that is almost black, like the bark of a tree just after sundown. Her eyes are a shade lighter. She has a lot of them. They cover her forehead and her cheeks. The trick to holding a conversation with her is to pick a pair and stick with it.

She brought the hot water over along with two cups and threw some leaves into each before filling them with water. Then she settled herself in across from me, and we waited for the tea to cool enough to drink. I told her about my brother who wasn't my brother, and she listened.

"How long has this been going on?" she asked quietly.

"Since August. It felt like he'd been around my whole life, though—like my mind was making things up to explain his presence and why I trusted him. And examining the memories for an instant was all it took for it all to fall apart."

"Human minds are rather gullible," she murmured. "You convince yourselves of things that aren't true so easily. But I can't get rid of him for you, if that's what you're here hoping for."

It was. It would be rude to say so, however, and I remained silent.

"There's more on your mind than just this Not-Brother," she continued. "You've lost people. You're trying to ignore your grief. But who are you angry with?"

"I'm not angry."

She waited, and under the scrutiny of all those eyes, I felt compelled to talk, if only to break the silence.

"I'm angry with those campers—they read the rules—"

"An easy target to be angry at."

I slammed the teacup down and stalked away from the table. I couldn't stand her staring at me, and that sat uneasily at the back of my mind, for her eyes had never bothered me before.

"I'm angry at April—she panicked—she would *still be here* if she'd just trusted me—"

"The anger hurts less than the grief, doesn't it?"

Coming here had been a mistake. But it was like the dam inside me had started to crack, and if I didn't bleed off the pressure, I'd collapse entirely. I'd thought that if I kept myself busy, I wouldn't have to think about anything, and I could push past my losses. But the Lady with Extra Eyes had nothing but time, and she was waiting for me to fill the silence.

"I'm angry the Old Sheriff went back in there—no—I'm angry that *I* didn't go with him—and..."

I took a deep breath.

"I'm angry that my mother isn't here to tell me what she knew about that house. And that I have to do all this alone."

I stood there for what felt like a very long time, my back to her and my hands balled into fists. Finally, the lady came over, and she touched me on the shoulder. I turned around and found that she was holding a candle out, balanced on her palm. The flame stood perfectly straight on the wick, not even moving from our breath.

"Take this," she said. "When it burns out, you'll know that the Old Sheriff is dead."

I took it with shaking hands. He was alive. The Old Sheriff was alive. I felt the weight of my guilt when I stared at the flame, pressing on my shoulders, and I heard the rain and saw that darkness bubbling out of the house and the sheriff's outstretched hands, shoving the woman to safety in a last, futile gesture.

He shouldn't have gone back in. One would have been enough.

Or perhaps I shouldn't have been so frightened; perhaps I should have stepped up on that porch, been closer, had better footing and been able to wrench her free before it was too late, and then his sacrifice wouldn't have been in vain.

I think it is more likely that I would have been swallowed up by the house as well.

The Lady with Extra Eyes wasn't done, though.

"I've helped your family from time to time," she said, returning to the table and tracing the rim of her teacup with one long finger. She had thin and delicate hands. "I stopped because, well, I think you know why."

"Grandpa," I said.

"Humans can be monsters too. You're just able to choose that for yourselves."

I shifted uncomfortably. I wasn't here to talk philosophy. I was here because I had something impersonating a brother I didn't actually have.

"I can give you some assistance," she sighed. "You will have to deal with the rest of this problem yourself."

She would give me the gift of sight. To see the Not-Brother for what he truly was, and in doing so, no longer believe the illusion he cast.

"You'll need to visit an optometrist to get this back out," she added.

And she took up a miniscule splinter from the table, rolled it between her fingers, and stabbed it into the sclera of my right eye.

I stumbled around her tiny one-room house for a minute or so, clutching at my face and bumping into the tables. I trusted the Lady with Extra Eyes, and so when she'd stepped up close to me, I hadn't thought to react until it was too late. She busied herself with cleaning up the teacups while telling me that the splinter would work if it was in the only eye open.

"One last thing," she said as I stared up at the ceiling, blinking rapidly as my eye filled with tears. "Keep both eyes open until you're out of the woods. There are things out here that aren't safe for a mortal to see clearly."

Now, I'm sure you're desperately curious as to what I could have seen in the forest with that splinter lodged in my eye. However, I have spent so much time and effort trying to convince other people to follow a set of rules that are designed to keep them from suffering a horrific fate, and I wasn't about to do the stupid thing and go ignoring the Lady with Extra Eyes's warning. Uncle Tobias took charge of getting us back so that I could carry the candle.

"Are you sure you want to do this at your house?" he asked

as we trundled through the woods at a sedate five miles per hour. Neither of us wanted the candle to blow out.

"It makes the most sense," I replied.

He was quiet for a moment

"I was the second person in the house that morning," he said softly. "I saw your mother."

"I dreamed about it. I know what happened."

I couldn't keep the annoyance out of my voice. I didn't want to talk about this. It had happened a decade ago. I'd learned to live with it.

"There's a big difference between a nightmare and actually *seeing* your dead mother, Kate."

"We don't know that's what I'll see." I wanted this conversation to be over. "It'll be fine. I'll deal with it, like I do everything else."

He sighed softly and continued driving to my house in silence. My uncle dropped me off on the front porch. I hesitated a moment before walking inside. Then I closed my good eye.

The light from the windows was brighter. There was a gold sheen across every piece of furniture, like it glowed with light from within. I went to the office, and the books on the shelves, the ones my father had collected and the ones passed down through the generations, they sparkled like stars. I cried, but not because of the splinter in my eye. I think I understand a little better what it means to be an old land. It isn't all bad. It isn't all dangerous. Some of it is beautiful, radiant with the life of those who came before us.

I didn't go into the bedroom, the master bedroom that I now claimed as my own, the one my mother died in. I wasn't certain what I would see . . . and I was afraid to know. Perhaps it would glow with the warmth of my family . . .

Or perhaps it wouldn't.

I suppose I'll never know.

I got on the radio and called for my Not-Brother to come by the house. I had more Halloween preparations I wanted him to take over, I said.

He was quick to respond. I waited in a chair, the shotgun loaded and resting over my knees, my good eye closed. I listened as the front door opened and shut behind him, listened to his footsteps as he rounded the corner.

I wish the Lady with Extra Eyes had warned me. As it was, I could only stare for a moment, my voice swallowed up by the cold terror settling in my stomach.

He was empty. His abdomen and chest cavity were open and hollowed out, the skin rolled back and neatly tied on either side of his body like one draws curtains. His sternum was gone, the ribs cracked so that they protruded like fangs. I could see clear through to the smooth muscles at the back of the cavity, to the bulge of his spine. He stared at me and asked what was wrong, why I'd gone so pale all of a sudden.

I stood, raised the gun and pointed it at his chest, and asked him what he was.

He was silent a moment. Then he lunged at me—I fired—and the blast hit him in the center of his mass, because that's where I'd practiced to hit, that's where my dad had taught me, but there was nothing left to destroy. It knocked him down, but he flipped to his feet, barely even stunned, while I desperately tried to reload. Then he sprang forward, his fingers closed on the gun, and he wrenched it from my hands and threw it across the room.

I found myself on the floor. Dazed, unsure of how this had happened, aware of a sharp pain in my knee. Then he was over me, snarling that this campground was rich pickings for him, and if he couldn't replace me, then he'd dispose of me instead.

I felt his nails against my abdomen and wondered what he'd do with my organs once they were removed.

That was when Bryan's dogs came in through the window.

My Not-Brother jerked to his feet as the glass shattered. I caught a glimpse of his face, his lips curled in frustrated rage, and then he turned and ran. The dogs pursued, knocking over furniture as they went, bounding over top of my supine body in one jump.

Bryan stuck his head in through the broken window. Shotguns are all well and good, but it never hurts to have a backup plan.

"I'm, uh, going to make sure they don't . . . eat him . . . in front of anyone," he said.

"Good plan," I said, picking myself up off the floor, my ears still ringing from firing a gun indoors. "Let's not traumatize anyone that's paid a camp fee today."

The dogs pursued my Not-Brother to the edge of the woods. There they stopped, barking ferociously as the creature vanished into the trees, and refused to pursue any farther.

Bryan tried to get them moving again but gave up after a few minutes.

"I don't know, Kate," he sighed. "They might know something we don't. With everything that's happened on the campground lately..."

He cast a significant look at the trees. It didn't need to be said. There were more threats than the Not-Brother in the deep woods, and they were turning their hungry eyes toward us.

And now I had one more threat to worry about.

> **RULE #11:** I only have one brother. He is younger than me, and his name is Tyler. If you meet anyone claiming to be my older brother, inform camp management immediately. He is not my brother.

Trick-or-Treating Hits Different Here

Our preparations for Halloween were rushed. I even had to swallow my pride and ask Tyler to come help, and he did, every day after he was done with his day job, and he stayed late into the evening. I'm sure his wife wasn't particularly happy with me, but I was here to run a campground, not to make friends. It was close, but we got it all done. I couldn't help but be proud of that. Between our defenses and driving the Not-Brother back into the woods, I was so bold as to allow myself to feel a little optimistic.

Then things started to go very wrong. Lewis came to me with an idea to put together a haunted house.

"Think of how much money we'd make," he said, which was certainly tempting.

Then he said the second part of his idea, which was to staff it with our other campground inhabitants, and if a couple of people went missing to sate their hunger, then oh well.

I immediately put him on a less people-oriented job, because apparently being a cashier in the camp store was damaging his perception of humanity.

Then, a day later, I had someone leave a one-star review on Google for my campground because—get this—the solar showers were cold during their visit earlier in the week.

It was late October, and it was overcast. *Solar. Showers.* What did they expect?

Lewis's idea about the haunted house felt a little more appealing after that.

And on the day before Halloween, the New Sheriff dropped by to see if we were all finished up with our preparations. I heard him out in the driveway berating Bryan, who was getting the second box of liquor out of the trunk while I put away the first. Look... I don't drink that much. A lot of that was going to be gifts for staff.

Anyway, Bryan was doing his job by trying to find out the reason for the sheriff's visit instead of just letting him blunder into my house—we've all been a little on edge about that since the Not-Brother incident—and the next thing I heard was the sheriff biting his head off because didn't Bryan know who he was?!

It takes more than that to rattle Bryan. I'm sure he was about to calmly explain that yes, he knew exactly who the sheriff was, and that it is campground policy to find out the reason for his visit prior to allowing him inside my office. His dogs, however, had raised their heads off the front porch and were growling low in their throats, like the rumble of a semitruck's engine right outside my windows. As much fun as it would have been to see the New Sheriff chased off by a pack of gigantic Irish wolfhounds, I figured I should do the responsible thing and defuse the situation.

I stuck my head out the front door and told Bryan to go sweep the hay out of the barn (which is code for GTFO) and then invited the New Sheriff in. He sprawled authoritatively in the chair opposite me and rested his hand on his gun, which I suppose was meant to be intimidating, but I've survived a direct encounter with the Thing in the Dark, and I just don't get intimidated by humans that easily anymore. I coldly asked him what I could do for him.

"There won't be problems this year, right?" he asked.

Referring to Halloween, of course. I'd already discussed my preparations with the local police force, and we had our points of contact established if containment failed at any time.

"There's always problems," I replied, and I wasn't able to keep the bite out of my voice. "But I'm sure all those procedures you documented will solve *everything*."

That was clearly the wrong thing to say, and I paid for it with an overblown lecture about his duty to protect the people and how my campground was a liability and blah blah blah. I tuned it out and fixed a solemn expression on my face, nodding occasionally, and let my mind drift until he seemed to be wrapping it up. Then I reassured him that yes, of course I understood, and we were doing all we could to ensure this year was uneventful.

When he left, I double-checked our preparations myself, cursing him under my breath the entire while. I also found Bryan in the barn, sweeping an already clean cement floor. I guess he's never realized that was a code phrase and has been taking me literally, which means I've been sending him to unnecessarily clean the floors for at least a decade. My bad.

I spent the night before Halloween like I always did—in the family cemetery. It's tucked in a grove of trees close to the house, sheltering it from sight of the campers, encircled by a wooden fence with STAFF ONLY signs. I lit candles and left them on each of the grave mounds and sat there in front of my parents' shared grave.

I keep hoping that someday, when the barriers between worlds are thin, I'll see them. My parents. But no one visited me. I stayed until the distant screams of the little girl signified that the beast had come and gone and it was dawn.

I wish I could say the rest of the day was uneventful. None of my staff were harmed, despite the Dancers deciding that they'd collect half my staff for their Halloween party. I think, after our last interaction, they were trying to fuck with me. They were gathering up everyone they passed, dragging them into the parade, and forcing a torch into their hands. I decided to go take a look in person, just in case my staff needed help.

I didn't make it far. I opened my front door, and someone was there, standing directly on the other side, their form looming out of the darkness at me. I screamed and stumbled backward, regaining my wits enough to grab the edge of the door in an attempt to slam it shut. The visitor put up a hand, and the door stopped short. I backed away, thinking of where my shotgun was stored, and then I saw the cup he clutched in his other hand. The white bone shone in the moonlight.

"Oh," I said. "You."

The Man with the Skull Cup nodded faintly. I let the door swing open again, but he did not enter, nor did I invite him in.

"I need to go," I finally said, as the silence between us grew awkward. "I need to check on my staff."

"They're fine," he said. I heard wry amusement. "Hospitality laws are in effect."

"Ah! So the Dancers *are* fairies," I said.

He shrugged, his gaze sliding away from the doorway.

"Fairies aren't the only things that follow hospitality laws. Even humans practiced them at one point, though that tradition has sadly waned in modern times."

"So they aren't fairies?"

He ignored my question and looked me up and down.

"It's Halloween. Aren't there traditions to be honored?"

I babbled an apology and went back to the kitchen to fetch the rest of my costume. I'm the same thing for Halloween every year. It doesn't take much work, just some black leggings, a black turtleneck, and a printed cardboard box to go over my head that I bought online.

Yes, I dress up as a video game monster.

Look. It's easy and kids love it.

I put the head on and took up a bowl of candy I'd prepared—just in case. I offered it to him, he hovered over it a moment, and then his hand dropped to the side and latched around my wrist instead. He pulled me out onto the porch. I let the candy bowl fall from my hands, protesting in sudden panic that I had work I should be doing. I needed to leave. He laughed and inquired as to whether I was confident that my preparations had been enough and whether I could trust my staff and family to do their jobs.

"I'm never confident," I said. "I live in constant fear that I'm not doing enough."

"See, that's the problem. You never relax. It's Halloween. Let's enjoy it."

He threw his arm around my shoulders, as if we were friends, but his fingers tightened, digging his nails into my muscle until I flinched.

"Let's go trick-or-treating," he said.

His tone indicated this was not a request that could be refused.

At the campground entrance, we paused. As our primary goal on Halloween is to contain the monsters, we reinforce the borders with bundles of all the materials known to ward off the supernatural. This protects the town. Then, since all those malicious entities are trapped here with us, we need to protect ourselves. We reinforce security on the various buildings, and staff only leave in pairs with their own personal protections, specifically, an orange safety vest covered in charms from every culture imaginable. Finally, we have cameras set up around the campground and run surveillance. If anything gets out, we notify the police.

The Man with the Skull Cup eyed the gate as I ran the

flashlight over it, and then he turned to me, his thin lips curling up into a smile.

"Would you," he asked politely, "open the gate?"

I stared at him a long moment.

"You can shut it behind us."

His words were very soft. The barrier was working. He couldn't leave without me allowing him to.

"I'm not obligated to," I replied.

I could stop him right there. Easily. He considered for a moment.

"I will owe you a favor," he said, "at a time of your choosing in the future."

A debt from an inhuman is not something you pass up, no matter the risk.

I silently went to the gate, removed the bundle, and swung it open for him to pass through. Then I replaced the bundle and joined him as he walked off down the road that led toward town.

My plan was to make the trip on foot, and hopefully that would take long enough that he wouldn't have time to cause too much mischief before midnight. Then someone going into town stopped and offered us a ride because she recognized me and clearly didn't recognize who was with me, and of course the Man with the Skull Cup accepted, smiling that soft, smug grin the whole time we were in her back seat.

There are still people in town who haven't read my rules. I don't hide the fact that they exist. I'm not sure what I'm doing wrong here.

The woman dropped us off at the center of town, where

the houses sit side by side for a few blocks. Old houses with wooden shingles and gnarled trees in their yards. This was the only place to trick-or-treat in town. Everywhere else had acres of land sitting between them and the next driveway. Kids ran past us, oblivious to the inhumanity of my companion. Their parents were a little more observant.

Everyone we encountered realized who I was, even with a cardboard box over my head. I've used this costume for years, so it's pretty apparent what's going on when a five-foot-four video game monster shows up on the doorstep with a man carrying a skull cup. Or woman. Or whatever people other than me see him as. His appearance is different for everyone he interacts with.

And the Man with the Skull Cup just solemnly intoned "Trick or treat" as each door opened for us and then stood there, his cup clutched in both hands, until the homeowner handed me the candy, not really sure what else to do. I hadn't brought a bag, so I took off my cardboard head and used that to store the candy in.

Then we reached a house, and after receiving our candy, the Man with the Skull Cup offered the person at the door a drink. I stood a pace behind the man, and I frantically pantomimed to the homeowner to take a sip. They did, their eyes wide and fixed on me the whole time. Then the Man with the Skull Cup walked away, and I followed him, casting nervous glances backward to the person who'd just been poisoned.

That wasn't the only person he offered a drink to. I started to sweat, despite the cold air. Drops of perspiration beaded up on the back of my neck, and I was flushed with anxiety, watching all this unfold.

After about an hour, I began to notice a trend in which houses he offered a drink.

"Are... are you only poisoning the people giving out shitty candy?" I asked.

"Maybe," he replied with a thin smile.

Now, while this may sound amusing, just think back to how I said the people in town haven't all read the rules. I'm sure some of them were hugging their toilets that night. But it wasn't until the last visit that I really ran into trouble. It was getting close to ten p.m., and most of the kids had gone home. The porch lights were starting to go out. The Man with the Skull Cup was walking quickly now, up to the last house on the edge of town. The streets were dark with shadows, as we'd left streetlights far behind.

"I'm sorry, I just ran out of candy," the woman who answered the door said, visibly growing more nervous as she took in who I was and who I was with.

"It is tradition to present all that visit with a gift," the Man with the Skull Cup said cordially, and he held out his cup in one hand and a knife in the other.

I understood what he was asking. I know how these things go. Behind him, I pantomimed to the woman cutting her palm open with the knife while mouthing the word "sacrifice" to her. I saw comprehension dawn in her eyes, and she nervously took the knife from him and put the point to her palm. She seemed surprised at how easily it cut through her skin. His knife is very sharp. Then I mimicked turning her hand over, and she did this and let the blood drip freely into the bowl of his cup. We stood there for a few moments, the woman growing pale, not from the blood loss, but from the sight of it, from the growing pain in her palm as the nerve endings finally realized what was happening.

Then the man thanked her, she snatched her hand back and clutched at her wrist as if she could hold back all sensation, and the man turned to go. I followed. Behind us, I heard the door slam shut and the heavy click of a dead bolt.

"Old blood from what was in the cup before," the Man with the Skull Cup murmured as we walked back to the street. "New blood freely given. I need only one more ingredient to refill my cup."

"Wait, refill? You have to refill it?"

He did, he said. I just hadn't noticed, or at least I hadn't made the connection when I found the bodies. The ones with their throats slit. And his eyes slid sideways toward where I stood beside him, slowly growing cold inside at the realization of what he was saying. The last ingredient.

Blood forcibly taken.

And I made to turn, to run, but he seized my hair and wrenched my head sideways, and I felt—briefly—the line of his knife against my neck—then I twisted and pulled, and I left behind a clump of my hair but I was free and running down the road, the line across my neck burning as it bled freely into my shirt, but it was intact, my artery was intact.

I was heading away from town by necessity. The man stood between me and the safety of the houses. I'd cut across the field, I thought desperately, and circle back toward town.

I'm in shape from all the work I do on the campground, but I'm not a runner. That's a different kind of athleticism. I quickly exhausted my stamina and was reduced to a fast walk, clutching a hand against the stitch in my side. My neck stung where his knife had broken the skin, but the blood flow was slowing. I angled my direction more toward the beckoning lights of the town.

Then I saw, somewhat behind me and to my right, the Man with the Skull Cup. He walked at an even pace, cutting a straight line between me and my destination, so that even if I sprinted, I'd run the risk of being intercepted. Even if I could sprint. So I changed tactics. I'd head back toward the campground. That was a straight line, and if I could reach the gate, I could get my hands on the bundle that guarded it and whatever it was that he feared inside.

Have you heard of persistence hunting? You walk an animal to death. You keep pace with it, so that every time it slows, you're right there, threatening it, spurring it to keep moving, keep going, step after weary step until it finally collapses of exhaustion.

I didn't have my cell phone on me; it had fallen out of my pocket in my struggle to break free of his grip. This is why women need real pockets on our clothing. My pants barely fit my cell phone in the best of circumstances. Worse, it was late enough at night that the road was deserted, and so, without any hope of rescue, I had no choice but to keep going.

And each time I looked back, the Man with the Skull Cup was there.

I collapsed long before I reached the campground. My thoughts were hazy at that point, worn thin by exhaustion and blood loss, and I remember thinking that all this was futile, that I was dealing with creatures far more powerful than me and my time was simply up. That it'd be easier to give in than to keep going for a minute longer.

That resignation broke as soon as I heard the gravel crunch under his approaching feet. I struggled to stand, my legs burning with pain, and I staggered blindly forward, driven only by an instinct to survive, pushed well beyond the limits of my endurance. His hand closed on my hair, right at the roots, and he jerked backward. I stumbled, fell, and then he was straddling my legs, pinning them in place, and he twisted his wrist to force my head back and expose my throat. His body felt cool against my back. Not cold . . . just . . . not as warm as a human should feel.

I clawed at his wrist as he raised the knife. I'm surprised at how clear my thoughts were—that I was going to die—and I wondered if this was how my father had felt as he walked out to meet the beast. Like floating. Like the world didn't exist anymore and it was just myself, alone with the beat of my own heart.

And here I always thought it would be the beast that killed me.

The knifepoint slipped along the line of my throat and there was no pain and I waited for my body to catch up, waited for the hot blood to soak my shirt . . . and then his wrist shifted again, and there was a flash of pain along my jaw.

He dropped the knife and picked up the cup, holding it just below my chin, and now I felt the heat of blood trickling along my neck, saw it dripping into the cup and mixing with the dark liquid already inside.

Then he released me and took the cup away. I pressed a shaking hand against the cut on my jaw and watched blood run down my wrist and soak into the sleeve of my shirt.

It was a long time before I could speak.

"I thought you were going to kill me," I whispered.

"Perhaps I was," he murmured. "Would it have been forcibly taken if you'd known you weren't going to die? Wouldn't you have simply acquiesced, knowing that it was easier to submit than to fight the inevitable?"

"But . . . why me?"

A selfish question, perhaps. But I've grown accustomed to others being the ones who die and me the one who lives.

"It's my gift to you. A reminder of the true dangers of your campground. You've grown complacent. That creature impersonating your brother might have succeeded in its plans if you hadn't gotten *lucky*. Think of how your mother died. I'd prefer you lasted a little while longer yet."

He walked away. I watched him go, dizzy with pain, shaking with exhaustion. When he was no longer within eyeshot, I simply lay down there on the shoulder of the road until my uncle came looking for me and took me back home.

Uncle Tobias had bad news on top of what had already happened to me, he said. They had found a break in the fence.

While not all of my land is fenced, there are still distinct boundaries, and the fence is part of what marks that. A break in the fence isn't just an annoying hole to fix, it's also a symbolic breach of our border, and inhuman things can take advantage of that. The fact it happened on Halloween was even more alarming. While the Man with the Skull Cup had taken a more direct route to being let off the campground, some other creature apparently had decided to be more covert about it.

The question was who had cut the fencing, and after hours of reviewing footage, my uncle had an answer. He showed me the video clip of someone walking along the fence, stopping and snipping out an opening big enough for a human to crawl through. They took the segment they'd cut out with them, leaving the hole behind to . . . weaken the boundaries of the campground, I guess? Because it doesn't take much to release creatures from the campground, especially when that is done by one of my staff.

The camera got a clear picture of their face when they turned around.

Jessie. It was Jessie.

And with her was a tall, lanky man with messy red hair and freckles. He pointed at where to cut the fence and then walked off with her, back into the campground. I didn't recognize him, but I recognized his lack of a shadow and that smug, confident smile he wore.

The Man with No Shadow and Jessie. I felt my chest tighten. This was it. This was the evidence I needed to prove to the town that Jessie was cooperating with an evil thing. Not willingly, but it didn't matter. Just like it hadn't mattered when I'd killed Laura.

And I was going to need the evidence too, because after the Man with the Skull Cup poisoned people, the town was in an outrage. The New Sheriff called for a town meeting. My presence was required.

Small-Town Politics

My family had stood before the town many times, and now it was my turn. It was a lovely day; the white wood siding of the town hall stood in stark contrast against the clear blue sky and the reds and yellows of the trees framing it. Inside, the atmosphere was decidedly less picturesque. The meeting started with the lady who had had to give blood to the Man with the Skull Cup talking about cutting her palm open and how it hurt so much more than the movies made it seem. Then it was a string of people complaining about spending all night puking after drinking from the skull cup. Finally, it was my turn.

My strategy was to avoid talking about the Man with the Skull Cup at all. Instead, I told them what I knew about Jessie—I even put the video of her cutting the fence on the projector—and pointed out the Man with No Shadow's presence.

"Yeah, so?" someone said from the back. "Aren't you supposed to keep us safe from creatures like that?"

His voice sounded familiar.

"And this only shows that Jessie cut the fence," the New

Sheriff said. "The person who *actually* let something out is *you*. Maybe we'd be better off dealing with the monsters ourselves, instead of counting on you."

Fine. I had tried to be diplomatic, like my father. It was time to be like my mother.

"You want to deal with these monsters?" I snapped. "You really think you're ready for it? Why don't we get Uncle Tobias in here to tell you about that ghoul my family dealt with? Or let's talk about how the vanishing house that took the Old Sheriff has been around for *decades*, but my mother was the only one trying to figure out what it was. My family has protected this town for *generations* and what thanks do we get—"

The doors to the town hall creaked open. I stumbled to a halt, the words falling from my mind.

Jessie walked in through the doorway. A hush fell over the room. Her footsteps lilted, one landing more heavily than the other, and it was like listening to a bell toll as each step landed, the dragging foot whispering on the wooden floor like a trailing rope. Her expression was distant, her eyes cast toward the heavens, and her mouth hung slightly agape. I knew, even before I saw what she carried, that this wasn't going to be good. That the Man with No Shadow had made use of his pawn far earlier than I'd anticipated, and whatever he'd done, it was going to be very bad for me, the campground, and everyone in town.

Jessie's arms swung loosely at her sides, and one hand clutched the hair of my uncle Tobias's severed head.

She threw it when she was halfway down the aisle, and it rolled across the floor and came to a stop at my feet. Then she fell face down onto the floor and lost consciousness.

The town hall erupted into pandemonium. There were people screaming, shouting, and Jessie's dad was somewhere in that mess, no doubt defending his daughter from the crowd that was slowly swinging toward anger. I didn't register anything. It was just distant noise, like the static of an old TV screen. I stood there, silent and still, staring down at my uncle's face, which was frozen into an expression of mute surprise. I thought about why now. Why my uncle. I thought on this for a long time, even while the New Sheriff (who for once had nothing to say to me) took me by the arm and led me away and took me back to the campground.

I remembered something else. Jessie's shadow, as I walked past her prone body. How the edges were tattered. Fraying, like an old scrap of cloth. I'm not sure anyone else noticed.

I didn't sleep at all that night. Instead I sat on my sofa staring at the wall as the little girl cried through my window. All I could think about was that I was too late. Always *too late*. Very little felt like it mattered. I was struggling to understand when I was at any given moment. This was shock, I suppose.

The New Sheriff showed up at the campground the next morning with a couple of police officers in tow. They wanted to talk to me. To Aunt Aleda, to my staff, to everyone they could.

THE MAN WITH NO SHADOW

It was an investigation, the New Sheriff said. They were doing their due diligence.

"What the fuck are you bothering to investigate?" I snapped. "We all know what happened. Bryan found Uncle Tobias in the camp office with a gunshot wound in his chest. *Obviously* Jessie shot him and then took his head—because she's been associating with a monster—and because you've been getting in the way of me *doing my job*."

"Isn't your job to keep this sort of thing from happening?" he asked stiffly.

"I can't save people when they insist on not following the campground rules. Whatever. I'm not playing along with your stupid investigation . . . and if you hassle Aunt Aleda while she's *grieving*, I'll kill you."

But he didn't leave.

"The town is out of patience, Kate," he said. "We need proof that you can do this job. Because right now, it looks like you're just sitting back making a profit off the campground, while monsters get out left and right to prey on innocent folks."

(I know the secrets of this town. Few of us are innocent.)

"Look at what happened to your uncle . . ." he continued softly.

"SHUT UP!" I shrieked.

Hatred boiled inside me, and I could no longer contain it. It coursed through my veins like molten iron. How dare he use my uncle's death against me.

I was on my feet, and my fist was in motion before I even

realized what I was doing. The New Sheriff jerked back in surprise, and my swing went past his face, and I staggered and almost fell over, stumbling sideways and finally hitting the wall of my office.

I was probably lucky I missed. The sheriff might not have let that slide. I could have wound up in jail for once. Instead, he tersely told me the town's expectations. No more incidents. Control the monsters.

It was not possible to do as they requested. Winter was coming. *Christmas* was coming. The powers of this world converge in the winter, and ancients walk the land and they go where they will and they do as they want. The long nights hide a multitude of evil.

Besides, I had no intention of following the sheriff's demands. There would be at least one more incident, this one caused by my own hand.

I would repay the Man with No Shadow with a gift of my own.

Jessie was unconscious for three days at the hospital. When she woke up, she was unresponsive. Dr. Henry took her home, and he'd had the audacity to show up at Tyler's doorstep in the city, asking my brother if there was something we could do to help her.

He knew better than to ask me.

I would have told him the truth. There was nothing to be done. She was no more than a puppet for a monster at this point. But he didn't want to hear that; he didn't want to know there was no way out of this. It always fell to my family to make the hard decisions.

So when he finally left to run an errand—he couldn't leave Jessie alone for long—I broke into the house through the back door.

It was just something that needed to be done. No different than putting down a rabbit that had been hit during mowing.

(But I was lying to myself, wasn't I?)

Then I went to the grove, my fingers clutching the hair of the severed head I carried.

The Man with No Shadow came to me, stopping just short of the grove's boundary. I hadn't got a good look at him when I was trying to save April. He looked just like I'd seen on the camera. Lanky, freckled, messy red hair. His appearance was different from when I was a child, but his smile had not changed. A thin half smile, smug, condescending. My heart raced upon seeing it. He dipped his head at me in greeting. He spoke sparsely when dealing with people who knew what he was. At his feet, the sunlight pooled unbroken.

"This is for you," I said, and I threw Jessie's head onto the ground in front of him.

His gaze flickered down to it and then just as quickly returned to stare at me.

"I don't care," he said softly. "I have more. This vengeance was for you, wasn't it? Do you feel better now?"

No. I didn't.

"You got April killed," I spat. "You told those campers to

follow the lights to the vanishing house, where the Old Sheriff never got out. And now you've murdered my uncle. What the hell do you have against my family?"

The clock was ticking. I had to end this conversation soon, before I fell under his control.

"What do I have against *you*," he gently corrected. "I'm going to take everything away from you, Kate."

"*Why?!*"

"I, like the town, would prefer new management."

"Over my dead body," I snapped.

"Seems more like it's over the bodies of the people you love."

His matter-of-fact tone was like being struck in the face.

"At this rate," he murmured, glancing down to the head at his feet again, "you'll turn out worse than your mother. She at least tried to save people from me. Even went so far as to strike a bargain—good thing the town never found out about that, eh?"

Something went cold inside of me.

"What bargain?" I whispered, knowing, but not wanting to hear it confirmed.

"Don't play dumb. You remember it quite well, don't you? The agreement she made to save your friends, all those years ago. Did she not tell you about it?"

I was silent, and he laughed.

"Of course not, she died before she could tell you everything. This is what she promised me. It isn't much dissimilar from the bargain *you* recently made."

He smiled, and my hand twitched, aching to cross the distance between us and punch him right in the mouth.

"Your mother would let me leave the campground three times of my choosing," he said. "Sadly, she died before she could fulfill my third request."

I said nothing more. The exchange had dragged on too long, and this was dangerous now. I walked away. I heard him laughing as I left.

The Man with No Shadow had left the campground twice.

This is a dark thought, but it came to mind unbidden, and I could not put it aside. What if . . . my mother had left the window open deliberately? To deny the man his third request?

And what had he accomplished the first two times?

PART 3

The Holidays

In November and December, camping is discouraged for everyone except people with extensive experience with cold weather. Plan for day hikes instead, to enjoy the snowy scenery. Campground closed around Christmas on account of high level of inhuman activity during the holidays.

Drowning in Christmas Spirit

I spent a lot of time before Thanksgiving holed up in my office, ostensibly trying to figure out a way to counter the bigger creatures of winter. Realistically, I didn't want to talk to anyone. No one accused me directly, but the town knew I was responsible for what had happened to Jessie. I felt their eyes on me every time I went to the grocery store, heard how conversations ended abruptly when I walked past. I wanted to scream at them that it wasn't my fault, that Jessie knew the rules, she knew to be careful who she talked to. And wasn't I hurting too? My uncle, my cousin, the Old Sheriff. Before that, my parents. Haven't I lost more than *any* of them?

It didn't help that the New Sheriff was making a show of "investigating" Jessie's death either. As if he'd actually dare to hold me responsible.

So I tried to stay away from it all.

But nope. I got a phone call from my neighbor, Kyle. He owns quite a bit of land, and over the years I've toyed with the idea of making an offer on it to extend the campground. He's willing to sell the lake and some surrounding acres. But the lake gives me pause. I'm not sure I want to deal with absorbing a lake into old land. I keep thinking of how many rules I'd have to add, and I reconsider. Anyway, he called me up and asked for help containing the Christmas demons that live in it.

They're called shulikun and are from northern Russia. Good luck finding info on them online; I haven't had much success, and the only reason I even know how to spell it is because in my parents' files is a typed handout with brief summaries of all the various Slavic creatures. Shulikun show up around Christmas by breaking out of frozen lakes using their pointy metal hats, and then they ambush Christmas revelers. Mostly they just play pranks. Sometimes they shove people into snowbanks or frozen lakes to freeze to death. They're banished by the celebrations leading up to Lent.

Needless to say, they're not a threat in late November or even early December. They're not much of a threat the rest of the Christmas season either, as we don't get deep snowbanks and people don't walk home, generally. Honestly, they were more of a joke around the town than a real danger.

I thought that perhaps a distraction was warranted, however, as I had spent the last few days in my office alone. My staff had been coming around with bullshit things they needed from me as an excuse to check on how I was doing, and I was suspicious as to who had orchestrated that plan.

I'm sure it was Bryan. He doesn't talk much, but he's damn perceptive.

I gathered some supplies and went over to my neighbor's property. It's becoming old land as well. The family timer got reset at some point through some shady business that caused it to change hands for a few years and then change back.

I took the car over and parked in his driveway. He came out to meet me while I popped the back and started unloading my gear. Thanked me for coming over. Told me that he was sorry about Tobias, and that whole business had him frightened and he wanted to try to contain the shulikun to the lake this year instead of letting them wander all over town. He was nervous. Kept tripping over his words. I wonder if that should have tipped me off, but I attributed it to his lack of experience with nonhuman entities.

The lake is quite large. There's a narrow strip of land leading out to an island off one bank. The landmass in the middle is too symmetrical to be natural, at least by my judgment, and I do wonder when and why my neighbor's family constructed it. It had to have taken a lot of dirt and work, as the pathway is big enough to accommodate a car, and the island could hold probably twenty campers, depending on the size of their tents.

Yes, I think of things in terms of campground usage. It's a habit.

I circled it once, hanging bundles of warding materials in the branches as I went. I don't know what repels shulikun—if they even can be repelled—so I just went with the full assortment of materials known to affect various other creatures from the same region.

I was walking back up the path leading to his house when I was stopped by the sound of something behind me. A noise that shot terror through my blood, freezing my muscles and robbing me of my breath. I stood there in horrified immobility, realizing that it was futile to run. And behind me, the horse walked closer, the thump of its hooves on the packed earth unmistakable.

Then a male voice spoke, and I almost wept with relief, before realizing that while it might not be the dappled gray horse, it was still something dangerous. I turned slowly, weighing what I would say in reply, knowing that my fate hinged on my response.

"It's . . . a little early, isn't it?" I asked weakly. "I mean, it's still November."

I suppose I could have done better.

Five shulikun were on the trail before me. Now, when I said that they prank revelers, perhaps you were imagining something a little more . . . benign. Mischievous gnomes? Christmas elves? Certainly not a warrior in chain mail with a pointed iron cap mounted on a warhorse, right?

He stared down at me, stone-faced, his lips and the corners of his eyes tinted with the blue of frostbite, and his gloved hand rested on the pommel of his sword. His four companions were arrayed similarly, straight-backed in their saddles, their stares cold and unyielding.

The shulikun don't just prank revelers. They are also the enforcers of the Christmas spirit and will drag anyone unfit for the season to a watery grave.

I sure as hell wasn't in the Christmas spirit yet. My uncle had just died, the town was questioning my competency, and we weren't even past Thanksgiving. How could I possibly be excited for Christmas?

I offered all this up as my excuse, and when I was finished, the lead shulikun kicked his horse forward and rounded past me, and as I turned to follow its course, the warrior reached down, grabbed hold of the back of my jacket, and spurred his horse into a run.

I was yanked off my feet, and then I was being dragged, half my body on the ground as the warrior leaned over in his saddle, allowing enough slack so that I didn't tumble under the hooves of his horse. I kicked, trying to get my feet beneath me—for all the good that would have done with a horse in full gallop—trying to get away from the stones and debris that tore at my jeans and bruised my flesh. I twisted in my jacket, clawing at the zipper, choking on the pressure just under my chin.

And then we hit the lake. Their momentum slowed some, the water supported my body, and I could breathe, but the warrior did not stop dragging me farther out, toward the deeper parts of the lake. I yanked savagely at the zipper of my jacket, and the damn thing got stuck.

"This isn't fair!" I shrieked. "Just because the stores are selling decorations already doesn't mean it's Christmastime!"

The warrior glanced down long enough to give me a disgusted look.

"You hold no joy in your heart," he rasped. "You anticipate the holiday with dread."

Make a movie out of this, Hallmark. Being carried away to

drown by a warrior on horseback for not eagerly awaiting the holiday season is certainly more motivating than watching a jaded CEO move to a small town where she falls in love with Christmas and her hunky neighbor.

The water was to the horse's chest. I began to take deep breaths of air, preparing myself to be pulled under. Maybe I could still break free. Maybe I could swim to the surface. The lake churned around me as the four other shulikun surrounded us, and then they plunged forward in one leap and I was yanked down, sharply, and there was nothing but water around me.

The cold of it almost shocked the air from my lungs. I held my breath through sheer force of will and continued to tug at the zipper, frantically, until it came loose, and I tore my jacket open and for one brief, exultant moment, I was free.

A hand closed over my throat instead. It forced me farther into the depths, and I could only claw helplessly at those fingers, my gaze locked on the receding sunlight above me. All I could think of was how unfair this was. My uncle had died. April was gone. What reason did I—or any of my family—have to be merry?

Finally, as my body strained to inhale, the warrior let go. I immediately started swimming up, toward the distant ball of sunlight that marked the surface. In my heart, I knew it was futile. He wouldn't have released me if I'd had any hope of survival. Still, I had no intention of dying quietly, and I kicked and pulled myself through the water, and then it was too late—I remember red spots dancing in my vision and then agony and then nothing.

I woke with one abrupt convulsion, like my entire body was crawling inside itself, and then I was shoved over onto my side as I began to vomit uncontrollably. I brought up everything in my stomach and then some, coughing and retching out dirty lake water until I was spitting blood. I dimly felt comforting hands on my back and voices telling me it was okay, I was going to be okay. And finally it was, and I could breathe again.

I began to shiver violently, soaked through. I looked around me and found that I was flanked on either side. To my left was Bryan. To my right was the Man with the Skull Cup.

I stared at him incredulously.

"Your aunt gave me permission to leave the campground to accompany Bryan on a small errand," he said tonelessly to my unasked question.

I turned to look at Bryan.

"He came and found me and said you were in danger," he explained quickly. "And that he'd be needed to save you. He led me here and waded out into the water and pulled you out. I thought you were dead. But he forced the contents of his cup down your throat, and that's when you started coughing."

I took a couple of deep breaths. I had done some dangerous things around here, but I honestly think this might have been the closest I'd come to actually dying. At least at that time.

"After what happened at Halloween," I said in a low voice, "what on earth made you think he can be trusted?"

Perhaps that was a little unfair. But I didn't want people getting hurt over me.

"I, uh, figured I could sic my dogs on him if he didn't come back to the campground."

Okay, fair, that would probably work. I looked back to the Man with the Skull Cup, and he didn't say a damn thing about that.

"Your cup is empty," I said uneasily, eyeing it. There were only a few drops left inside. Old blood from what was there before. My blood.

"So it is."

He considered it a moment before his hand shot out and seized Bryan's wrist. Bryan shrieked, half in fear and half in outrage; then the Man with the Skull Cup sliced his palm open with his thumbnail and held the open wound over the cup long enough for a few drops to fall inside. He let go, and Bryan clutched his hand to his chest, pale, panting, and visibly relieved. When he turned to me, I obligingly held out my own hand to provide him with "blood freely given."

"Surprise counts as taking blood by force?" I asked as I bled into the cup from a small wound on my palm.

He gave me a pained look.

"It does when I'm in a hurry," he said. "Could you not be difficult about this? I'm helping you here."

I told Bryan to head back to the campground and fetch me a change of clothes. I'd wait at the neighbor's house to keep warm. He seemed happy to leave after that, cradling his injured hand. As he left, I told the Man with the Skull Cup that his task was done and that he should be returning to the campground as well. He nodded softly and acknowledged that yes, the terms of his agreement were fulfilled. However . . .

"There's something else you should consider," he said. "Do you truly believe your neighbor would have missed them being out of the lake already?"

The Man with the Skull Cup stood and walked away, leaving me alone with that question. I considered it, feeling anger bubbling inside me, and finally, when it was roiling and my blood was hot and I no longer felt the cold, I stood and walked toward my neighbor's house.

Kyle was shocked to see me, alive and dripping wet on his doorstep. Courtesy demanded he invite me in. I stood in the entryway while he ran to fetch towels, and when he went to hand them to me, I slammed my arm against his chest, pushing him until he was pressed against the wall and there was nowhere to go.

They know I've killed people before. They all know this. They try to forget, so that they don't have to be afraid of me.

"You knew," was all I said.

He tried to deny it. Made a weak joke about how global warming is why the shulikun are out early—until I pressed my arm up against his throat. Then he started to cry and admitted that yes, he knew, and he also knew that so soon after the death of my uncle I'd be easy prey for them.

"I'm sorry," he whimpered. "I'm so sorry."

I stared at the wall beside him so I wouldn't have to see the snot dribbling down his face. My eyes caught the edge of his shadow.

Tattered. Like a sweater coming undone at the hem.

I released him and backed away, trying to keep my expression neutral.

"Okay, I accept your apology," I said. "Forgiveness is keeping with the Christmas spirit, right? Wouldn't want the shulikun to come after me a second time."

Kyle slid down the wall to sit on the floor, babbling his thanks. I left him there and stalked out of the house, heading home to commit the unforgivable sin of putting up a Christmas tree before Thanksgiving was even over.

A Very Special Gift

As November gave way to December proper and the first snow started to fall, I did my best to embrace the Christmas spirit. It seemed prudent. I put an assortment of cookies on a plate in the kitchen, and there was a carton of eggnog and a jug of apple cider in the fridge, ready to be warmed up at a moment's notice. Not that I expected any visitors. Kyle had told the gossips in town that the shulikun had almost drowned me, and the rumor mill was churning about how Kate couldn't even fight off those silly spirits on horseback. And it seemed that now everyone was also hearing from a trusted friend that Kate was planning to sell the campground, but even with the help of Bryan and my extended family, I couldn't pin down the source of the rumor.

But much to my surprise, on the night before Christmas Eve, there was a knock at the door.

I opened it and was taken aback at the sight of a horse skull looming in the doorway, green ball ornaments shoved into the eye sockets. A white sheet covered the person holding the skull down to their ankles. For a moment I thought my visitors were from the town—although no one I knew practiced the Mari Lwyd tradition—and then I saw a familiar face grinning at me impishly from the edge of the crowd. The Dancers.

I shifted nervously, and they began to sing. Then, at the end, they fell eerily silent and waited for my reply so that the battle of wits could begin. We'd go back and forth, answering in rhyme, until finally one side couldn't reply fast enough and either had to leave or had to invite the entire party in for food and drink.

"There is no way I'm winning this one," I sighed. "Just come in."

And I threw the door open and the entire party stomped inside, tracking snow all the way down my entryway. The musicians, mercifully, were masked and considerately kept their hoods on as well. I focused on the kitchen for a bit, warming up the apple cider in a Crock-Pot and getting out the paper plates while the Dancers demolished the cookies.

"I have to ask," I said to the lead dancer, once everyone was occupied with food and beverages. "That skull. Is it . . . one of the horses buried in the field?"

"We'll put it back," she replied primly. "Rumor has it that you went to the Lady with Extra Eyes for help a while back. You got what you wanted . . . but you didn't like what she told you."

"The campground monsters are gossiping now; that's just lovely," I muttered snidely.

She pivoted to face me squarely.

"Monster? You sure you want to use that term, considering you've *also* decapitated someone?"

THE MAN WITH NO SHADOW

She had a point there.

"I notice no one has come by your house lately," she murmured. "You're not going to survive without allies."

"What am I supposed to do? The Man with No Shadow has been eliminating everyone I care about."

"Then go get someone back." She glared at me, unblinking, while I tried to comprehend what she was saying. "The Old Sheriff. *Go get him back.*"

I stared blankly at her for a moment, and she heaved a long sigh and asked if I wanted a hint. Obviously I wanted a hint. I had no idea what she was going on about.

"The rule of three. You need three things. The candle is the first."

She nodded toward the bedroom, where the candle burned, indicating that the Old Sheriff still lived. I was in shock. No, I thought frantically. I didn't want to hear what she was telling me. There was nothing I could do about the Old Sheriff. He was gone, just like my parents were gone, just like my uncle was gone.

"And the other two?" I asked unwillingly, knowing that this was my only opportunity to ask, and I couldn't let myself get in the way of information.

One would come to me, she said. Indeed, it was already en route. The other I would have to request. Then she flashed me a wink and trotted off to make sure she got some of the cookies before they all vanished.

I woke up on the sofa the next morning and found that my pantry and refrigerator were empty, my trash was full of wrappers (how do you go through four sticks of butter in one night?), and there was an eviscerated deer on my kitchen table. I had a vague memory of one of the Dancers telling my fortune using its entrails, but I didn't remember what she'd said. It was something momentous. I remember being afraid, emotional—I think I cried. I wasn't sure if it had been some kind of spell, or if I had just been hilariously drunk. They'd certainly spiked the cider at some point, because my Crock-Pot smelled like the contents of my now barren liquor cabinet.

I was becoming convinced the Dancers were fairies.

I stumbled into the kitchen to get some water, just in case a hangover was the reason I felt like crap, and that's when Bryan burst in through the front door.

"Yule cat," he panted. "Near town."

I got a couple of answers out of him, between his ragged gasps for air. Where it was. Whether he thought the cat was hunting or not (it was). And then I was running out the door. I wasn't certain what I could do, but I knew that I had to try, because otherwise the New Sheriff would get the incident he wanted.

I hate the Christmas season. You'd think it'd be a lovely, peaceful time of year, but no, it's absolutely brimming with monsters.

I drove as fast as I dared until I reached the road Bryan had indicated. There was only one house along it, a squat one-story of tan brick, set near the top of a low hill. I stopped halfway up the driveway, my tires throwing gravel. I got out and ran toward the house, just in time to see a large cat backing out of a broken window.

When I say "large," I'm not talking about something like your grandmother's cat that she swears is a Maine coon, but it doesn't have long hair, and you're certain it's not actually a Maine coon, just obese. I mean that this was a picture window, and the cat was barely making it out. The frame was completely filled with its ass, its hind legs braced against the wall as it ponderously heaved the rest of its body back through the opening, tail aloft to prominently display its butthole in perfect feline fashion.

Which all sounds hilarious, except this was the Yule cat, and the Yule cat is one of a handful of Christmas creatures that roam the world purely for the purpose of brutal murder.

It dropped out the window and onto all fours. If not for its size, the Yule cat would look like an ordinary fluffy house cat. Its coloration is that of a gray tabby, and its coat is long and bushy, giving it a majestic mane around its neck and enveloping its legs and body. In its mouth was an arm. The owner was at least still connected to the arm, a bit bloodied from being pulled through the broken window, but otherwise still alive. Screaming in terror, but alive.

The Yule cat hunts only under very specific circumstances. It roams the countryside during Christmastime in search of people who haven't received new clothing before Christmas Eve. (Don't worry, I'm pretty sure presents of clothing not opened until Christmas Day count). I guess this poor resident hadn't received a new shirt or gloves and hadn't thought to buy any for himself before Christmas came.

The cat released the man, and he began to crawl away, struggling to get to his feet. I ran for him, thinking that if we couldn't stop it, perhaps we could flee. Behind him, the cat dropped low to the ground, tail lashing furiously. It was growing in size—it was bigger each time I blinked—and by the time I crossed the short distance to him, the tips of its ears were even with the roof of the house.

I seized the man's arm and pulled him to his feet. I screamed at him to run. The car, I said. We just had to get to the car.

The cat pounced right as we reached it. It landed over top of us, the impact knocked both of us off our feet, and there was a screech of twisting metal as one of its paws came down on the front of my car and crushed the hood. Then the cat snapped a paw out and slapped the man away, sending him tumbling across the yard. It hunkered down to the ground, eyes intent on the man's prone body, waiting for him to get up again.

Panting, I got to my feet. My arm was bleeding from hitting the gravel, but I didn't feel anything under the adrenaline. My car was ruined. At least the cat was still playing with its prey, and as horrific as that was, it bought me more time.

For a brief moment, I thought about the shotgun in the back of the car. Guns so rarely worked against the inhuman, though, and I didn't have time to be wrong. I cast about desperately for something else that might deter the monster. Then I saw it. Coiled alongside the house was a garden hose.

If it was going to toy with the man like a cat, then perhaps it would react like a cat to this, as well.

I cranked the spigot open and ran. Since it was ignoring me, I would get as close as I could and hit it at point-blank range. I aimed the hose up, between legs as thick as tree trunks, and sprayed a stream of ice-cold water right onto its belly.

The cat yowled and jumped straight up, legs flailing as it twisted in midair, tail lashing. Then it hit the ground and spun, hissing with its ears flattened against its skull. There was a blur of movement—just a flash, an impression of something dark headed at me, and then I was airborne—I hit the ground on my shoulder, and the resulting burst of agony blinded me for a moment. I rolled and wound up on my stomach, dazed from the blow.

I raised my head again just in time to see the Yule cat holding the man down with one paw on his legs. Its teeth were sunk into his torso. I could hear his screams, and then the cat simply... raised its head... and the screams were abruptly silenced.

The cat opened its mouth and let the upper half of the man's body fall to the dirt. It sniffed at it, daintily plucked up a loop of intestine and ate that, and then immediately lost interest. I was too late. Someone had died, and yes, it wasn't my fault, but did that really matter? The town wasn't going to tolerate another dead local, and the New Sheriff would be there, ready to lay all of this at my feet. I groaned.

The cat turned its head and stared down at me. It put its ears back.

"Oh fuck off," I said to it. "I got new clothes, you don't get to eat me."

It dropped to the ground, its belly a mere foot above the grass. It took one slow step forward. I nervously began to stand.

Had I gotten new clothes? It wasn't like I'd opened my presents yet. Normally I bought myself some new socks, just in case, but I hadn't been getting out much, and my most recent trip into town had been a frantic, last-minute ordeal where I just got presents for my family and called it a day. But even without my yearly socks, Aunt Aleda always was sure to give us something, I desperately thought as the cat continued to stalk closer. A scarf. A handknit sweater. It was kind of her thing.

My aunt.

Who had just lost her husband.

I couldn't recall her showing up at my house to drop off a package yet.

For as much as I go on and on about the rules, I find it ironic that I would finally forget about one myself. I suppose it's inevitable. I know it seems like such a simple thing—just read the rules and follow them—but there are so many things to remember and life crowds them out and the years blur together and we grow complacent. And eventually, we all make mistakes. My mother left a window open. I . . . forgot to buy a new pair of socks before Christmas Eve.

I turned to run. I didn't get far. A massive paw hit me in the back and sent me flying, landing face-first in the gravel, barely getting my arms up in time to shield myself. I scrambled to my feet, slipping on the loose stones, my mind consumed with replaying the memory of the cat toying with the man before finally ripping him in two. My chest was so tight with panic, it was like my lungs were twisting together and I couldn't even inhale.

A hand seized the back of my jacket. For a moment I was lifted clean off my feet and the world spun as I was twirled around, and then something heavy and warm fell over my head and shoulders. A strong arm wrapped around my back and pulled me forward, burying my face into a thick wool shirt that smelled like pine.

"She has new clothing," a voice boomed over my head.

Whoever this guy was, he was tall. I twisted my neck enough to look up, and all I could see was a mass of curly white hair.

A shadow fell over us. The cat, looming above me and my rescuer both. I felt a gust of air as it flicked its tail in frustration.

"It's my gift to her," my rescuer continued.

And somehow that sounded like a threat. The cat gave a little growl that made the hair on the back of my neck stand on end, and then the shadow over us withdrew. The man holding me let go, and I stepped back, glancing fearfully to the side to where the cat had been standing. Nothing. Just the driveway, the house with the shattered window, my crushed car, and the corpse.

I stood there for a few moments, stunned into incoherency. Then, as my heart rate slowly began to wind down, I turned my attention to my rescuer. A tall man, dressed in jeans and a red plaid shirt, with a long, curly white beard and hair to match. His expression was stern, and his eyes were cold. A simple silver cross hung around his neck.

"Saint... Nicholas?" I ventured.

A faint nod. I was rendered speechless. I'd heard the stories, of course, but I'd never thought...

There are many creatures in this world. Old things and ancient beings that are both god and not and many that lie somewhere in between. Not all of them are predators.

On my shoulders rested a thick wool mantle, hanging almost to my waist. The hood and hem were trimmed in white fur. I fingered it for a moment, then made to take it off and return it to the saint. He shook his head.

"It's a gift," he said firmly. "That's what I do."

"You do a lot more than give gifts," I replied. "You save people. I didn't think you'd save me, though. I'm not a good person."

"I help the good and the wicked," he said. "It's why I'm a saint."

There are plenty of saints who punish the wicked, but I felt it would have been rude to point that out. Saint Nicholas is known as an embodiment of mercy who helps anyone in their time of dire need, and I guess I qualified.

"Can you bring him back?" I asked, pointing at the man.

But Saint Nicholas just patted me gently on the arm and walked away.

The New Sheriff arrested me a few hours later. I'd barely returned to my house before he showed up on my doorstep, claiming I was responsible for the man's demise. Because my car was there. That's it. My car.

"The Yule cat ate him," I said, indignant. "This is bullshit, and you know it."

Anyway, he just grabbed my shoulder after that and threw me against the wall to handcuff me, and I let him, because I didn't want to give him a reason to escalate on the grounds that I was resisting arrest. I spent Christmas Day in a jail cell until my brother showed up to post bail.

"I was wondering why you didn't come over for Christmas," he said. "I was so worried."

"Did the New Sheriff not tell you where I was?"

"Well, he did, but he wouldn't let me post bail until today."

"Wow, *that's* a dick move there."

Tyler drove in tense silence until we reached my house. I stayed in the car after he parked in the driveway, sensing that there was something he wanted to talk about.

"Danielle is pregnant," he said. "And I think she's going to divorce me."

"Wait, *what*?"

That's a lot to have dropped on you.

He kept talking, the words spilling out. I tried to focus on the whole "I'm going to be an aunt" part of the conversation, but Tyler was too distraught. They'd fought over the campground—repeatedly. Danielle was afraid that their child would be pressured to carry on the family business. It wasn't like I was going to get married and have kids of my own.

"Okay, that's not how this works," I finally snapped. "We've moved the campground around in the family before, and we can do it again. We've got cousins—"

"Like April?"

I didn't know what to say to that.

"Maybe she's right," Tyler sighed. "Maybe she should just take our kid and leave. Maybe we need to keep our child as far from the campground as we can, because otherwise they'll *want* to take it over."

"They'll turn out like me, in other words," I said, quietly seething.

"Why does our family have to do all this?" he said in obvious frustration. "Why *you*?"

I laughed bitterly. I'd missed Christmas, spent the night in a jail cell, and now I was stuck having a conversation I really didn't want to have with my brother.

"Who else will do it?" I asked. "Uncle Tobias is gone. April wouldn't have been able to, and she's gone now too. And you have *never* wanted any part of this."

I got out of the car and slammed the door shut behind me before he could say anything else.

I was deeply grateful to whoever among my staff had cleaned up after the Dancers, because coming home to a days-old disemboweled deer carcass would not have been a pleasant experience. If I find out who it was, they're getting a bonus in their next paycheck.

It was probably Bryan. He probably let the dogs eat it.

Unfortunately, despite my efforts, the damage was done. The town now believed I wasn't qualified to protect them, and maybe they were right. I'd learned how to contain these creatures growing up, how to maintain the status quo, but the situation was rapidly moving past that. This was a bad year. Everything was more active—more aggressive—and containment was no longer working. Perhaps I would have learned how to fight this from my parents, but they weren't here, and it was just me, against the Man with No Shadow, who clearly had a plan to remove me from the campground.

I needed a plan of my own. I had to rescue the Old Sheriff.

The Dancers had said I required three things. I had the candle, and now I had the saint's mantle. I needed to find the third item and then figure out where the house was going to appear next. The dark days of winter are when the boundaries between our worlds are weakest, the dead walk the earth, and the devils and malicious spirits are loosed upon us to roam free until the day of Epiphany. I could use that. The days before Twelfth Night were my window. This is when divinations are best performed and what is lost can be found.

This isn't just my land—it's also my home. I was ready to fight the New Sheriff and the rest of the town and anyone else who tried to take it from me, be they human or otherwise.

Seamstress of Slaughter

I had a visitor on New Year's Eve. He showed up on my doorstep, looking for the camp office. A skinny, earnest man, likely in his early twenties. He reminded me a little bit of Tyler, if Tyler had been crossed with an anxious Chihuahua.

"Hi," he said, sticking out his hand. "I'm Curtis. I'm interested in buying the campground."

I stared at him blankly for a moment.

"Did . . . the New Sheriff tell you I was coming by?" he asked.

"He . . . did not," I replied. I did not shake his hand.

He stood there, stammering, and the anger I had stashed away for occasions like this just couldn't be roused. He looked bewildered. Hurt, almost.

"Sorry—it's just," he said, "I was told you'd be selling at the end of January? Something about the town council finalizing the decision? And that I didn't need to come by until then, but I had some time off and was just excited to see it. . . . My mother always talked about how beautiful Goat Valley is. . . ."

I forced a smile on my face. I felt bad for him. I had no idea how the New Sheriff had dug him up, but clearly he'd been duped. So I took him for a tour. Showed him the woods, fields, and even the family cemetery. Nothing out of the ordinary. Then I escorted him off the property and reiterated that I wasn't selling, that there was clearly a misunderstanding here.

"Okay, well, I've got quite a bit of vacation time," he said, "since I figured wrapping this up would take a while. So I'll stick around. I've got the finances lined up if—"

"That's nice," I replied curtly. "But I'm not selling."

As soon as he was gone I alerted my staff to keep an eye out for Curtis in case he came back. I did not want him wandering around unescorted.

A half hour from midnight I got out my tarot deck. I laid out a Celtic cross with the cards, as that was the first search result on the internet. Whilst I know my folklore, I'm really not an expert in this witchy stuff. I was sitting on the floor of my living room with the guidebook open on my phone, trying to figure out if the Devil represented the sheriff or the Man with No Shadow and whether there was any significance in so many cards being from the oak suite, or if I was just bad at shuffling. I'd just finished reading up on the Chariot and was thinking, *Well that's promising*, when the front door flew open.

It smashed into the entryway wall and hung there, letting in a gust of cold air that stirred the cards on the floor. Framed in the doorway was a woman, beautiful, with pale skin like winter frost and hair like snow.

"Uh, hello?" I said tentatively. "And you are?"

She wasn't inside yet. This was a good sign. All manners of

creatures roam the world on the eve of the new year, but most of them cannot enter the home without permission. There are stories of even the devil itself being repulsed for lack of an invitation.

"I am Perchta," she replied. "Don't trouble yourself to get up; I'll invite myself in."

She stepped through the open doorway. This was not a good sign. And worse, I knew that name. She was an old entity. One who could go wherever she willed, regardless of whether she was welcome or not.

For good children, she would leave a silver coin. For the wicked, she would cut open their abdomens, remove their stomach and guts, stuff them full of straw and pebbles, and sew them back together again. So a little bit like Santa Claus, but with murder instead of coal.

Perchta had not visited our town for a long time. Not in my lifetime, but she had in my parents', before I was born. They told me of her when I was young and could be frightened into obedience. They said a young man had done something terribly wicked, and one night, in the days leading up to Twelfth Night, his neighbors had been woken by his screaming. They broke into his house through a window, and that entire time he had not stopped screaming. They entered his room to find a beautiful woman with long white hair standing over him, knotting and snipping free her thread. She turned to them, smiled, and vanished.

He died in the hospital. His abdomen had been sewn neatly up in a straight line, the stitches so tiny they were almost invisible, and when the surgeon snipped them open, bloody straw and stones bulged up through the incision and spilled out onto the floor of the operating room.

Now I stared at Perchta as she stood framed by my entryway, holding a needle between the pinched fingers of one hand and thread wound around the fingers of the other.

I grabbed my deck of tarot cards and scrambled to my feet to run. Some cards fell from my hand as I sprinted toward the kitchen, but I knew better than to stop and grab them. I could hear her footsteps crossing the living room as I fumbled with the dead bolt on the door leading to the garage.

"You have been wicked, haven't you, Kate?" Perchta said from behind me, her voice a lilting singsong. "Saint Nicholas saved you, but I am not nearly so kind."

How many did I kill this year? Was it only two? The camper who died in the hospital, writhing and vomiting blood? And Jessie, who died when I took her head? I've had worse years.

"I did what was necessary!" I panted, throwing myself through the door, then slamming it shut behind me and locking it.

It jolted as Perchta struck it, and I was thrown backward. I dove for the door leading outside and got it open just as the other one was ripped off its hinges. I ran out into the cold air, letting it fill my lungs, fighting through that initial shock that threatened to rob me of all ability to breathe. I was running, down through the yard, toward the edge of the driveway. I had no idea where I could go to get away.

Perchta was once a goddess. Perhaps she still is. I don't

know if ancient beings can lose their divinity, or perhaps divinity is merely a word that only has meaning for humanity. Her status as a "former" goddess had certainly done nothing to lessen her power.

I reached the end of the drive, and at first I thought to cut toward the road, but there was something standing on the asphalt. Multiple somethings. Their heads hung sideways at odd angles, and their limbs swayed in the wind. I veered wide around them, confused, unsure of whether I should go past or go the other direction entirely.

Then my eyes adjusted to the darkness, and I realized what they were.

Scarecrows.

All their heads snapped up, still hanging sideways on loose necks, but the empty spots where their eyes should have been were fixed on where I stood, hesitating, keenly aware of the woman with white hair making her way steadily down the driveway at a confident, unhurried clip. The pace of a predator that knows it is only a matter of time.

I began to back away, and then—in the corner of my vision—I saw a large shape lunging at me out of the darkness. I dodged to the side, almost falling. Its arms passed over my head, and I smelled damp straw and a foul stench, the smell of rot, and then I was sprinting across the frosty field and leaving the scarecrows behind me. The tree line rose up before me. The darkness was impenetrable between the trees, but it was the darkness of my childhood, and there was a sense of safety in the forest. I just had to reach it.

My reprieve was short-lived. I heard a noise from behind my right shoulder, and I risked a glance backward.

The scarecrows were racing across the field after me. They ran in great, loping strides on all fours like animals, and their limbs seemed elongated, thin, more like gangly canines than human forms now. They were rapidly gaining. I hit the tree line, and the grass gave way to dead leaves.

I stumbled through the underbrush, and then one scarecrow hit me, a bodily impact that took me off my feet, and I landed on my side, felt a weight fall over top of me, pinning me to the ground. I struggled, kicking and punching, and my fingers clawed straw from the back of its head and my knee connected with something soft, something that came free with a sickly sound, like the last bit of jam releasing from the bottom of a jar. Something like rope, but slick and wet, landing on my legs, and I gagged at the stench of bad meat.

Now I know what Perchta does with the intestines of her victims.

I seized the scarecrow's arm with both hands and wrenched, and the straw parted and I tore it clean off. The scarecrow's body lilted, and one last blow to its side knocked it away from me. It writhed on the ground, trying to stand, more intestines spilling out of the hole in its midsection. I rolled and pushed myself up.

Then another blow, and this one slammed my back against a tree trunk. My chest seized up at the impact, and for a moment I could only feel the agony radiating from beneath my rib cage, and then that was buried under the ice of terror. Perchta's hand was around my neck, and it was she who held me pinned, my feet straining to touch the ground. My tarot cards lay strewn across the forest floor.

"Necessary? That's debatable," she said, answering my earlier plea for understanding, "and certainly no less wicked."

A twist of her wrist and her bone needle shone ivory in the moonlight. She pushed my shirt up and out of the way, and I felt the point of it against my skin, just above my belly button. The goddess leaned in close to me, and her breath on my neck felt like frost.

"What else am I to do?" I said. "I'm trying the best I can, but I can't save everyone."

"You *can* save them all," she hissed in my ear.

She released my neck and let my feet hit the ground, but I remained pinned with my back against the tree, the point of her needle digging deeper into my stomach. I whimpered low in the back of my throat. She bent over languidly, and her thin fingers plucked one of the fallen tarot cards from the ground. She held it up in front of my face. Justice.

"I don't know what you're trying to tell me," I whispered. "I don't know what I'm doing."

"Figure it out," she replied grimly.

Perchta punished the wicked. She cut them open, replaced their guts with straw and stone, and sewed them back up again. And I had killed two people in the past year with my own hands.

The needle pierced my skin—I yelped with pain, but it wasn't as bad as I'd expected—and then it exited somewhere else, creating two bright points just above my belly button, and then she was knotting the thread and snapping it with a jerk, eliciting another brief moment of blinding agony as the stitch pulled tight against the wounds.

Then she let me go.

I pulled my shirt up and stared at my stomach in the moonlight. There was a faint line of white against my skin, a single stitch that she'd sewn into my flesh with her needle. I fell on my hands and knees and vomited. Perchta was gone when I got up. I limped home, holding my stomach.

The night was waning. I was running out of time to get my answers, and I didn't know what I was doing with tarot cards. However, there were other methods of divination.

I took the candle from my bedroom—the Old Sheriff's candle—and poured some of the wax into a spoon. I then poured that into a cup of cold water and stared down at the resulting image. It coalesced into a blob with two empty spaces like eyes.

A skull. Floating in a cup of water.

The third item. I wandered the campsite for hours, and just before sunup I found him. The Man with the Skull Cup. I told him I was here to claim my favor, and he held very still while I spoke. He looked pleased when I said what it was I wanted.

"To save the sheriff," he murmured, running a finger along the rim of the cup contemplatively.

"Have you been reading Reddit or something?" I demanded. "Or gossiping with the Dancers?"

His eyes flicked up to stare at me in unspoken reproach.

The Man with the Skull Cup merely tolerates my sarcasm. The silence between us stretched on until my nerve broke, and I coughed and awkwardly changed the subject.

"So, what am I going to find inside the vanishing house?" I asked.

"I cannot tell you. I have no more ability to read the future than you. I see patterns and possibilities, and perhaps I see ones that you miss while you struggle in this web not of your own making, but even I do not know what the house's master is."

"I'm getting tired of puzzles," I muttered. "What web?"

He sighed softly and shoved the cup into my hands.

"You continually disappoint me, Kate. The Man with No Shadow has you ensnared, and you focus on a single strand of his plans."

"Would you help me fight him?"

A question asked on impulse, born of a wild hope that the Man with the Skull Cup had no fondness for his . . . neighbor. His expression went carefully blank, and while he only displayed the emotions he chose to—disdain, typically—this felt even more controlled than usual.

"This is all the help I will give you," he said dismissively. "Our agreement is concluded."

He told me I could have the cup until the next full moon. I must be careful not to spill it, he said sternly, for it would take a heavy cost to fill it again.

The cup sat on my dresser, between the candle and the folded mantle.

I was scared. But I was as prepared as I could be and there was one last thing pushing me forward. A faint glimmer of hope, that maybe, just maybe, this time I could save someone.

As for finding the house?

I had an idea.

Some Rules Are Meant to Be Broken

Remember the one thing I said you shouldn't do? Yeah. I followed the lights.

At first they tried to lead me into danger a handful of times before we reached the edge of my property. They took me to the Dancers. The lead dancer looked at the mantle I wore and the cup and candle I carried and smiled. She asked me in a low voice where I was going. To the vanishing house, I said. I asked if they knew the way, hoping to circumvent having to follow the damned lights all over the campground. But they did not. After that, the lights took me to where frost hung on the leaves and coated the ground, but I wore the mantle and the cold could not touch me, and I moved on unscathed. They took me past the lair of the Thing in the Dark, but it was dormant, and I passed by. Finally, they took me to the edge of the property.

They stopped just shy of the border, marked only by my memory and a few scattered NO TRESPASSING signs. Beyond that was the road and beyond that . . .

The vanishing house sat before me, just as it had months before, a squat thing of wood and shingles with that front porch and the barely open door. Inviting me in. I made a call to Aunt Aleda and told her where I was, in case I needed a quick getaway. I did not want to go inside. I'm not entirely sure how I forced myself to move. The mantle was heavy on my shoulders, and that was some comfort, it and the light cast by the candle and the feel of the skull cup in my hand. Were the heroes frightened, in the stories? I think they were. Of course they were. But they had their protection, their three items, their rules, their helpers, or whatever it was that would see them to safety. They only had to trust and do as they were told.

I didn't have any rules to follow. Not here, on the threshold of the vanishing house. My mother hadn't figured out a pattern to it; there was no information in my books about what I would find inside. It was up to me to figure out the rest, and all I had were my three items and my courage, which was sadly lacking. But I had to go inside.

The door swung open at my touch. The flicker of the candle struggled to light only a few feet of the unnatural darkness. Within the bubble of its glow I could see weathered floors covered with a layer of dust and wooden walls devoid of ornamentation. There were squares where the color of the wood was darker, untouched by the sun's light, where pictures had once hung. After that . . . nothing. Just a darkness so deep it was as if nothing existed at all and I had reached the end of reality. I felt a tinge of panic merely looking at it, the instinctive terror you experience when you stand on a precipice. I tore my eyes away and focused instead on what was directly in front of me, what was real and stable.

The door creaked shut behind me. Gently. I heard the latch catch.

"I'm here for the sheriff," I said to the empty house.

Nothing. If the house had a master, it wasn't inclined to converse. I took a shallow breath and pressed forward. The house unfolded before me as the candlelight touched it. I took the first doorway, entering a living room. Two windows were against the front wall, one of them the very same window that the young man had stared out at me from. There were dark rectangles on the floor, clear of dust, where furniture had once sat. Only a single chair remained, shoved into a corner. My breathing quickened.

A woman sat in it limply, her head lolling to the side so that her ear almost touched her elbow. Black blood coated her side and pooled on the floor, having poured out of her missing arm and the gaping cavity that was once her lung. It'd long since dried into something resembling ink.

"Do you know my name?" she asked as I moved closer.

She raised her head, and it flopped over to the missing shoulder. Black bile dribbled out of the corner of her mouth and her nose. It fell in viscous drops to the floor.

"I'm afraid not," I said. "I didn't ask. Sorry."

"It's okay. You've seen so many die, I imagine. What's one more name?"

I walked around the edge of the room, to the windows on one wall, covered with heavy curtains of a pale brown loose knit. I looked outside and saw my aunt's car parked on the shoulder of the road, but there was a pall over the scene, as if a black mist had settled around her vehicle.

"Are you dead?" I asked the woman, if only to hear my own voice.

"Quite. You feel guilty, don't you?"

"I wish I could have saved you."

She didn't answer, just continued staring at me.

"Can you tell me where the sheriff is?"

"I cannot. He was dragged away from me, cursing, fighting to get to me the entire time. The house took him, and I was left to die alone. I was so scared. I was choking on my own blood, and I just wanted someone to be there, to hold my head up so I didn't have to taste it in my mouth, to tell me it was all going to be okay."

She paused for a moment, a thin stream of black liquid trickling down her chin through pale lips.

"I suppose it wouldn't have mattered, though," she said contemplatively. "We all die alone and afraid, don't we?"

I thought of April, screaming for me to save her. I thought of my father, dragging the little girl by her hair out into the yard. We die alone and afraid . . . or angry. Angry was also an option.

I walked past the young woman toward the next doorway. I couldn't help her. I had to keep moving. I had no idea how long the house would remain in one spot, and I didn't want to risk being trapped in here.

The next room was a kitchen. Cupboards were along the far wall. All their doors were removed, and the shelves were barren. A table with no chairs was shoved against the other wall, and the young woman lay upon it. She was on her back with her remaining limbs splayed and dangling over the edge. Her head also dangled, her long hair almost touching the floor.

I glanced back into the first room. She was still there, sprawled in the chair. And she was here, laid out on the table.

"Is this the house's doing?" I asked. "Are you here to distract me? Or . . . are you the master of the house?"

She laughed, and black liquid frothed at her lips until it filled her mouth and she began to choke on it. She spat a thick clump like a clot out onto the floor and regained her voice.

"I'm not the master," she said bitterly.

I edged past her. I pressed my back against the cabinets, not wanting to get any closer to the dead woman than I had to. Her eyes tracked my every movement. She spoke again when we were directly even with each other.

"I died." More black liquid dribbled down her chin, bubbling forth every time her lips moved. "You killed me."

"I tried to save you."

I continued edging past her, my heart hammering. I watched her remaining arm. If it so much as twitched, I was going to bolt.

"You could have done more. You've always been able to do more."

Now that just wasn't fair. First Perchta and now this . . . dead girl.

"Like what?" I snarled.

"You could leave the campground for good."

A giggle, punctuated by the rasp of liquid obscuring her throat.

"Like hell I will," I muttered.

I crept down the left side of the kitchen wall, sighing in relief once I was out of reach. She stretched her hand toward me as I reached the doorway, rolling on the table so that she stared at me from her side, the swell of her broken rib cage luminescent white in the light of my candle.

I stared into the next room—a hallway with a staircase at the end.

"Is it pride?" she whispered from behind me, almost to herself. "I think it is. You're too proud to admit that you're killing all of us."

I'd had enough. I whirled on her, stalked back through the kitchen to where she lay, and plunged the candle flame into her body. I'm not sure what I thought would happen. I was blinded by anger and acting on instinct.

She caught like paper, her skin curled and blackened and burned, and she screamed, the remains of her body thrashing and that black liquid fountaining sluggishly out. It swallowed up the candlelight and the flame both, and all light vanished just as she finally fell silent. I realized what I'd done too late, panic seizing at my chest as I strained to see anything.

Then I felt the lap of cold thick liquid at my feet. I moved, quickly. I put one hand out, the hand with the candle, and stretched out two fingers to feel for a wall. There were stairs. I remembered seeing stairs. I had to find them.

The liquid was at my ankle. It was so cold.

I stumbled forward. A wall. I had to find a wall. My hands touched something fibrous, like the surface of a dry leaf. I desperately traced along it, running my hand up and down its height to see if it turned into a staircase at any point. It continued on, and then it turned sharply. I stretched out my hand, trying to find the other wall to indicate a doorway. Nothing.

The sludge was up to my knees. I was beginning to shiver, and I clenched my teeth to keep them from chattering. I followed the wall, and it turned again, and again. This exceeded the bounds of the house, I realized. I'd been walking for too long. I'd made too many turns. Where the fuck was I?

And then the water was at my waist, and I struggled to move, for its consistency was akin to mud and it dragged at my body, pulling me back. All I could think was forward, forward. Keep moving, keep feeling for a wall with trembling fingertips.

The water was at my chest. I remembered what it had felt like, when the shulikun had pulled me under. When I'd almost drowned. And I began to properly panic, my breath came so fast I was dizzy, and I staggered on, consumed with the desperate thought that I just had to keep going because there was nothing else I could do.

The water got to my chin, and that was when the floor vanished. I began to tread water, trying to keep my head above the surface, but it began to rise so quickly, like it was trying to pull me down, and I then was dragged under. It felt like falling, I was tumbling in a current that was taking me deeper into the morass, and I curled around the cup I still had clutched in my hands. I clamped my fingers over the improvised cover for it—layers of plastic wrap and rubber bands—because that was all I could think to do in my panic. I couldn't spill the cup. He would be so angry. I couldn't let it spill.

Then I remember nothing else until I woke in a strange place, wrapped in blankets and lying next to a fireplace.

The Master of the Vanishing House

The room had wooden floors and beige striped wallpaper. The fireplace was brick, and a handful of logs burned heartily inside its mouth. An iron poker and shovel hung on a squat stand next to it. I sat up, slowly, letting the faded quilt fall off my shoulders and onto the floor. The cup was still clutched in my hands, and Saint Nicholas's mantle was over my shoulders, the clasp securely fastened between my collarbones. I had lost the candle.

"You were caught out in the rain," a voice from behind me said. It felt familiar. "Do you remember?"

"I do," I whispered.

It'd been raining. The campers had taken shelter on the front porch, and I'd gone looking for them.

"You were out in the cold so long you were hypothermic," the voice continued gently. "Just sit by the fire a bit longer. I'm here for you. I'll always protect you."

Something stirred in the back of my mind. Never in my

life had anyone said they'd protect me. I remember my own mother, the strength of her arms, the lines of her muscles as she held something down against the ground, her grip taut on a knife handle.

"We can't protect you forever," she'd said. "You'll have to learn to do this on your own."

And she'd slit the monster's throat and let it bleed out into the dirt.

I wondered who this voice was, then, that it would make such a promise to me. It no longer felt as familiar as it had, more like a voice I'd heard in a dream. I could feel the edges of my memories fraying the more I tried to examine them, struggling to place who it was that was behind me.

"You were so cold and exhausted when I brought you inside," it continued. Its tone was soothing. I felt heavy, listening to it, and it was an effort to keep my eyes open. "Do you want to sleep some more? You don't have to fight anymore, not in my house. You can finally rest."

I lay back down on my side, and I stared at the fire. It blurred before my eyes and I teetered there on the verge of sleep, but then I shifted, trying to get my head into a more comfortable angle, and the pin of Saint Nicholas's mantle pricked my collarbone.

The voice was over me. I couldn't see it, it remained just out of my eyeshot, but I felt its presence hovering over my body like a shroud. I felt it draw the blanket up and lay it against my shoulder. Its touch reminded me of dry leaves.

"Do you love me?" the voice whispered.

Something was off. I fingered the edge of the mantle I wore. It was the source of my warmth, I realized. Not the fire. I stretched my fingers toward the flames and felt no heat.

"You don't want my love," I murmured. "Everyone I love dies."

A hiss and the presence recoiled. I continued reaching out, until my fingers touched the flames, and then my entire hand was in the fire and it licked at my skin and I felt nothing but cold air. I felt the drowsiness slipping away, and I pushed myself up; then I stood, taking the skull cup as I did.

I turned. The room vanished into darkness beyond the edge of the firelight, and I heard a creaking noise, like a strained rope swaying back and forth, and ragged, uneven breathing. It paused, I heard the catch in the back of its throat, and it spoke again.

"If you will not love me," it hissed, "will you worship me?"

I reached to the side, and my hand closed on the handle of the iron poker. It felt real enough. I took it with me and stepped forward, to the edge of the light.

"I worship no god and no power," I murmured mechanically. "Worship demands obedience, and the only obligations I will carry are to my land and my family."

I walked into the darkness. I pressed on, straining to place the movement of the rope and the ragged breathing. Somewhere above me. I hefted my improvised weapon uneasily.

"Do you fear me?"

The fire sputtered and died. I felt its breath stir the hair on the back of my head.

"I fear death," I snarled. I whirled and swung, and the poker passed through empty air. I backed up. "I fear failure. But I don't fear you! Show yourself, master of the vanishing house!"

The quality of the air changed. It thinned. It left a faint, metallic taste on my lips, and then I could see. There was no light source, merely a lifting of the darkness, and before me hung the master of the house. A human torso with the legs and head of a deer, hanging limp from the rope bound tightly around its legs. The fur was stained with black blood from where its bonds had cut through its flesh. Its eyes were empty, black hollows where they once were, and dead moss hung off its antlers. Its wrists were bound together, the arms dangling lifelessly before it. It rotated slowly upside down on the rope that held it aloft.

A line bisected its human belly. Then it split open, the upper body tipping back to reveal the insides—a mouth with a black throat and a tongue and white teeth slick with something like ink. The liquid dribbled down its torso as it spoke, ran along the grooves of its antlers, and dripped onto the floor.

"Do you fear me now?" it rasped.

Of course I did. But that's what anger was for.

"Buddy, you are asking the wrong person," I snapped. "I have a dead girl knocking on my window every single night, and every morning I get to listen to her be dragged off by a monstrous beast. And that's probably among the least of the horrific things I've witnessed. Now, *where is the sheriff?*"

I brandished my iron poker for effect. I'm not sure it made a difference.

"He didn't love me," the mouth said. "He wouldn't worship me. And he certainly didn't fear me."

"He's alive, though."

The candle had still been burning, up until the moment I set someone on fire with it. I didn't think that extinguishing the candle would actually kill him; it was a representation of his life, not his life itself.

"I kept him. I keep all of them. Even the ones that die."

"For what?"

It told me, its words rolling out of its mouth like the toll of a bell. They echoed in my ears, sharp like needles, and I scratched futilely at my own skin to dislodge them. The inhuman things of this world can die, it said. We humans can kill them. But there are always more—another river spirit to drown the unwary, another hunter to stalk the lonely caught out after sundown. They exist because at some point, long ago, someone had made them persist. So that they would not fade away when the sun rose and banished the terrors of the night like the morning fog.

Someone loved them, like the saints. Or someone worshipped them, like the gods. Or someone feared them, like the monsters.

"It is so hard," the creature lamented, and its sorrow was like a wave. I might have wept, if I hadn't come to kill it. "So hard to move my house. So hard to make you humans find it."

The rope continued to twist until the mouth rotated to

face me, and then it stopped. It stared at me with dead eyes in the deer's tattered skull. It hung there, immobile, until the belly split open again, the torso bobbing with every word.

"I will make you fear me."

It began to sway, the body jerked on the rope, and the line curved as it reached for me, those bound hands suddenly full of life, and it stretched its fingers out to where I stood. The mouth gaped, the tongue running across its oily teeth, and more liquid spilled forth to land in thick clots on the floor like tar.

The darkness closed in again, robbing me of my only advantage: mobility. I swung wildly into empty air, turned, swung again. *Keep moving*, I thought, because while I could no longer see the monster, perhaps I could keep it at bay if I just kept moving. I felt the brush of air touch my cheek, I swung, and the iron poker continued its arc without ever meeting resistance. The creak of a rope, from somewhere to my right. I turned abruptly, swung again, stumbling because panic had not given me the presence of mind to catch my balance first.

A hand closed on my hair. A jerk—sudden bright agony—and I was suspended in midair. My feet kicked wildly at nothingness; I clutched at the fingers holding me, gripped the ropes that were bound around its wrist, trying to get purchase enough to take the strain off the back of my head and give me leverage to fight. My fingers slipped off the ropes, wet with black blood, fastened so tight that it was like they were simply part of its skin. I felt liquid splatter on my forehead and slide down past my eyebrows, and I closed my eyes tight, desperately hoping it wouldn't get in my eyes. My skin was numb along the path it traced. More fell onto my shoulders, like rain on the mantle I wore. The pin stabbed into my collarbone.

"Fear me," the monstrosity hissed, more black liquid splattering on my neck and face. "Fear me!"

I let go of its fingers, and my hand closed on the pin of Saint Nicholas's mantle instead. It came loose at my touch. I stabbed the heavy metal needle into the creature's wrist.

It shrieked. Its arms went slack and I fell, landing hard on the floor. My left foot struck the poker, and I seized it and scrambled to my feet. From all around me came the frenzied shrieks of the creature and the groan of the rope as it struggled to support its frantic writhing.

The darkness lifted a fraction. Enough that I could see its writhing silhouette, jerking like a fish on a line. It was weak. It'd admitted as much. The house was so much to maintain, and it wasn't getting the prey it needed. And while it suffered here in the darkness, starving and desperate, the sun continued to rise each morning and banish the terrors of the night once more. It knew its end was near.

Back when I'd decided to rescue the sheriff, I'd sworn that I would bring him out, even if I had nothing but my own will to drag him free with. It seemed that the time had come.

I am my mother's daughter, after all.

I said nothing. I felt nothing but a cold, smoldering rage. An old anger that was kindled to life long ago, perhaps when I was helpless to save my friends, or perhaps when I came of age by strangling my childhood friend, or every time I failed to save anyone and was only there to clean up the pieces left behind. I hefted the poker in one hand and walked up to the master of the vanishing house. I raised it, let it fall, throwing my shoulder and hip into its path to lend it the mass of my body.

The meaty impact of each blow traveled up my arm, past my elbow, and into my shoulder. I felt the resistance of bones and then the softness of when they shattered, the sickening crunch echoing through the chamber. The pin fell free from its shattered arms and landed at my feet.

"Fear me," it gasped, and this time, it sounded like it was begging.

I continued to swing until my arms ached and I was panting, covered in sweat and black blood, and still the monstrosity made its demands, even as its head caved in and its body split and splattered like overripe fruit. Its legs and pelvis dangled from the ropes, and the rest of it lay in a puddle of meat and blood and bone at my feet, and still it cried out, barely a wet gurgle, but a cry nonetheless. And while it could no longer speak intelligibly, its words still echoed in my mind.

Love me.

Worship me.

Fear me.

Make me last.

I don't think that what I did next came from my own knowledge. I think I was guided, and considering the source, I'm okay with that. I knelt beside its broken form. I whispered to it, gently, that it was okay, that this was the end and that it was time to go. The mantle had slipped from my shoulders, and I picked it up and draped it out over the creature's body. The white fur flattened, melted into a single strip of cloth, and the whole of it elongated into a thin white sheet. A shroud. A funeral shroud. It fell over the monster's body, black bile soaking into the cloth, and then the master of the house was still and silent. And the words I spoke over it were not my own, but they were a blessing, a rite, and then it was dead. The darkness lifted.

The house shook around me. It went still a few seconds later, groaning ponderously, and then another tremor shook it. I glanced around me in panic. I was in an attic. The roof was close by overhead, and the floors were roughly hewn wooden slats.

In the corner lay the sheriff.

I ran to him and dropped to my knees. He was breathing, but he did not stir as I shook him. Around me, the house creaked and moaned, and another shudder sent a shower of dust and wood splinters over my head and shoulders.

The cup.

I hastily ripped off the covering and forced the cup up to his lips. Tipped it, and most of the liquid ran out and onto his chest, but some of it went into his mouth, and I saw the movement of his throat as he swallowed. I gave him all of it—I had to—just to get some inside him. He stirred, right as a beam collapsed, taking part of the floor with it as the house shook yet again.

The Old Sheriff came to and vomited black liquid onto the wooden floor. I threw his arm over my shoulders and yelled that we had to go, we had to move. He was dazed, but my words stirred him into action and he stood, shakily, and staggered along with me even as his body continued to convulse and bring up more and more of that sickly liquid, thick as tar.

We just made it outside when the house collapsed behind us. I put the sheriff on the ground by the road, and he continued to vomit into the grass. I went to the trunk of the car, got out a can of gasoline, and Aunt Aleda and I, we soaked the remains of the house and then burned it into ash.

The Beast Within

We kept the Old Sheriff's rescue quiet for a few days. He needed some time to come to terms with what had happened before putting himself into the spotlight of the town's rumor mill. I suspect he'd said that more for my sake, because he had no memory of his time inside the vanishing house, and his wife seemed completely unbothered by the whole ordeal. In fact, she showed up the very next day on my doorstep with a casserole dish in her hands.

That's how small towns are. Whenever something happens, people show up with food. New baby? Casseroles. Death in the family? More casseroles. Rescue someone's husband from a massively haunted house? Hope you like casseroles.

"I knew you could do it," Sorcha said as she handed the dish over. It smelled strongly of tuna.

"I'm glad you believed in me, because I sure didn't," I replied.

"Going against your upbringing is hard, isn't it? You either disappoint your parents or, in your case, their memory.

Which is probably worse—at least people can change. Memories can't."

I had no idea how to respond to that, so I invited her in as a clumsy attempt to talk about literally anything else. She declined. She was only here to drop off the casserole. I realized, watching her walk off, that she hadn't brought a car. I supposed she'd just . . . walked all the way here and intended to walk all the way back. I shook my head and shut the door.

A few days later the Old Sheriff stopped by to plan and pick up the casserole dish. "So everything goes back to normal now, right?" I asked. "You'll talk to the New Sheriff and get your job back."

"There was an election, Kate—"

"We can undo that! It's not like this town doesn't turn a blind eye to a whole lot of other stuff; we can ignore election laws. You can tell him to step down and—"

"Kate." The Old Sheriff's voice was firm. "I'm not going to be sheriff anymore. I wanted to retire long ago. I stuck around because after your parents died, I didn't want to leave you without help."

"So you felt sorry for me? Is that it?"

Even to my ears, my words sounded high and desperate.

"You needed help," he said, his voice slow and patient. "You don't need that anymore. You went into that house and got me out. You'll be fine."

I stood up and started pacing the living room. Of course it wasn't that simple anymore.

"Are you upset because I'm retiring," the Old Sheriff said quietly, "or is it something else?"

"I almost lost you!" I snapped, rounding on him. "I thought I *had* lost you."

He sat there on the sofa, his hat sitting on the table in front of him. He looked old, I thought.

"I'm sorry," I said. "It's just . . . after you vanished inside, I looked through my mother's journal again. She'd been tracking the house. The Man with No Shadow told those campers to follow the lights to it, I think to try and get rid of you, or me, or us both. Did Mom ever talk to you about the house?"

"She didn't. Your mother kept a lot of things to herself."

"My parents planned to teach me the rest of it after college. . . . I was never going to have a normal childhood, but they didn't want to burden me with *everything*."

I knew how the creatures on the campground worked and how to manage a payroll. I knew how to shoot a gun, what charms worked against what monsters, and which contractors around town were reliable to do construction on the campground. But the hard things, the *really* hard things, like the town demanding that I protect them in one breath and cursing me for letting someone die in the next, or lying to someone about how their friend died, or letting some creature take someone I cared about because I was only human and couldn't kill all the monsters . . . these things I had to learn by myself.

"And I keep thinking that it was an accident," I continued, unable to stop myself, "because she planned to tell me everything, so of *course* it had to be an accident. Why would she leave the window open?"

"Kate." The Old Sheriff's voice was firm. "It doesn't help anything to dwell on that."

He was the person who had responded that morning. Aunt Aleda had called him, after they heard my father's screaming. Then she blocked Uncle Tobias from leaving the house, because they'd heard my father's scream cut abruptly short and they both knew what that meant, that it was too late, it was *always* too late when dealing with the inhuman. All my family can do is pick up the pieces. And that's all the Old Sheriff found of my dad, a piece of him. His hand.

The Old Sheriff had to work backward on what had happened. Start on the outside of the house and work inward, to the open window that started it all.

He saw it as he approached the house. A window in the master bedroom, still open, the curtains drifting softly in the morning breeze. He came close enough to see the bloodstains on the wall.

He made the paramedics wait outside while he went in. The house was silent and stunk of blood, of filth, and he held a handkerchief over his face as he entered the master bedroom. That's where he found my mother, lying in bed in her nightclothes, her eyes wide open and staring at the ceiling. Her expression was of surprise. That was all. Astonishing, considering her abdomen was torn open, two hands forced in just above the belly button and then pulling the skin and muscle apart. Her intestines were strewn all across the bedsheets, slipping off one side to pile on the floor. There were flies in the room from the open window, but they buzzed around aimlessly, refusing to land on the body.

And my father... the Old Sheriff saw the tangled sheets on his side of the bed. The bloody handprints on my mother's face. And most tellingly, how the back door had also been left ajar and how my aunt and uncle were woken by angry shouting—my father, yelling that she was a curse on this family and she wouldn't take any more of us—and then it was dawn and the beast arrived.

I know this next part. I know it because that morning I woke in my college apartment, miles away, sobbing, knowing that the dream I'd just had was the campground reaching out to me, telling me what had happened.

My father had woken beside the body of my mother with the little girl between them, sitting cross-legged, my mother's intestines still in her bloodstained hands. She just stared at him, her expression solemn and remorseless, and then my father—normally so careful and so unwilling to harm anything unnecessarily—snapped.

He grabbed her by her hair and dragged her outside. She screamed at him, as she screamed every morning as the beast dragged her away to be devoured. For him to stop, for someone to help her. But my mother was dead, and he had forgotten about me in that moment, forgotten about everything but his rage at being so *helpless* to stop these creatures from taking and taking and taking.

THE MAN WITH NO SHADOW

I knew how that felt.

And my father waited the last few minutes until the sun appeared on the horizon and the beast appeared.

I only saw its eyes in my dream. A multitude of them, shining like stars as it towered above my father.

He threw the little girl to it. She screeched, there was a crunch of bones, and she was silent.

And then it was my father's turn.

He screamed, he clawed at its eyes in futile anger, and there was a crunch of bones and he, too, went silent.

That is the first and most important rule any child in my family's line learns. Do not open any door or window after dark, except if a human guest is visiting. And do not go out at dawn. Wait inside while the beast drags the little girl away. Wait until she stops screaming and begging for help. Only then is it safe to go out.

Some people keep roosters to wake them up. My family has incomprehensible horrors instead.

"I just feel like I got lucky with the vanishing house," I said, "and I might not get lucky a second time."

"Look, I'm only *retiring*," the Old Sheriff sighed. "I just won't be the sheriff anymore. It's not like you can't ask me for help."

"Can you help with the town wanting to take Goat Valley from me? The New Sheriff is forcing me to sell."

He stood, grabbing his hat.

"Let's go have a chat with him. And we can talk about your situation with the Man with No Shadow on the way."

I hesitated, then said I'd be a moment, and I ran to my office to grab two things. The first was a decent-sized pocket knife. The second was the empty skull cup.

I didn't dare return it to the Man with the Skull Cup without refilling it first. And I couldn't think of a better candidate for "blood forcibly taken" than someone who needed a reminder of what family he was picking a fight with.

I'm sure it was a hell of a shock when the Old Sheriff walked in the door behind me. One minute, the New Sheriff was wearing a shit-eating grin seeing me in his office, thinking that I was here to talk about selling the land, and the next minute he was white as a sheet, thinking he'd seen a ghost. Which was a reasonable thing to think. But no, the Old Sheriff was back, and he sat himself down in the only chair opposite the sheriff's desk, and I stood at his shoulder.

And the Old Sheriff went on a lecture. Real calm and collected about it. Gently explained that the campground brought in a lot of money for people around here. That my family were upright citizens and an asset to the community, and he'd done us a real disservice by bad-mouthing our names. The sheriff's job, he explained, was to make our lives easier by lending his assistance. Sometimes that was mere paperwork, sometimes it was cleaning up a body or two, and sometimes it meant a little more—like risking one's life to drag someone out of a vanishing house.

The New Sheriff squirmed uncomfortably at that. We all know that he wasn't the type to put himself in danger. He thought I wasn't either, but then I'd gone and proved him wrong. Then the Old Sheriff leaned forward and got to the most important part of his talk.

The threats.

"You got this position because you were the *only person* available," the Old Sheriff said. "So don't go thinking that you've got it all figured out. I made you my deputy because you don't know shit. If you keep going around making a mess of things like this, I might just have to come out of retirement, and it's going to be ugly. That happens and you can kiss your job—and your reputation—goodbye."

"And if you try to interfere with my ownership of the campground," I added, "I'll show up at your office and blow your brains out. And I'll tell the town that you were working with some nasty evil thing, and maybe you are or maybe you aren't, but the town isn't going to question it, not if the Old Sheriff is backing me up."

The New Sheriff blanched at that. I grinned smugly, thinking that was all it would take. I'd put the cup on the table now, get an involuntary blood donation, and we'd go on our way.

"You're too much like your parents," the New Sheriff spat. "The town is better off without them. Damn shame they willed the campground to their psychopath of a daughter."

Something went white and hot in front of me, and it felt like my body was moving of its own volition. The Old Sheriff remained where he was, because everything was still going according to the plan to his knowledge.

I walked around the desk to where the sheriff sat. He recoiled from me. I slammed the skull cup down on the desk in front of him.

"Blood from what was already there," I said. "Blood freely given. And blood taken by force."

Then I changed the plan.

I stabbed the knife into his neck instead of his arm.

He went rigid with a gasp, then twitched violently as I yanked it free, grabbed his hair, and held his head over the cup.

I didn't get much. Not before the Old Sheriff seized the back of my shirt and threw me off, slamming me into the wall of the office. He grabbed the sheriff's radio and started yelling for an ambulance to be sent. Then he yelled at me to get out.

So I did. And I took the cup with me.

PART 4

Late Winter

In January and February, frequent cold snaps mean this is a poor season to be outdoors. Use the time to plan for camping season in the spring instead! Be mindful of seasonal depression and creatures who are hungry from lack of prey.

Pancake Saturdays Are a Problem

I found myself looking through my mother's journal in the days following. I still seethed at the New Sheriff's words whenever I had a quiet moment with my thoughts, and perhaps I was trying to refute them in my mind. All those pages of notes, cryptic phrases known only to my mother, evidence that she and my father were trying to keep the monsters at bay harder than anyone else in this town.

And I was searching for information.

I found what I was looking for in the corner of a page filled with dates. Some I recognized. Tyler's birthday. Mine. Their anniversary. Many were unlabeled, their significance lost with my mother's death. But three particular lines stood out. *The Man with No Shadow* followed by two dates.

I shared them with the Old Sheriff. He noticed something interesting about the second date. It was the first time that the New Sheriff ran against him for office, roughly five years ago. He hadn't won, but he ran every year after that. It struck the

Old Sheriff as odd at the time, because he'd never really thought that the man was someone who would ever want the job.

The other date was twenty-one years ago. The Old Sheriff couldn't think of anything significant that had happened that year but promised to look into it for me. I had enough on my plate, after all. Normally the weeks after Twelfth Night are fairly laid-back for me. The latter half of January and all of February are still too cold for camping. I do a lot of planning for the coming year, mostly renovations or upkeep. I don't worry so much about the creatures inhabiting the campground. With the holidays behind us, the majority of the things in the woods go into dormancy until spring. Until the campground has prey again.

I'd asked Bryan to patrol the woods with his dogs. The rest of my staff were taking time off, partly because it was the quiet time of the year, partly because I didn't feel comfortable putting them in a position where they might encounter the Not-Brother or the Man with No Shadow again. I'd already killed one of my staff members with my own hands, and the memory of it prickled uncomfortably, like a needle sliding under my skin.

It was a crisp and clear day in late January when Bryan radioed me, his voice tense. We'd agreed that he would check in every hour, and I immediately glanced at the clock when my radio crackled. Forty minutes past the hour. Not yet time for a check-in.

"I might have a problem," he said, and I was alarmed at the

anxiety in his voice. "My dogs took off after the Children with No Wagon."

"The *children*? Why would the dogs care about them?"

"They, uh, were yelling that it was 'pancake time.'"

He sounded embarrassed. I was already putting on my winter jacket and grabbing my shotgun to join him out there.

"Why would the dogs care about pancakes?" I asked as I headed for my four-wheeler in the garage.

"My mom makes them pancakes every Saturday," he said miserably. "It's their favorite thing."

Well, that explained why he'd insisted he wasn't available for Saturday-morning shifts.

"I'll be there as fast as I can," I said. "We'll go find the dogs together."

I didn't like this. The children had been incited to cause problems on the campground once already, and it seemed they were at it again. I drove along the packed snow covering the roads as fast as I dared until I reached where Bryan was waiting for me.

He was on the ground, curled on his side in the snow, his hands clutched to his chest and his shadow stretched long in the sharp afternoon sunlight.

And nearby crouched the Man with No Shadow, his hair shining like embers. His hand was splayed, the fingers vanishing into the snow—no—they vanished into Bryan's shadow.

I killed the four-wheeler and stumbled off it, running toward them with my shotgun tucked under my arm. With the engine off, I could now hear Bryan's soft cries of pain between each sharp intake of breath.

Slowly the Man with No Shadow locked his gaze with mine; he pulled his hand free. Bryan let out a shuddering sob and twitched, but did not try to get up.

"Didn't I warn you?" the creature said quietly. "I said I'd take your campground from you over the bodies of those you care about."

In the distance, I heard the baying of dogs, furious, growing rapidly louder. They were coming to protect their master. But I was here, I was ready. I raised the gun and fired.

It hit the Man with No Shadow right in the chest. He pitched backward, eerily silent save for the thud of his body hitting the ground. I fumbled to reload the shotgun, backing away as I did. And the Man with No Shadow . . . stood up.

Brushed the dirt off his jeans. And then raised his head and smiled at me. There wasn't a single mark on him from the gun. It was like the bullet had vanished when it hit him.

"Not so confident now, are we?" he asked mockingly. "I'll take them all from you. You have so many people to protect and there's only you, but there's so many monsters, and they're all willing to help if it means they get a chance to *feed*—"

I kept the shotgun trained on him. And as the sights settled over his torso, I thought of how his hand had intersected Bryan's, and I dropped the aim lower, toward the ground.

I shot him in the space where his shadow *should* have been.

The bullet hit the ground in a cloud of dust. And the Man with No Shadow shrieked in agony, his body spasmed, and he fell heavily to his hands and knees, one hand clutching at his ribs. Blood leaked between his fingers and fell in beads to the dusty ground beneath him.

I hastily began reloading the shotgun. I was fast, but it took precious seconds, seconds that I couldn't afford.

The Man with No Shadow twisted, face contorted in rage and agony, and he raised his bloodstained hand in my direction. Gripped the air tight, his knuckles white, and I felt something grab hold of my shadow. Like a shiver up my spine, but sharp as a knife.

He pulled. Something gave. I dropped the gun. And white agony blinded me, drove me to the ground, and all I could do was scream, digging my fingers into my shoulder as my body told me that my arm was gone, that there was nothing there, even as my fingernails clutched at numb flesh.

I'm not sure how long it took for me to regain my wits. Pain has a way of distorting time, narrowing your thoughts so that it is all you know, so that everything is driven from your mind except a desperate desire to be free of it. I next remember being on my knees, my forehead pressed against the ground, my fingers clutching a shoulder that I could barely feel.

My shadow's arm was gone. Only a tattered end remained behind. The Man with No Shadow was also gone. I found a trail of blood that led into the woods. I didn't dare follow it, not with my right arm hanging limp at my side.

I suppose I'm lucky that he didn't do worse. That his priority was to get the gun out of my hand and taking the arm was the fastest way to do it.

The dogs arrived shortly after. They crowded around Bryan, sniffing at him and whimpering, and I tried but I couldn't convince them to go after the Man with No Shadow. They refused to leave Bryan's side.

Somehow we both staggered back to the house. Bryan was struggling to breathe. I stared down at his shadow. It lay slanted along the floor, and in the center of his chest were five holes. I could clearly see the color of the hardwood through them. Like the Man with No Shadow had stabbed his fingers straight into Bryan's lungs.

"I'll be okay," Bryan groaned, sitting down on a sofa. "I can breathe . . . it just hurts."

"I'm so sorry, I was too slow—I'm always too slow; my whole damn family has always been too late—"

I was babbling. I took a deep breath and tried to focus through my pain. Bryan was quiet for a moment.

"I can't do this," he finally said. "I'm not—like you."

Most people quit the campground pretty quickly if they couldn't stomach the danger. Bryan had been here for a decade, though.

"Are you . . . quitting?" I asked.

Insensitive? Yes. But Bryan was my best employee.

"No, I—I can't. But the dogs—if they can be fooled—I can't do this."

He turned his head away from me so I couldn't see his face and took a deep breath.

"I'm sorry, Kate," he said quietly. "But the Man with No Shadow isn't going to stop. I'll help if I can ... but I can't come back to the campground."

Not until the Man with No Shadow was dead.

Flash Mob

The next day my arm had at least stopped hurting enough that I could function, although I couldn't move it. I put it in a sling and took advantage of the empty campground to see if I could shoot a shotgun one-handed. I could not.

As I was putting the gun away, the security camera at the front gate pushed a notification to my phone. I get a lot of false positives with the camera, but I dutifully checked the feed anyway. I almost dismissed it with barely a glance out of reflex. Thankfully, the array of colors from the mob's jackets registered as unusual in some part of my brain, and I looked at my phone again. Then I radioed Aunt Aleda and told her to get in contact with the police while I went to the gate.

I think the mob hadn't expected me to actually show up. They'd brought a reporter from the local newspaper (easily recognizable on account of there are only a handful of people on staff), and he was busy taking photos from angles where the signs would block the view and make the crowd seem larger than it was. There were perhaps a dozen people present. The signs were about what you'd expect. THE CAMP MUST GO and KATE IS THE REAL MONSTER.

Not gonna lie, that second one made me a bit angry. After all, they had a literal monster leading them.

The Not-Brother stood in the front of the mob, well-dressed with his hands in his pockets and a smirk on his lean face. At least, that's what I saw before I closed my left eye. Through my right, the one that itched under my lower eyelid, I saw a cavernous abdomen and the bone of his spine. The mob unconsciously formed around him, clinging tight as if he pulled them into his orbit.

I walked to the gate and leaned on it, staring him in the eyes.

"How the hell did you get out?" I hissed, keeping my voice low so that the others wouldn't hear.

"Jessie cut the fence during Halloween," he smirked. "That did the trick. Maybe you should have decapitated her sooner—"

"Or maybe I should have decapitated *you* months ago. Still, now's just as good. You wouldn't be the first monster I've killed with my own hands," I snapped.

He leaned in so that we were close enough that I could feel his rancid breath. My focus was entirely on him, my heart hammering, knowing that this was dangerous, that I was mere inches from a predator. Behind him, the mindless shouting of the mob fell away, meaningless in my ears.

"In front of all these witnesses?" he chided. "You'd really show them your true colors?"

"Everyone will see what you are when you're dead. You know what they call people that kill monsters? Heroes."

"They won't think that way about you. You've got too much blood on your hands. They're starting to realize that you're as dangerous as the creatures in the woods—and worse, you can't be kept at bay with an evil-eye charm and a couple of herbs."

His eyes flicked to the crowd around them, landing on one sign in particular: KATE IS THE REAL MONSTER.

"I didn't suggest that," he murmured. "They see you as a monster all on their own. No influence from me."

He straightened, still smiling, but I saw the rage in his eyes. One of us was going to end up dead before this was over.

The police arrived shortly after. One cruiser with one officer, and he didn't have much luck dispersing the crowd, as they were too riled up. The Not-Brother didn't even have to do anything, he just stood in the back, looking satisfied while the crowd surged forward and hit the gate, shaking it violently. I was suddenly grateful for the heavy iron chain that held it closed. I knew the town didn't like us, but to see the naked ferocity of their anger was startling.

The mob didn't leave until the New Sheriff turned up to disperse them. The Not-Brother was the last to go, walking backward slowly, staring at me the entire time. The New Sheriff stood on the other side of the gate after everyone was gone, and I went over there to thank him, because I felt obligated to, and he just looked at me with undisguised loathing.

"Don't mistake this for help," he said tightly. "I'm just doing my job."

He glanced at the sling.

"The hell happened to your arm?"

"Tripped in the garage," I lied.

His eyes narrowed and tracked downward . . . toward my shadow. I hastily turned so that it wasn't apparent that my shadow's arm was missing—but then—why would he know to look for that in the first place?

The New Sheriff had gone very pale when I'd threatened to claim he was working with an evil creature, back when I'd stabbed him in the neck. Perhaps that wasn't a lie. I glanced at his shadow in turn, not trying to disguise what I was staring at, and he stood there in silence and let me take a good long look.

It was riddled with holes. The edges pitted like an insect had nibbled at a leaf.

"I'm sorry," I said after a minute of uncomfortable silence. "I didn't realize you were under his control."

The line of his jaw tightened as he clenched his teeth in helpless anger.

"Yeah, well," he muttered, "I think I'd still hate you. You're not a very likable person."

Then he left. And I stood there for a moment, wondering how I was going to deal with the Not-Brother with one arm and no allies left on the campground.

No. Not quite. There was the Lady with Extra Eyes.

I packed an appropriate bribe and started wandering in the

deep woods. I count the money I spend on fancy tea leaves as a business expense. I didn't have to walk for long before I came across the house in the woods with its front yard carpeted with white flowers. The Lady with Extra Eyes was waiting for me on the front step. She invited me in, brewed some nettle tea, and told me my gift was appreciated, but it was not the reason she'd allowed me to find her today.

"The Man with No Shadow," I said.

A faint nod as she raised her teacup to her lips and took a small sip.

"He cannot succeed. *All* will suffer," she said.

The Thing in The Dark had said the same thing. But to hear it repeated now, with every single one of the lady's eyes fixed on me with such intensity, gave me pause to reconsider the words. *All will suffer.*

All.

"Does his plan . . . affect *you* as well? The other inhuman creatures on the campground?"

"There's a reason some of us are choosing sides."

My teacup was halfway to my mouth when she said that. I set it back down on the table and stared at the steam wafting off its surface. The Not-Brother was on the Man with No Shadow's side. The Lady with Extra Eyes seemed to be on mine. But were there others?

"Do *you* know what he's planning?" I asked.

She fixed me with a steely glare.

"I am not omniscient," she said. "Nor does the Man with No Shadow partake in—as you put it—*gossip.*"

Honestly, that was one of the more straightforward answers I've gotten from inhuman things.

"I just know his nature," she continued. "If he had his way, the whole of the campground would be his puppets, and I would have no visitors."

The Man with the Skull Cup had said something similar. If everyone died, he wouldn't have anyone to share his drink with. I didn't care if they were helping me for selfish reasons, though. I would take what I could get.

Unfortunately, help from the inhuman almost always comes with a cost.

"You're short on staff, I noticed," she said calmly. "Where is Jessie?"

"She belonged to the Man with No Shadow," I replied mechanically. "Something had to be done."

"And the New Sheriff?"

It's hard to maintain eye contact when over a dozen pairs of eyes are staring at you accusingly. I dropped my gaze and didn't reply.

"You've taken your grandfather's approach to dealing with problems," she sighed.

Why did she sound so disappointed? My hands tightened on the teacup. There was anger roiling in my chest, anger that had not subsided since I saw my uncle's head on the floor in front of me. Killing Jessie had done nothing to appease it.

"I'd burn this whole forest down if I thought it'd bring them back," I said tightly.

"That's what I am afraid of," she said with a sad smile. "I'll help you this one last time. And after that, I will never help you again. Is that a price you are willing to pay?"

She couldn't fix my arm, she said. That would only heal with time. Instead, she gave me nettle tea, mixed with the earth from around the roots of the tree in her backyard. If I drank it each morning, she said, I would be immune for that day from the Man with No Shadow's silver tongue. This magic would only work for me.

Would she still help my campers, I asked. Yes. She would. But I . . . I would be on my own.

I don't know why this was the cost. I don't know why these creatures make the demands they do. I could only consider my options, weigh the more immediate threat against a future that has never been certain of anything except the little girl and the beast, and then decide.

Forgive me, but I said yes.

What the Doctor Didn't Order

There is an old anger inside me. I can't remember when it was first kindled, but it was an anger born of helplessness, and that is the worst anger to harbor. It has no target, no direction, and it can smolder for a lifetime until the coals are white hot and all they lack is a scrap of fuel with which to ignite and scorch everything to ash.

I pretended I was the master of my anger. That my rules were there to keep everyone safe, that I did what I could, and if someone broke them—if someone bought ice from the Children with No Wagon or was disrespectful of one of the entities on this land—that they deserved my anger. These are the consequences after all, the results of a world that is both cruel and unfair.

It was a false justice.

I kept the thread that Perchta had stitched into my abdomen on my dresser. Brittle, stained crimson with my blood. Perhaps her sense of justice is similarly skewed (keeping a messy house is deserving of death, in her book), but I could not help but wonder about her warning. If you'd asked me this when I took over the campground, I would have said that it was necessary. That I'd seen what happens when people try to evade their fate, and there is always collateral damage. The innocent suffer alongside the culprit. I merely chose the lesser of two evils, and that is the closest I would ever get to virtue.

I didn't feel so confident anymore. Perhaps it was Perchta's thread, or perhaps it was from wearing the mantle of a saint, but I'd begun to doubt. Silently, insidiously, and then the Lady with Extra Eyes confirmed all my fears that perhaps I was as bad as the monsters I claimed I was protecting the town from.

This is what happens when I'm indoors by myself for too long. I spend too much time thinking.

A few days into February, the Old Sheriff showed up on my doorstep. He invited himself in and conspicuously eyed the unwashed dishes and the pile of blankets on the sofa.

"Haven't been getting out much, have you?" he asked gruffly.

"I've been injured," I replied defensively. Then, because it was the Old Sheriff, and he'd been there when my parents had died, I added the rest. "And I'm . . . feeling a bit lost right now. I've done some awful things, and . . . is there something wrong with me?"

"No. Well, no more than the rest of us."

I stared at him until he sighed.

"Yes, you have done some reprehensible shit, Kate," he said. "But you can't change that. You just have to keep moving forward, otherwise you wind up here—having a crisis of confidence at the worst possible moment. Do you know what fixes it?"

"What?"

"Getting out of the house and doing your damn job. Let's go."

And somehow, his gruff rebuke did make me feel more normal. I brushed my teeth and then followed him out to his pickup.

The New Sheriff wasn't able to do anything in town anymore, now that we knew he was under the control of the Man with No Shadow. The Old Sheriff was watching him too closely. Unfortunately, the town's anger against the campground was going strong without his help. No doubt the Not-Brother had a hand in keeping it going.

The Old Sheriff wasn't intervening but instead had been focusing on investigating who might have been in contact with the Man with No Shadow. His diligence had paid off. He'd unearthed someone who might know something, and he was willing to speak with us. He was frightened, though, and so we were going to meet him someplace discreet. Someplace where none of us would be recognized by the locals.

Outside a bowling alley in another town, to be specific. The sheriff pulled up next to a young man wearing a bright-red T-shirt and he got in the back seat, and then the sheriff drove off. I glanced back at the man. He looked scared and avoided making eye contact with me. I introduced myself, just to relieve the tension, and he said that he knew who I was. Or at least he knew me by reputation.

"I work in the hospital," he said. "I don't want to tell you my name. But I need to tell you about something that's been going on for a long time now."

It had started years ago. I pressed the young man for an exact date, and he couldn't give me one, as he'd only pieced the timeline together from records. But roughly speaking, it was around nine years ago, shortly after I'd taken over the campground. The man worked in the ER as a nurse for a while, but he'd transferred to another department after he'd noticed what was happening. He suspected it was still going on.

"Every now and then we'd get someone from the campground in the ER," he said nervously. "No physical injuries, but the patient's heart rate would be erratic, their oxygen count was low . . . and then they'd go into cardiac arrest and die."

"How often did this happen?" I asked.

"Perhaps twice a year. I only noticed because I started looking through the records and then tracking the cases going forward."

The hospital had recorded their deaths as being from underlying health issues. He'd accessed the health history of one such patient and didn't find anything to indicate this had been the case.

The nurse hesitated a moment in his story, staring out the window and fidgeting.

"I see a lot of weird shit," I gently said. "Nothing you say will be unbelievable to me."

"There was one patient I treated," he continued. A young man. Looked healthy, not the kind you'd expect to find gasping

THE MAN WITH NO SHADOW

for air on a gurney. They'd given him epinephrine, thinking it was an allergic reaction. Then, right before his heart had stopped, the patient had sat straight up in the bed and grabbed him.

"I'm scared," he gasped, clutching at the nurse's arm. "There's something—in the woods."

And the nurse noticed—just before he collapsed again and before the heart monitor sounded its alarm—that the young man's shadow wasn't right.

It was almost gone. What little remained was tattered, like it'd been torn to shreds.

After that he began to look at the shadows of all the people who died of natural causes in the ER. Most were normal. A few were not. And of those few, he noticed another pattern.

The final cause of death was always written by the same doctor. It didn't matter who had actually been present. The record was always entered or amended by the same person.

The Old Sheriff thanked the nurse for his courage. It was hard enough to recognize the patterns, he said, and even harder to jeopardize his position by coming forward. He gently suggested the nurse look for a position elsewhere. In another county, perhaps. Just to be safe. Then he dropped him off back at the bowling alley, and we sat in silence for a while as he drove back toward the campground.

"The Man with No Shadow has a doctor under his control," I said. "So what? I think we know by now that he's gotten to people in town."

"Look at the big picture," the Old Sheriff replied gently. "Think of the timeline. This happened after your parents died, so he couldn't have gotten to the doctor by being released from the campground. He's been trapped since then."

I was quiet for a moment. His words conjured a terrible reality, one that I did not feel ready to confront.

"If I look in my camp records, I'm going to find the doctor's name, aren't I?" I asked miserably.

"I reckon you are. He's not local, either. Moved here from out of state."

The Man with No Shadow was collecting my campers. Rearranging them like pieces on a chess board. I knew sometimes someone fell into his sway, but I thought we'd caught most of them and banned them from coming back. No. We caught the ones he wanted us to see talking to him, the ones he used to make me think I had the situation under control.

I didn't. It was slipping through my hands, no matter how hard I tried to hold on. His reach was far broader than I thought, and he'd been planning for a long, long time.

I glanced sideways at the Old Sheriff suspiciously. He didn't take his gaze off the road, but he noticed nonetheless.

"He can't control me, Kate," he said gently.

"Are you like Bryan, then? Some distant ancestor that wasn't human?"

"No. But let's just say there's someone that protects me and leave it at that."

His wife. Of course. I left it alone. There were plenty of these open secrets around town that we didn't talk about. Not every supernatural creature was only out for murder. Despite my family's closeness to the inhuman world, though, we didn't have any such secrets. I'm ordinary. Just a girl with a gun and a list of rules.

"Let's go visit the doctor," the Old Sheriff suggested.

"And . . . kill him?"

"No." He paused. "Well, maybe. But let's keep that as the last resort."

Thirty minutes later we were pulling into the doctor's icy driveway. It was a long drive, winding through a grassy yard to a big, expensive house set up on a hill. We have clusters of these sorts of homes in scenic areas. You know how groups of animals have their own names? A murder of crows. A conspiracy of ravens. What do you call a group of rich people with big houses sporting too many gables?

Around here, they're called easy targets, especially when the Old Sheriff has made a call, and the police will ignore any alerts from the security system company.

We went in through a window when the doctor didn't answer the door. The Old Sheriff had taken a rifle from the back of the truck and bashed in the glass with the stock. That set off the alarm, as we expected, but the Old Sheriff ignored it and tossed his jacket over the ledge to cover the broken glass. We climbed in.

The interior was dark. And the furniture . . . it looked ransacked. Everything was pushed away from the windows, to the far end of the room. The living room furniture was piled against the wall, sofa upended to make room for chairs, possessions stacked on top of seat cushions and littering the carpet underneath the end table to leave the rest of the floor bare.

"This is . . . weird," I whispered uneasily.

We cleared the ground floor. Every room was the same—all the contents stacked as far from the windows as possible. Then we went upstairs. The stairway ascended into darkness. It was an unnatural gloom, deeper than merely having the lights off. The Old Sheriff shone his flashlight into the first bedroom. The windows were covered with layers of black plastic, the edges sealed over and over with duct tape. No sunlight was able to get through. He cleared that room while I stood watch at the doorway, and then we made our way through another bedroom and a bathroom. There was no furniture. The rooms were completely empty.

We found the doctor in the second to last room. The Old Sheriff hesitated before entering, only because he was looking through another doorway into the master bedroom. It appeared to contain all the furniture in the second floor. It was stacked up to the ceiling, beds and bedside tables, lamps and storage boxes. The piles cast long, jagged shadows on the far wall as the flashlight beam played over the interior. I admit that I was being careless—I was looking too, wondering what had driven the doctor to do such a thing. Neither of us was watching the room we were about to enter.

The doctor emerged from the darkness at a run. He bodily hit the sheriff, who staggered back with a grunt. The doctor's eyes were wide and unfocused. His hands were wrapped around some kind of weapon that glinted in the flashlight. He waved it wildly in front of him, panting desperately with fear.

"Get out!" he shrieked. "GET OUT!"

The Old Sheriff backed away, telling him easy, easy, just calm down. We weren't here to hurt him. The doctor lunged again with his weapon, screaming that we had to get out, that we were going to get him killed. And all the while, the Old Sheriff was trying to talk him down.

I didn't feel we were getting anywhere with that.

I took careful aim and kicked, driving my heel into his knee. He shrieked and went down, and then the Old Sheriff smashed his flashlight on the back of the man's head. A box knife fell from his hands and onto the carpet.

The sheriff handcuffed him while he recovered his senses, and I took the opportunity to tear the plastic off the windows. Sunlight poured in. And the doctor began to shriek, screaming that the shadows were going to devour him. The sheriff ignored his terror and grabbed him by the arm.

"Let's go," he said.

We hauled the doctor downstairs and to the yard. If it weren't for Perchta, I might have slit his throat and dumped his body within eyeshot of the Man with No Shadow's grove. I had to be content with merely kicking him a few times while he was down, just to hear him yell. I was wearing my work boots too. Probably cracked at least one rib before the Old Sheriff gruffly told me to knock it off.

"He made a lot of trouble for me," I complained as we wrestled him into the car.

"If I beat the shit out of everyone that ever caused me trouble, I would not have this cordial of a relationship with your family."

I didn't really have a way to reply to that.

We took him to the Old Sheriff's property and dumped him in an empty shed in the backyard. Sorcha stood by, holding the door for us, sipping from a cup of coffee in her free hand as if this was a very normal thing that happened around here. Maybe it is.

"Okay, let's give it a few minutes, and then we'll go inside and talk to him," the Old Sheriff said.

"Am I bad cop? What do I do?" I asked.

"Just stand there and look like yourself. You don't need to say anything. In fact... please don't."

I felt a little offended.

The doctor was huddled in the darkest corner of the shed. All the fight was gone from him. He was willing to talk. Unfortunately, it was a lot of hysterical babbling. Something about how the shadows were watching him and how he saw their faces. I can only assume that the faces were of the people who'd died and whose records he'd falsified and his guilt had finally broken him. After a lot of prodding, the Old Sheriff got some useful information from him.

Years ago, the doctor had gone camping at Goat Valley. He'd gotten to talking to someone else there, someone who was curious about his job. That was all. He didn't go back to the campground again. Just that one time. But shortly after, he felt an intense need to move to our town. Like a hand was on the back of his neck, guiding him to where he needed to go.

"That man didn't have a shadow, did he?" I asked.

I felt the Old Sheriff glance at me in irritation, but I kept my eyes glued on the doctor.

"He's angry," the doctor sobbed. "I feel it. So angry. He thought you'd be easy to remove, but you *aren't*, you keep *fighting* him, and you won't just do as he wants you to."

My breath caught in my chest. Selling the campground. That's what he wanted, because it would get me out of the way for . . . what, exactly? Were my rules too effective? Had I robbed him of his prey? I didn't think so highly of myself to believe that. Besides, he'd started planning all of this long before I inherited the campground.

After that, the doctor settled on one thought, and that consumed what was left of his mind.

"He eats them," he whimpered, over and over. "He's going to eat me, too."

That's it. That's all we could get from him. As we were leaving, the doctor begged us to seal off all the cracks and leave the lights off. No light could get in, he babbled. He's powerless in the darkness. The Old Sheriff obligingly stuffed a bunch of ragged towels under the crack of the door to block out the light, which was far more courteous than anything I would have done.

"Is it safe to leave him here?" I asked, as he did this. "What if he gets out and you're not around? What about your wife?"

He laughed in amusement.

"She'll be fine," he said.

When I got home, I brewed the tea from the Lady with Extra Eyes, and then I went to the grove. I took my shotgun. I still couldn't fire it one-handed, but hopefully the Man with No Shadow wouldn't know that. I had no doubt that he'd know I was coming. The doctor belonged to him, after all.

The Man with No Shadow was not alone when I arrived. A woman I didn't recognize lay at his feet as he sat upon a rock, absently running his fingers through her hair. She wasn't moving, and I was too far away to tell if she was breathing. I stopped well before the edge of his grove.

"Who is that?" I asked quietly.

"Just a little snack I had tucked away, not far from here," he replied. "I don't like to go hungry, so I've made . . . preparations."

"How many?" I demanded.

His eyes shone in the late afternoon sunlight.

"I've lost count," he replied quietly. "I can't even tell them apart anymore. I call . . . and a meal delivers itself to me."

I took a deep breath, trying to steady my nerves. The shotgun hung heavy in my hand. I tried flexing the fingers on my wounded arm, felt them respond sluggishly, felt the weakness of my grip.

"So you called this person here," I said evenly, "because you knew I'd be coming by your grove. Why? What's the point?"

Perchta had said I could save them all. I seethed. What a cruel joke.

"You don't like me talking to you," he said. "So I thought I'd answer your inevitable questions by showing you what you want to know."

And he reached down and ripped her shadow away from her torso, pulling a chunk of it out with his hands, right where the heart should be. Her body shuddered once and then slumped motionless to the ground. My gaze returned unwillingly to the Man with No Shadow, hunched over his meal, devouring the murky darkness in his hands with the sound of ripping meat.

He didn't just control my campers. He had been eating them as well.

I was angry at myself for missing the signs. The Man with No Shadow had been preying on my campers all along, and I never realized it. I thought we were losing people to normal reasons: severe allergies, dehydration, heart problems. And perhaps we were, but there were also some who were being devoured. I thought about what it was like when he ripped my shadow's arm off. I remember how much it hurt.

I can't imagine how they suffered before they died.

Before this was done, I was going to burn his grove to ash, with him in it. Maybe that would bring some peace to the people he had killed there.

The Man with the Skull Cup Kissed Me

I'm sure, dear reader of this guidebook, that some of you are inwardly celebrating this development, but I am afraid I must crush your hopes and tell you that it's not what you think. Not that it'll stop any of you.

But like any bad romance, it does start at a courthouse.

The Old Sheriff had done a bit of investigative work on his own. He'd borrowed a police cruiser and pulled Curtis over for speeding. He'd checked the man's driver's license and then let him off with a warning.

Curtis's birthdate was seven months after the first date in my mother's journal. Seven months after the Man with No Shadow was let out of the campground for the first time.

"So it's a dead end," I sighed.

"Kate," the Old Sheriff said firmly over the phone. "Seven months. That's an important amount of time."

"Because . . . ?"

"A pregnancy lasts nine months. The Man with No Shadow

might not have gotten to the buyer, but he could have gotten to the buyer's *mother*."

"What? It's not six months?"

"How do you not know this?!"

"I don't plan on having kids! I slept through health class in high school!"

The Old Sheriff sighed. "We need to get at the records room in the town hall. They might have a birth certificate. Are you up to doing some breaking and entering?"

My arm was not fully healed, but I had mobility back, if not strength. It would have to suffice. I could at least drive myself now, as Tyler had lent me his old car. The Old Sheriff would stay at the station to run interference with the New Sheriff in case anyone called in about what I was doing.

Our courthouse is connected to the town hall building, and across the street is the library. There's a handful of stores—some places to eat, a general store, and a hardware store. And that's it. That's downtown.

Early on Valentine's Day morning, before the town was awake, I broke in through the back entrance and took an immediate left down the stairs leading to the basement. They creaked on every step, and the building seemed to sigh, like the entire structure was vibrating with my presence. I knew this was a quirk of the old building, but after the experience with the vanishing house, I was unnerved by the sound. The basement was dark, but I did not dare turn on the lights. I wanted to get in, get the file, and get out totally unseen.

So I descended into the darkness, and it swallowed me up.

I told myself it wasn't the same. It wasn't the vanishing house. My heart still hammered in my chest until, finally, my feet touched concrete and I felt safe turning on my flashlight.

I went up and down the rows of cabinets, searching for the year Curtis was born. I opened the drawer and fished through the records. I found what I was looking for just as I heard the creak of footsteps on the stairs. Someone flipped on the lights. Fortunately, my years of dealing with dangerous monsters have given me some capacity to think quickly in urgent situations, and I snatched the document out of the folder, folded it a couple of times, and stuffed it inside my bra.

I shut the file cabinet and turned around just as the New Sheriff came around the row of cabinets. With him were two police officers, neither of them in uniform. That didn't bode well. The New Sheriff was supposed to be at the station. I closed my left eye, and the splinter in my right itched. My heart lurched in my chest. The Not-Brother stood there, the two officers flanking him to block the path to the exit. His abdomen was a pit in the dim lighting, the pale ghost of his spine barely visible to connect the two halves of his body. It was like his chest was floating in the gloom. I reluctantly tore my gaze away from it to look him in the eyes.

He smirked at me. I detested the sight of that smug smile.

"Shouldn't you be hiding at home?" he asked, showing his teeth.

"Needed some fresh air," I replied. "Shouldn't you be trying to start another riot?"

"Don't need a riot if we can force you to sign over the campground right here."

One of the men held up a pile of documents and a pen. I eyed them and then carefully spat on the floor at his feet.

And the second man hit me. Right on the side of my mouth. I just remember the impact when I hit the floor—so sudden that I didn't even register the pain until I was on the floor, watching blood splatter on the cement from a split lip. I was dazed, and I didn't comprehend that they'd surrounded me, not until one of the men hoisted me back to my feet.

"Does it really count if I sign that under duress?" I finally said, spitting again, but this time to clear a thick clot of blood from my mouth.

"It does," the Not-Brother hissed. "Maybe not in your courts, but the intention matters for us, and that intention can be you wishing for the pain to stop."

He considered for a moment.

"I think I'll start breaking your bones," the Not-Brother said thoughtfully. "We'll see how many I can get through before you sign. I'll leave your hand alone, of course. You need to be able to hold the pen."

I shifted slightly as he stepped closer. Slid my feet farther apart. Widening my stance. And then I twisted, hooking the man who held me by his ankle with my own, and I threw.

People don't realize how strong I really am. They forget I

do a lot more than just management. They forget that I do manual labor as well, that I don't sit at home all day letting my staff do all the hard work. I dig holes. I carry things. I clear brush and trees. I build.

I kill monsters.

The man behind me was surprised by my sudden show of defiance, and he tumbled forward and into the gaping abdomen of the Not-Brother.

He went in headfirst, and the Not-Brother's face registered first with shock and then with outrage and then... hunger. He shuddered, throwing his head back, and his throat bulged as a ripple ran through his entire body. Then he doubled over, clamping his chest down on the man, who was trapped halfway inside the Not-Brother's body. The man's legs kicked in the air futilely, and the Not-Brother wrapped his arms around the man's waist, greedily shoving him farther inside his empty abdomen. The skin of his back began to distend, stretching outward as his victim frantically tried to claw his way free. I heard muffled screams.

The other man dropped the paper and the pen, his eyes clearing, and he stumbled away from the Not-Brother in horror.

I didn't waste any time. I grabbed his arm as I ran past the Not-Brother and dragged him along with me toward the stairs. He didn't need much encouragement. He was right behind me when I risked only one backward glance. Past him, I could see the Not-Brother still doubled over, the man almost entirely engulfed now. Only his ankles protruded, and his struggles were growing slower. The Not-Brother's abdomen was horribly distended, like a tick. I looked ahead at the stairway and kept going.

I could at least save one of them.

The man followed me to the car. I yelled at him to get in and he did, almost falling into the passenger seat. Then I turned the key in the ignition and peeled out of the parking lot.

I got on the county road heading toward the police station. I'd take him to the Old Sheriff, I reasoned.

"That was my *partner*," the man whispered. "It *ate my partner*!"

"Yeah, that's what monsters do," I replied tersely.

"You're supposed to keep them away from us."

He turned to look at me. His gaze was wild and unfocused, like an animal in a trap.

"I want out," he gasped, his voice thin with panic, grabbing at my arm. "I want away from you!"

"Fuck! No! We're going to the Old Sheriff, and you're telling him what you know!"

"Let me *out*!"

And he grabbed the wheel and pulled. I only had a few seconds in which to process what was happening and I tried to correct the car, but I was too slow; we swerved, there was a catch as the car hit the snowbank on the shoulder, and then I felt the back tires slide sideways. There was a violent lurch to the side—I remember feeling like I was floating. My vision shut off as my brain blocked out all else, and then there was nothing.

Like the lights had been turned off.

They switched back on when the paramedics were pulling the door to the car open. I didn't understand how they'd gotten here so fast, not until much later when I was sitting in a bed at the ER and the concussion symptoms showed up. Then I understood that there was a gap in my memories because I'd been knocked unconscious. The car had rolled. They scanned my brain and didn't find any bleeding. A concussion, the doctor said, and put me on "brain rest." Lying around in a dark room doing nothing, basically. They assumed the bruises and cuts on my face were from the crash. I didn't correct them.

My passenger had died, they told me. He hadn't been wearing his seat belt and was ejected from the vehicle. Such a polite way of saying it. Ejected. I called the Old Sheriff and asked him to pick me up, because I wasn't emotionally ready to tell Tyler that I'd wrecked his car.

"You got lucky," the doctor told me as he was finishing up my discharge paperwork. "That accident could have killed you. I have to admit we'd always figured it'd be one of those things on your campground that'd do you in."

I did not appreciate his dry humor about the situation. I snatched the script for painkillers out of his hand and let the Old Sheriff escort me to his car.

We stopped by the pharmacy to fill my meds on the way home. I took the first dose straightaway. Neither of us talked much. I told him that the Man with No Shadow had clearly been recruiting more people from town, not just the campers. The police, too. The Not-Brother might be helping with that, he suggested. Coercing them onto my land. There were plenty of ways onto it through the woods, through the parts that are not fenced.

"We need to kill the Not-Brother," I said grimly. "And I think I know how to do it."

"But not until you're off brain rest," the Old Sheriff said as he pulled the car into my driveway. "Concussions are serious."

I didn't answer. I was staring at the Man with the Skull Cup, who stood on the walkway leading up to my front porch.

The Old Sheriff stayed with the car and let me approach on my own to see what he wanted. "I am concussed and on pain meds," I said wearily as he approached. "Please make this quick. Why are you here?"

"You refilled the cup," he said slowly.

"Yeah, and? Did I do it right?"

For a brief moment he looked exasperated, and then his expression went cool and unreadable again.

"I knew you were injured," he said. "I came to see how bad it is."

He reached out and grabbed my chin, turning my head to the side to inspect the bruises darkening one side of my face. I whined in the back of my throat so that he knew he was hurting me, that his thumb was pressing into the bruises.

"Poor thing," he murmured. "Here. Drink."

Maybe it was the drugs or maybe it was the concussion, but I did something I'd never done before.

I refused. I resisted.

His grip on my chin tightened, and when I opened my mouth with a cry of pain, he forced the cup up to my lips and poured the contents down my throat. I choked on it, swallowed on reflex, and only then did he release me. "What the hell?!" I demanded weakly, wiping at my lips with the back of my hand. "I can't take my pain meds now!"

"Yes. The medication."

His eyes narrowed, and he looked at me with naked calculation for a moment; then he grabbed my throat. I cried out, instinctively, as fresh pain blossomed as his fingers tightened in my bruised flesh.

Then the Man with the Skull Cup kissed me.

Due to the nature of my upbringing, I am not really "into" other people. I made a half-hearted attempt at boyfriends in college, briefly dated a girl, and once made out with a guy in a nightclub in a vain attempt to understand what I was missing out on. The stranger's lips on mine were awkward, I was repulsed by his tongue, and his gum falling out of his mouth and sticking to my blouse finalized my opinion that the answer to my question was "not much."

This experience was more terrifying than awkward, and instead of mint, I tasted the metal of his tongue piercing.

My first Valentine's Day kiss and it was with a monster.

Then he released me, and I collapsed at his feet as my stomach convulsed and I vomited repeatedly onto the snow covering my front yard. I suppose swapping spit counts as ingesting something.

After my stomach was empty, I sat there, crying, until the Old Sheriff came over and gently urged me inside. I think he also told the Man with the Skull Cup to "fuck off," but maybe that's wishful thinking. I eventually cried myself to sleep.

When I woke up, there was a note from the Old Sheriff

saying that he'd come back after dinner to take the night shift, and that he had taken the pill bottle because it seemed off.

He texted me that night.

Pills came up positive on toxicology screening. You should be fine, though. One dose isn't dangerous on its own, and you probably threw it up before it had fully dissolved in your stomach. Police are on their way to arrest the person who filled your script.

Yes, he really does type everything out with proper punctuation and no abbreviations. We should all learn from his example.

And then when I replied back with *wtf I hate this town*, he reminded me that I was on brain rest, and now that I had checked my messages, I needed to put the phone away.

I must admit that I cheated a little. I still had the birth certificate on me. I turned the lights on and read it. The Old Sheriff's gamble had paid off. Curtis's mother was a local who had moved away shortly after his birth. I remembered her because there were rumors that she was pregnant, but those all died away quickly after she left.

But his father . . .

His father was Uncle Tobias. My uncle had had an affair.

Now I know why the Man with No Shadow was interested in this woman and her son. He's family. The buyer is my cousin.

The Man with No Shadow isn't just trying to take my campground away from me. He's trying to claim it, using my own family against me.

I'll be damned if I let that happen.

I Saved Someone. Sort Of.

A week later, when my concussion had finally begun to ease, I received a call from the Old Sheriff that he was on his way to my house and that he had a problem we needed to deal with. I didn't ask questions, just got my "dealing with" kit together. Charm vest, shotgun, and some heavy duty trash bags that can double as body bags in a pinch. Then I waited by the front door until I heard the Old Sheriff's car pull up. He waved me over as I walked out of the house, and I followed him to the back of the vehicle.

He popped the trunk open. I'll be honest—I was not expecting who was inside.

It was the New Sheriff. His wrists were handcuffed behind his back, and his ankles were tied together with rope. His knees were tied as well, but despite this, he continued to struggle, a strangely rhythmic rocking back and forth as his hips shifted and his knees tried to bend. Dried blood crusted his face from a gash directly in the middle of his forehead. His eyes were heavy with exhaustion and fear, and he weakly turned his head toward us, squinting at the sudden sunlight.

"Help me," he gasped.

I was bewildered as to why he would ask me to save him from the Old Sheriff. I turned to the man beside me, who only stared grimly down at his captive, one hand still on the lid of the trunk.

"So . . . are you looking for somewhere to dump a body?" I asked. "Because honestly, we could just drop him in my neighbor's lake and blame it on the shulikun. Lent hasn't started yet. I don't think they've been banished for the year."

Look, I may have been reconsidering my violent ways, but I trust the Old Sheriff's judgment, and if he says someone needs to be disposed of, I ain't questioning it for an instant.

The Old Sheriff only sighed softly and reached down, grabbing the man's arm and hauling him out of the vehicle. I took his other arm as best as I could, and together we dragged him from the car and into my house.

Then the Old Sheriff pulled a sizable pocket knife out and set to sawing through the ropes that bound the New Sheriff's legs. Surprisingly, he began to fight back, shaking his head violently and begging not to be released. The Old Sheriff refused to be dissuaded, and the ropes snapped free, leaving the man on the floor with only his hands handcuffed behind him. And he began to weep. It was a broken sort of crying, deep within the chest, and there were no tears. It was a paroxysm of despair, the hopeless weeping of a man who had nothing left in him with which to fight.

He stood. His legs jerked mechanically, as if they were on strings. And he began to walk in a straight line and didn't stop when he hit the sofa, just continued to go forward and slowly, slowly, the piece of furniture began to budge. Inch by inch, being resolutely shoved forward and to the side with each impact of the sheriff's knees. After a minute of this, the Old Sheriff intervened by taking the man by his shoulders and forcibly turning him in another direction.

And off went the New Sheriff, like a mindless toy, and it was only the Old Sheriff's intervention that kept him from walking straight into the wall of my living room.

"I have an idea," I said. And I went to the garage.

I don't keep pets. After the horse incident (some other time), we decided they were just a bad idea to have around. However, at some point I acquired a dog tie-out—a long spiral stake that went into the ground with a swivel on the end and a long wire lead. It was probably left behind by a camper. I tend to keep any lost property I think might come in useful. We took the New Sheriff out into the backyard and struggled to shove the stake in the icy ground. Then we put the lead around one of his elbows. He walked in one direction until he was out of slack, and then, tugged to the side by the off-center pull of the lead, he began to walk in a long circle, tracking a path through the snow.

"Well, that's a solution," the Old Sheriff sighed. "He's going to walk himself to death, though, if this keeps up. He's been at this for hours. He's already exhausted, and I'm afraid he's going to keep going until he simply drops dead."

"The Man with No Shadow?" I asked, watching the sheriff make his slow, torturous lap around my yard.

A faint nod. "I guess he's done with him."

He wasn't much use with the Old Sheriff watching over his shoulder, now that we knew who he was really working for.

They had found the man caught on a fence on some farmland. The farmer saw a figure struggling at the far end of his field. He went out there to investigate—armed, of course, that's just how we are around here—and was surprised to find the sheriff. Walking. Just . . . walking. Straight ahead, directly into the wooden fence. He must have been out there for some time, for the snow was melted, exposing the frozen ground, from his feet repeating the same steps over and over and over.

The landowner took him inside and called the Old Sheriff. While he was on the phone, explaining the situation, the New Sheriff proceeded to walk into a wall and keep walking into it until he'd bashed his head enough times to split the skin open. That was where the head injury had come from. The landowner found the sheriff moaning in pain with blood running down his face, and still his legs continued to carry him forward.

After that, the farmer tackled the New Sheriff and held him down until help arrived. That's when they tied him up, and the Old Sheriff brought him to me.

I went over to the sheriff, once I was caught up on what was happening. I matched pace with him as he continued walking in his long circle.

"What did the Man with No Shadow tell you to do?" I asked.

"Walk," he panted. "Just . . . keep walking."

Without turning or stopping. Just walk until his heart gave out or he blundered into something deadly—like the highway. My heart sank.

I told him I'd think of something. He stared hopelessly straight ahead and replied that I shouldn't bother, that he knew something like this could happen from the moment he became a pawn to a monster. He suggested bringing my shotgun out here, just to speed things along a little. He was so tired. He just wanted it to stop.

I went back to the house, but I did not get the gun. I stood with the Old Sheriff on the back porch, and we watched for a little bit in silence. I suggested taking him to the hospital and having them sedate him. He agreed that we could try that, if there weren't any other options. It could buy us a little time. Or the drugs would simply not work, subsumed by whatever foul power was keeping his body moving. He asked if there was any other remedy I knew of. Something that wasn't normal medicine.

I knew some things, I said. Ways to protect against powers and ways to banish powers. The problem was that a lot of them didn't work against the greater entities on my campground, like the Man with No Shadow, or I would have gotten rid of him already. And worse, a lot of what I know is focused on protection. There wasn't too much in my repertoire to undo the damage, once done.

And the stories? What happened to people who were cursed in the stories?

Well, I explained, they usually had to have some other being of power intervene. And the Old Sheriff just looked at me for a moment until I realized what I had said.

So we took the New Sheriff into the woods. I walked to his right, and the Old Sheriff walked to his left; we each held one of his arms to guide him between us, so that he wouldn't keep going straight into a tree. He didn't speak. He was beyond exhaustion, nearly senseless, but unable to do anything about it, not with the Man with No Shadow's words coursing through his body. I told the sheriff that we were taking him to see the Lady with Extra Eyes, and that while she wouldn't help me anymore, I hoped that she'd be willing to help him.

We didn't find the Lady with Extra Eyes.

The Dancers found us first.

The young woman greeted us on the road. She stood in the middle of the path, barefoot, wearing jeans and a garish hot-pink bikini top, despite the cold. Guess fairies don't fear frostbite. We had to adjust our path to go around her, and she fell in beside me as we walked.

"You're looking for me," she said.

"I was looking for the Lady with Extra Eyes," I replied somewhat tersely. I was not in the mood to deal with the Dancers today.

"No, you were looking for a cure," she corrected.

"Bargains with fairies always have a price."

"Did I say I was a fairy?"

I stopped. I let go of the New Sheriff's arm and let him and the Old Sheriff continue on. This needed my full attention. I stared at the woman in front of me with her round face and her black hair and that faint grin on her lips.

"You dance," I said slowly. "There's some beliefs that a group dancing in a circle around an afflicted person will remove a curse."

"Give him to us. You will not get him back. He will join our company and live as long as he chooses to."

I ran to the sheriffs. Took the New Sheriff by the elbow and turned him around. I told him I had a solution, that he had to go with the Dancers. They'd make him one of their own and that would save him. It would break the Man with No Shadow's hold. He'd be free. He couldn't fight back, his body no longer under his control, just as he'd been unable to even raise his arms to stop himself from slamming his head into the wall, over and over until he bled. All he could do was beg, as his legs carried him inevitably forward to the waiting dancer. She watched him with bright, eager eyes.

"They kill people," he cried weakly. "I can't do that! I'm not—like—you!"

My chest felt tight at hearing his cries of protest. But I kept going. He screamed that he would rather die as a human than be one of the monsters on my campground. That he hated me—my whole damn family was evil. That I didn't have the right to make this choice for him. But he couldn't stop me. The Man with No Shadow had told him to walk and so he did, straight toward the dancer who stretched out her arms to him.

I delivered him into her waiting hands. He wept and the

lady shushed him, telling him that he'd fought hard but now his fight was done. And she glanced backward at where I stood with the Old Sheriff on the road.

The Old Sheriff didn't say much on the walk back to the house, other than he would try to head off the fallout when people noticed the New Sheriff was missing. Keep them from blaming it on me. He didn't sound very hopeful—everyone knew we had bad blood, what with the stabbing and all—but I appreciated him trying.

A few days later, at sundown, Aunt Aleda was making the final rounds through the campground to make sure all our protections were still in place. She saw a group of people in the woods and stopped at the edge of the road to see if they were trespassers or something else.

The Dancers. They were setting up wood for the bonfire. The sheriff was there, stuffing dead leaves and small branches in at the base in preparation for lighting it. One of the Dancers touched his shoulder, and he looked up, to where my aunt sat on her four-wheeler, and he waved. Then he went back to work.

The dancer had said he could choose to die, so I guess he was okay with the arrangement.

I kept telling myself that maybe this is a good thing. He never wanted to be sheriff. I don't know what he wanted. I didn't pay much attention to the New Sheriff in school and never found out, and now it was too late. The Man with No Shadow dictated his future for him, took hold of his life and discarded whatever hopes and dreams he'd once harbored.

And then I took him by the arm and delivered him to another fate that he hadn't chosen.

I hope he's content with them. I hope he someday stops hating me.

I hope he never has to kill anyone.

I think a few months before this I would have simply killed the New Sheriff and justified it as a necessary evil. Putting someone out of their misery. Removing a pawn from the Man with No Shadow's grasp. Perhaps I'd have blamed the sheriff for his predicament, even though the Man with No Shadow had sought him out in that one day he was free from the campground's borders.

A freedom my mother had granted. To save my friends.

I can't blame the New Sheriff for hating my family.

I wish there had been a better way to save him. But when an opportunity to save someone presents itself, it is often the only opportunity. This is a cruel world, and mercy is a rare commodity, doled out reluctantly, and to reject the dancer's offer very well could have meant there would be no other.

PART 5
Early Spring

As February moves into March, be prepared for rain. Bring extra changes of clothing, as being wet in the early spring chill can be dangerous. Watch out for any lingering holiday monsters that haven't been banished yet.

Blood Forcibly Taken

The situation in town deteriorated rapidly with the New Sheriff gone. People started saying that I was responsible (true), and it was clear I'd already started getting rid of my detractors (false). We had to make our move. It was time to put our plan in motion. I was anxious, as we didn't have a lot of time, but to make this work, we needed to set the stage. While the Man with No Shadow would likely know some of what we were planning from his many spies, he wouldn't know that it was a trick.

Also, we'd been communicating all of this by text so that no one or nothing could overhear. That's the one advantage we have over these creatures. Technology.

For the first step, we needed to convince the Man with No Shadow that he had me cornered. That I was afraid of losing anyone else and that my fear was causing me to drive people away. The sheriff's idea was to stage a highly visible blowup at one of my staff. Yell at them over something trivial. Make it look like I was stressed to the point that any little thing would set off a collapse. I was still considering which staff member to target—who would be the most resilient to being unexpectedly yelled at—when Tyler came over.

It wasn't an intentional change of plans. It just . . . sort of happened.

I don't like making our family drama public. Due to the nature of what we do around here, we tend to keep our problems to ourselves, and we certainly don't involve outsiders. But I've told you some personal things already, and maybe it's only fair that I tell you this as well, no matter how ashamed I am.

He came by to drive me to the grocery store, as I didn't have a new car yet and he was out of spare cars to loan me. While we were at the store, he glanced around at how everyone was avoiding looking at us and mentioned he'd heard some people talking in town.

"They were saying you're selling the campground," he said.

"Didn't you know already?" I snapped. "Aren't you one of the ones who want me to sell?"

"What?"

I knew at that moment that I'd made a mistake. He wouldn't have sounded so startled if it had been true.

But I was angry—no, worse, I was *hurt*, and I couldn't stop myself from continuing. I needed him to feel as bad as I did. To understand what I felt.

"You *never* wanted the campground," I said. "I'm sure you wouldn't be too upset if the town runs me off my own land."

"Kate, I live an hour from here! I had no idea this was going on!"

"Well, it is. There's a monster inciting the town against me. So you can tell Danielle—"

"Don't you fucking dare bring my wife into this—"

"That she might just get what she wants, and your family will be safe from the campground forever, once I'm gone."

"Damn it, Kate!"

His tone made me catch my breath. All around us, the store had fallen dead silent.

"Yes, I hate the campground!" he shouted, then took a breath, struggling to bring his voice down. "It took our grandfather, it took our parents, it took Uncle Tobias and April, and I swear every time I get a phone call from Bryan or the Old Sheriff, I think it's them calling to tell me that it's taken you, too."

I was breathless for a moment.

"And I know," he continued, breathing hard from his outburst, "that if the campground changes hands, all those monsters scatter into the community, but you know what? Fuck this town."

Then he stormed out, yelling over his shoulder from the parking lot to call him later when I could have a conversation without being an ass.

Which is pretty rich, considering he's the one who left me to walk all the way home.

There were a couple of other incidents we orchestrated, nice and visible, to demonstrate that perhaps Kate wasn't keeping it together after all. I blew up at someone whispering behind my back at the hardware store—which admittedly was *very* satisfying. I "happened" to run into Bryan in town on another instance and shouted at him for abandoning the campground—though I cut that one short because his dogs were staring me down and it was rather unnerving. And then I "confronted" the Old Sheriff about how he wasn't doing enough to keep the town off my back, and the Old Sheriff yelled back that I made everything "so damn difficult" and "threw me out" of the police station.

We gave the small-town rumor mill plenty of fodder.

However, I wasn't as confident in our plan as the Old Sheriff was. There was one additional assurance that I wanted. I hadn't told him what I planned to do. He would have deemed it too risky. He might have tried to stop me.

We would have fought for real, if that had happened. I will sometimes listen to suggestions, but I do not take kindly to being told what to do.

I went to see the Man with No Shadow.

The bruising from being punched in the face was still visible, purple and yellow with spots of magenta red, blotches that covered the entirety of one side of my neck, down onto my collarbones, with lingering patches on my jaw. It was tender and hurt like hell if I touched it. My arm, thankfully, was almost recovered. My shadow was close to fully regrown. The edges were uneven, and my arm itched a lot, but that was all.

I skipped my pain meds that morning. The less acting I had to do, the better. Then I took my shotgun and went to the grove.

He watched me approach, sitting on a large stone, one bare foot tucked up close to his body, the other stretched out to touch the grass. He conspicuously eyed my gun a moment and then lazily glanced up to meet my gaze.

"Fancy another try at me?" he asked. "Good timing—I was feeling peckish."

He dropped his eyes down to the shadow at my feet and slowly smiled. I dredged up the memory of the pain of having my shadow torn apart. How I'd collapsed, screaming. I let my voice tremble. His smile deepened. "I'm here to negotiate," I replied. "Tell me what I can do to make you stop hurting people."

The Man with No Shadow laughed.

"Kate," he sighed, hopping off the stone. "Oh, Kate. I thought you were smarter than this."

He walked toward me. I hoisted my shotgun, letting my hands shake, and he hesitated only briefly at the edge of his grove. Then slowly, deliberately, he stepped out of his territory and continued to advance toward me. I pointed the gun at him and he paused, barely a foot away from the barrel.

"You already know what I want," he murmured.

Then he jerked a hand up, so quickly I might not have been able to react if I hadn't been expecting it. It was an effort to not squeeze the trigger. I almost did. My hand twitched reflexively, but I fought the urge down and let him grab the gun and rip it out of my hands. He tossed it aside onto the forest floor.

I cried out in surprise and stepped backward, but he wasn't letting me escape. He lunged forward and grabbed the front of my shirt, twisting the fabric between his fingers, and he pulled me close. I was forced to tilt my head back to look up into his eyes, and the bruises on my neck were clearly visible. He traced them with one finger of his free hand, and I did not have to pretend as I trembled in fear.

"Or maybe you're not being stupid," he said, his finger stopping just at the edge of the cut across my lower lip. "Maybe you're desperate."

"The Not-Brother almost killed me," I whispered.

"Is that the closest you've come to dying? Poor thing. Humans aren't really cut out for this sort of thing. Wouldn't it be a relief to let it all go? Is your family's legacy worth this?"

He gently brushed a lock of my hair behind my ear, the tenderness of the gesture offset by how tightly he still held my shirt, pinning me in place. I shuddered, and he seemed pleased by my reaction.

"I have ... some ... authority over the mimic who was posing as your brother," he said, studying my face. I dropped my head and avoided eye contact. "I can tell him to stop hunting you. Give you a little peace in which to make your decision. But, Kate ... he is my subordinate, not my slave. Wait too long and I may not be able to restrain him entirely, nor the town. They won't kill you, but neither will they leave you ... intact."

The threat was not unexpected. Even though I'd mentally prepared myself for this, I still felt sick hearing the words and understanding their full implication. My words stuck in my throat, and I was unable to reply. The Man with No Shadow took this to mean I was truly cowed—and perhaps in that moment I was—and said that he would tell the Not-Brother to spare my life. As a gesture of kindness. He didn't actually want me dead, after all. That wasn't necessary.

It all sounded very convincing, and I think without the lady's tea, I would have believed every word.

"You want me to sell," I said, finally finding my voice again. "That's why you're leaving me alive. Why? Why take the campground away from my family?"

I didn't want the Man with No Shadow to realize I knew Curtis was my family. Fortunately, I have a lot of practice from lying to my campers.

"You are all *far* too competent. Even your brother would be an issue, should he take over."

"But it won't be old land if Curtis—"

"You don't have to worry about that," he snapped. "You just have to do what I want. Sell it, or I'll take everyone you've ever cared about."

He smiled broadly and patted me on the check. Then he let go of my shirt and briskly walked away, casually putting his back to me. I eyed the distance between myself and the shotgun. I admit it was tempting. I wasn't sure I wanted to gamble all of this on having better reflexes than him, though.

"This was a good talk," he called back to me. "It was nice to have a civil conversation for once"

He laughed. That was enough for me. I couldn't stay any longer. I scooped up the shotgun and turned to leave, walking quickly, eager to put the sound of his laughter behind me.

The next day, a town-hall meeting was called, just as I expected.

Curtis would be there. He was going to be introduced as the new owner of Goat Valley Campground. The Man with No Shadow was giving me some space . . . but was using that time to further box me in with the town. And the Not-Brother would be there, appearing as someone they all trusted, to tell them that if Kate wouldn't sell, well, then the town council would just need to force my hand.

And they'd do as he said.

Unless, of course, someone killed him first.

Since I was still without a car, the plan was that Bryan would pick me up shortly before the meeting was scheduled to start. The Old Sheriff was already in position. I'm not sure what it says about him that he knows how to get a good angle on the town hall with a scoped rifle, but I'm glad he's on our side. I was armed with a knife and my shotgun. The Not-Brother was resilient, but I only needed to make a symbolic gesture.

Bryan called to tell me that he was waiting at the front entrance. I grabbed my shotgun and hurried to the door, only to nearly fall backward in surprise at finding someone directly on the other side.

The Man with the Skull Cup was on my doorstep.

"Uh, this is a bad time," I finally said after a long moment of awkward silence. "Can we talk about that kiss some other day?"

"What makes you think I came here to talk about that? Perhaps I am here because of how you tried to refuse my offer of a drink."

I froze, like every muscle in my body was shot through with

ice, locked up in terror. Some part of my brain gibbered that I was going to die—horribly—and while I heard what he said next, I didn't register the words. Not until he said my name to get my attention and repeated himself. He wasn't going to kill me, not after all he'd done to keep me alive. But I would have to atone for my mistakes—and there had been many as of late.

He sighed and traced the rim of the cup with one finger, his eyes half-closed.

"I told you to be careful with the cup in the vanishing house," he murmured. "It is easy enough to refill when it runs low. Refilling it after it is emptied is another matter. The conditions are harder. More exacting. The normal sources will not suffice. I honestly would have preferred you let me refill it after you saved the sheriff, as I could have managed it properly. But what's done is done, and now you need to finish what you started."

His voice sounded weary, and this time, it wasn't the condescending exhaustion he adopted when I was—in his opinion—being dense. I peered at him intently, noting how stark his cheekbones were and the shadows under his eyes. He looked ... gaunt. Pale. Like he was sick.

Did I do this to him?

He looked me dead in the eyes, and with a flat, emotionless stare that never wavered from my face, he turned the cup sideways until the liquid spilled out and puddled on the porch. He tilted the cup upright before the last few drops fell. Blood from what was already there. Then he lifted his hand to his mouth and bit down hard on a knuckle. The skin split open, and brilliant drops of red beaded up. He tipped his hand so that they collected together and spilled out and into the cup. Blood freely given.

The Man with the Skull Cup handed it to me, along with his knife.

"Blood of an enemy, forcibly taken," he said. "Don't screw it up this time."

I had had the right idea but the wrong source. The New Sheriff was never my enemy.

But the Not-Brother sure as hell was.

I called up the Old Sheriff and told him there was a change in the plan. He didn't like it but grudgingly agreed.

"The town isn't going to like how you're handling this," he said.

"My family isn't here to be their friends," I replied. "We're here to protect them."

And then I was at the gate and Bryan was waiting for me, the back of his pickup truck loaded with dogs, and I climbed into the passenger side and buckled myself in. He asked where my gun was, and I told him about the change in plans.

"This is going to be messy," he sighed, backing the car out of the driveway.

Messy was fine. Maybe a veritable bloodbath would remind the town exactly what they were dealing with. Both what my campground was . . . and what I was.

Yes, I was trying to save people instead of letting them suffer the consequences of their choices, but that didn't mean they could just forget that I was willing to slit my share of throats.

After Uncle Tobias's death, I hated the sight of the town hall. My heart sped up as Bryan parked within eyeshot of the building. I took a shallow breath and let it out slowly, trying to calm myself, and then gave up on that. Screw it. I didn't need to be calm. I needed to be angry. Anger had carried me through every hard thing I'd done, whether it was just or not, and it would carry me through this as well.

I slammed the door of the pickup truck behind me. The dogs watched me go, lined up at the edge of the pickup's bed with their tongues hanging out. I walked alone to the closed doors of the town hall, took a breath, and then shouldered them bodily open.

Kicking them open would have made a more impressive entrance, sure, but I didn't want to risk spilling the contents of the cup I carried.

The Not-Brother stood behind the podium at the front of the room. It was a lovely building that used to be a church, and while the stained glass was gone, it still sported tall, arched windows that let in the last of the fading sunlight. Beside him was Curtis. My unwitting cousin looked nervous, his eyes wide and his forehead shining with sweat. He seemed ready to bolt at any moment, and for a brief second he looked relieved by the interruption. Then he saw the knife in my hand, and he went pale. Opened his mouth to say something, perhaps to yell for someone to call the police, and then that died when he realized that no one else was moving—like this was normal.

I guess it is, around here.

I stopped halfway to the Not-Brother, who had not moved

from the podium. He stared at me in shock. Clearly our plan had paid off, for he hadn't expected me to be here. I raised the knife and pointed the tip at him.

"That is not your friend," I said in a clear voice that carried easily throughout the room. "That is an abomination, no different from all the other monsters that I keep trapped on my land so that you all can sleep safely in your beds at night."

"Kate," the Not-Brother sighed. "Didn't you get a concussion recently? Maybe you should see your doctor about these . . . outbursts you've been having lately. Is your brother speaking to you again yet?"

The Old Sheriff had picked up some things during his tenure. Things about surveillance. And he'd wired up the podium so that he could listen in while he was in his sniper position. At the moment when the Not-Brother paused, before anyone in the room could react, a bullet came through the window and into the side of the Not-Brother's head.

The force of it knocked him over. Curtis shrieked and threw himself to the floor. The rest of the room stirred, some stood, some dropped to the floor for cover among the chairs. Then everyone went still and silent again as the Not-Brother slowly picked himself up.

See? Stupid. He could have just played dead long enough for the police to escort me out.

But now . . .

They all saw him for what he was.

"Fine," he snarled, blood dripping down from the bullet hole in the side of his head. "FINE. This plan was annoying anyway. I don't like being around humans. I don't like pretending to be your friend. Or your brother. I just . . . want . . . to FEED."

He knocked the podium aside with one sweep of his arm. It smashed sideways to the floor. People were on their feet now, someone screamed, and they bolted to the edges of the room, crowding near the walls, desperate to get away from the creature that was stalking down the aisle to where I stood. I had both eyes open, but I saw his empty abdomen stretched wide, ribs dripping with fluid, and there was raw hunger in his eyes.

I felt elated. They saw him as the monster he was.

I held my ground. I've dealt with plenty of monsters on my land. We have a simple strategy.

Guns and dogs.

The rest of the people in the room made for the exit to escape the chaos, but before they could reach it, the doors were violently thrown open, slamming into the walls with enough force to shake the ceiling.

And Bryan's hounds came through the doorway, rolling past in a black, angry pack of fur and fangs. They hit the line of people trying to escape the room in a heavy collision, and they all went down, a veritable barricade of flailing and fighting. There were screams, and I couldn't tell if they were rage or pain, for the dogs had cleared a pathway between me and the Not-Brother and I was running forward.

The Not-Brother ran to meet me, arms spread low to his side, ready to pull me into the void of his abdomen. I gripped the knife tight. And just before we collided, the Old Sheriff took his second shot, and the Not-Brother's knee exploded into red ruin.

The knife went up and into his chin as he fell. He landed hard in front of me, his body held up by one knee and the strength of my arm, his head twisted back as he dangled from the blade, gurgling as blood flooded his mouth and throat.

The room went quiet. The people who hadn't managed to escape just yet were on the floor, knocked aside by the weight of the dogs. They just stared, wide-eyed, breathing fast. The only sound was the desperate choking of the Not-Brother. Then that, too, went quiet, replaced by the steady drip of blood onto the wooden floor.

I held the cup under the wound until it was full. Blood of my enemy, forcibly taken.

Then I ripped my knife free and let him fall to the floor. And I left. Behind me, the dogs turned their attention to the Not-Brother. They savaged him, ripping into him and tearing the skin from muscle, severing tendons, pulling the bones free. The Not-Brother shrieked—in impotent rage—and then that dissolved into a wet, gurgling sound accompanied by the crunch of bone between a dog's jaws. Someone was sick in the corner of the room. I didn't care.

They'd made a deal with the devil. They shouldn't have been surprised by the results.

Paradise Lost

The next time I went to the grocery store, everyone scurried out of my way and no one made eye contact. They were afraid of me. As they should be. And I, buoyed by my victory, was ready to try something new.

My family's focus was containing the inhuman. We reacted to it. But I'd gone into the vanishing house, and now I'd killed the Not-Brother. Merely reacting to the situation hadn't worked ... but fighting back *was* working.

So I was on the attack.

Getting the materials I needed was easy. I already had plenty of gasoline, some old rags, and empty bottles. Then I had to wait for it to not rain for a few days. I needed the ground dry enough to burn. Enough to drive the Man with No Shadow out of his grove, and then we'd deal with him ourselves, the same as we'd dealt with the Not-Brother.

We knew how to hurt him now, which meant we could also kill him.

The Old Sheriff was willing to help. We planned to go in daylight. We didn't see a way to completely deprive him of his ability to access shadows, not without broadcasting our intentions and giving him an opportunity to escape. Going at night might have limited his abilities somewhat, but it would also have hindered ours. The Old Sheriff feared that our visibility would have been too impaired to get a good shot in on the Man with No Shadow.

Unfortunately, the weather did not cooperate. I don't know what I expected—we were moving into spring. It rained a lot that week, and there were still patches of melting snow. Finally, after a few days of sunshine, I went down to the tree line to check how dry it was and was, yet again, sorely disappointed. However, I noticed something else when I turned back to the house. There were cars out near the barn. This was odd, as the gates were shut and the campground was still closed to campers. I warily made my way toward the barn. There were a LOT of cars.

I recognized a handful of the vehicles from town, and my heart sank. There were cars with out-of-state license tags too. Previous campers.

The Man with No Shadow had said he had people waiting nearby, stockpiled as his food for when he needed them.

It was painfully apparent what was happening.

My childhood all over again. My friends, called out to the woods and held as hostages for the Man with No Shadow's demands. Who else could have brought this many people here?

I'd wondered if he'd bring reinforcements to the campground at some point. Except . . . I'd expected perhaps a handful of people. Those ringleaders whom he'd roped into leading the campaign against me within the town. People who . . . wouldn't be missed as much as others.

Not this many. Not the campers.

But of course it was them. It had to be them, because it was my job to keep them safe, even though they were the ones who disobeyed the rules and talked to the man who didn't cast a shadow.

But what could I do? What the hell could I have done about this? I couldn't abandon them to their fate. That would have been monstrous.

I hastily brewed a cup of the tea the Lady with Extra Eyes had given me. While it steeped, I called the Old Sheriff. I told him we needed to delay another day. It was still too damp. I did not tell him what was happening. He didn't deserve to be dragged into this, and there was little he could do to help me.

Then I drank my tea and went to the grove.

I think I understand a little more of my mother, how she must have felt walking alone to the grove so many years ago, knowing she would have to give something to save my friends. She couldn't have known what it would be, only that it would cost her dearly, because that is how bargains with the inhuman always turn out.

I already knew what the Man with No Shadow wanted from me.

I felt light. Like I was floating. The sun was too bright in my eyes. The forest around me didn't feel entirely real, like I was separate from myself and the world.

We don't always get to kill the monsters that hunt us. Sometimes we can only delay. In the end, they are still the predators, and we are only the prey. I've known this my whole life, and it was folly to think a few minor victories would change that.

Perchta said I could save them. She hadn't specified *how*.

I finally reached the grove. There must have been at least fifty people there, all kneeling, each paired up with someone else. They were knee to knee, facing one another. One was passive, hands resting on their legs, staring straight ahead without movement or emotion. The other held a gun to the forehead of their victim.

They were of all ages. Some looked like teenagers, trembling and crying but unable to move the gun away from its intended target. Others were older, white-haired and resigned, eyes empty with despair. I recognized some of them. I work closely with the people who organize the big events on-site, along with their volunteers, sometimes the same people year after year. I saw a few of them, scattered in among the crowd. There were a couple of people from town, too, some people who had never liked me, some others who I'd never even spoken to. At the fore of them all, between two trees that bowed over to each other, forming a gateway of sorts, was the Man with No Shadow.

"Kate!" he cried, as if he were happy to see me. Perhaps he was. He threw his arms out in welcome.

"So glad you came. I didn't have a way to send you a message, so I just had to hope you'd figure it out. Perhaps you are a bit clever after all."

"This is crueler than the last time you took hostages."

I glanced at the pair nearest to the border. Two men, one as immobile as a statue, the other shaking while he held the gun, terrified, hopeless, his shoulders rising and falling with his panicked breathing.

"Well, you are older now," the Man with No Shadow said cheerfully. "I didn't want to traumatize a child. But I'm not entirely evil. You see, only half of them die if you refuse me."

He snapped, to illustrate his point, and the man closest to the border pulled the trigger. I flinched at the gunshot and then kept my gaze averted as he began to cry out in wordless anguish, horrified at what he'd just done. Some of the other people around the grove began to cry more audibly, whimpering in terror.

"That was ... unnecessary," I said stiffly.

Reluctantly I glanced at the body. At the bits of bone and brain matter spewed onto the grass.

"Just making sure you understand the consequences," he murmured. "Perhaps you think you can still find a way to fight this. That's your nature. I realize that now, after you killed the Not-Brother. That was well-played, although I confess I hadn't been paying him the attention he needed. His usefulness was coming to an end."

"What did you promise him?"

"Prey." He shrugged indifferently. "I told him if he helped me, I'd be able to replace you with someone easy to control. Someone that wouldn't stop him from feeding whenever he wanted. So he infiltrated your staff, and when that failed, I sent him out into the town."

"So you could turn them against me," I spat. "Force me to sell. So is this your backup plan?"

"It is," he sighed. "I could have done this at any time. I could have called to all those unwitting campers that didn't pay attention to my lack of a shadow, and they would have come. But I wanted the town under my control, as it would have made what comes next a little easier... but I'll improvise. After you're deposed."

After I was deposed. The phrase rattled around in my head, and then I grasped his meaning—he wasn't done. This was only one step in some larger plan.

The Man with the Skull Cup was right. I was caught in a web, and I couldn't see the whole.

"What are you trying to do?" I whispered.

He smiled and held out his hand to me.

"Step inside my grove," he murmured, "and perhaps I'll tell you. And then I'll let everyone go."

Let me tell you something, as someone who has gone through some shit. We, as a species, will sacrifice for others. This is our nature. When we sacrifice ourselves, it feels like the right thing to do, and the burden we carry is made lighter. It is easy to be the one who suffers for the sake of others.

Helplessness, however, will destroy you.

It is a poison. We ingest it unknowingly, and it eats at us inside; it clouds our souls; it breaks our hearts bit by bit, the cracks so tiny we don't understand why we hurt. Perhaps we see the signs—we cry when we shouldn't, we cannot focus on the things we love—but we shrug them off and keep going, because our wounds are invisible. We're dying in silence.

I was helpless there at the entrance to the grove.

I have been helpless for a long time. My courage is merely the flight of the hunted deer that knows all it can do is run until a misstep spells its doom. I wonder how deep the poison has sunk, if perhaps it is now in the marrow of my bones.

And part of me just wanted the hurting to stop.

I gave my hand to the Man with No Shadow. His fingers closed over mine and he pulled and I followed and he led me into the grove.

I next remember being back in my own house. Hours had passed. When I ran back to the barn, it was empty. All the cars were gone, and I was alone on the campground.

I was not the Man with No Shadow's pawn—I knew that much. The tea from the Lady with Extra Eyes had held. However, I was bound to my agreement with him, just as my mother was. The details floated in my mind like mist and faded away when I came close, no matter how hard I tried to force them into clarity. I knew a few things, at least. That night, at midnight, I would be at my house, and the Man with No Shadow would come and bring a contract, and then I would sign it. I tested this agreement. I tried to leave the campground land and was overcome with sickness, a weakness that nearly took my ability to walk.

The hours until midnight were my own, however.

I desperately tried to take matters into my own hands. I drafted up a contract transferring the campground. I took the language from my will, hoping that would be enough to be legal once it was signed and notarized. I hesitated at filling out the recipient, however. I didn't know whom to trust. The obvious choice was Tyler—that's who was in my will—but . . .

He'd never wanted the campground. I'd destroy his marriage . . . his life away from all this . . . and leave him to finish what I'd failed to do with the Man with No Shadow.

There was at least one person on this campground who was solidly opposed to him, whose advice I could rely on. I printed the document with a blank spot for the name. Then I folded it, stuffed it in an envelope, and started out into the woods.

I walked for hours. I traversed the entirety of my campground, walking through the woods, off the roads. Trying to remember every piece of my home. Straying from the road for too long is an invitation for trouble, but I was desperate. I needed to find the one person on the campground who had never given me any doubt as to their intentions toward me. Surely they'd know what to do. They had helped me so much already, after all.

Instead, I found the Man with the Skull Cup.

He stood blocking my way, a few feet in front of me, and I wondered how I hadn't seen him sooner. Like he'd stepped out from between the slender trees and thin air, or perhaps I simply hadn't been paying attention in my distress. His expression was severe, harsher than his usual blank disinterest. The corners of his mouth were creased with his frown, and his eyes were narrow slits.

"Should you be wandering the woods like this?" he asked.

"They're my woods," I replied testily.

"I was not questioning that. I was questioning if this was the most productive use of what time is left for you."

He knew. Somehow he knew.

"I'm looking for the Lady with Extra Eyes!" I snapped. "I don't know who else to trust."

His gaze dropped to the letter that I clutched in one hand. I warily took a step back.

"Do you know what this is?" I asked.

He nodded faintly.

"Then tell me what name I should put on it!"

I waited, breathless. I don't know if I intended to take his suggestion. I truly didn't know who was on my side anymore. He'd helped me, but perhaps that, too, was a ruse. Maybe he only protected me to lead me to this point. I just wanted to hear him say it, if perhaps that would confirm or deny some wild theory that bubbled half-formed in my head, the product of my self-doubt and fears.

Instead, the Man with the Skull Cup snatched at the letter. I jerked my hand back in surprise, and his fingers closed on my arm instead, and then he squeezed, and my fingers went weak and the letter fell from my hand. He grabbed it out of the air and stepped back. I hesitated, my hand halfway to the gun at my waist, but reason caught me. It wasn't worth it. I could always print another if he didn't give it back.

"I need a name," I continued. "If I'm going to lose this campground, I should at least lose it to someone who isn't one of his pawns. Someone who can fight him. Tell me who you want to manage this land."

He tore the letter in half, then half again, and let the pieces fall to the ground.

"I chose you," he hissed, staring me in the eyes. "Don't disappoint me."

He turned abruptly and began to walk away.

"But... help me!" I cried.

"Save yourself this time, Kate," he called back to me. "Did you not kill the master of the vanishing house?"

"That was different! It was already dying!"

"Then perish. Old land is no place for the weak."

I was truly on my own.

The Family Curse

The Man with No Shadow came at midnight. I'd given myself one last sunset, before going inside for the evening. It was muted by clouds, a wave of mauve, deepening to puce along the ridge of the ebony trees. I watched from my front porch, wondering if it would be the last sunset I would see, here in my family's house where I was raised and where my parents died and where all my ancestors had sheltered from the terrors of the night.

Then I waited inside by the window, watching.

Two figures approached from the road. The Man with No Shadow's hair shone, catching the moonlight. Beside him was a shorter figure, unrecognizable in the gloom, his shadow stretching long beside him. The little girl waited for them at the fence, and the Man with No Shadow spoke to her, and she turned and left around the side of the house, her steps dragging reluctantly in the damp grass. Then he came and knocked on my front door.

"Invite us in, Kate," the Man with No Shadow said gently.

I did. I suppose that was part of our agreement from the grove.

With him was Curtis. My cousin. He glanced around him in delight, taking in the aged wooden crossbeams of the ceiling, the dated wallpaper, and the photographs of my family from when I was a child that I didn't have the heart to replace.

"This is quaint," he finally said. "It's very charming. I can see why you've been so reluctant to part with it, Kate. But I think it'll be for the best. Someone in town told me all about how this will reset the campground, and then everyone will be safe. No more monsters! You can have a fresh start!"

For a moment I could only stare. Curtis had no idea what was really happening here, no idea that the land wouldn't reset, because it was going to a blood relative after all. He was just being duped into thinking he was being a hero.

Behind him, the Man with No Shadow gave me a thin, warning smile. He set a stack of paper and a seal on the table.

"Let's get this all signed," the Man with No Shadow said. "I normally don't work this late."

"Of course, of course."

Curtis hastily sat down at the dining room table and waited patiently. I joined them more slowly, my back to the wall. The Man with No Shadow flipped over the first page and shoved it toward me. I took it, mechanically, and there was something tight in my chest, and my fingers were numb.

"It's all pretty standard sale of a property," the Man with No Shadow said tonelessly. "Give it a read and then initial at the bottom."

He pushed a pen in my direction. I took it. I initialed. I

couldn't *not* initial. Like a hand was over my own, guiding my motions. I wanted to scream, I wanted to weep, but I only stared stupidly at the papers that the Man with No Shadow was handing me, one by one, dryly explaining what each one was before asking for an initial and then collecting them to form a second stack of completed paperwork. Across from me, Curtis waited anxiously, excited in his ignorance as to what was happening here.

"So how do you two know each other?" I asked.

The words came with difficulty. It was like my mouth was full of sap and my tongue stuck to the roof of my mouth. The Man with No Shadow's eyes narrowed with annoyance.

"Oh, we don't really know each other," Curtis said. "He just met me at the gate. I got a call from your lawyer saying you'd decided to sell after all and wanted it done as fast as possible. So I needed to get down to the campground as soon as I could. And sure, it's midnight, but she said you and the notary were both fine with it."

My lawyer. Bullshit.

"It is late, isn't it," I sighed. "Do you want some coffee?"

Curtis happily agreed. I got up and went into the kitchen. Behind me, the Man with No Shadow excused himself to help. I forced myself to focus on filling the kettle, even when he came up behind me and stood at my back, mere inches apart. I felt his breath stir my hair.

"You're stalling," he hissed.

"Damn right I am," I replied.

I stepped back, forcing him to move lest I step on his toes. He hovered close by, looming over me as I turned on the stove and began pulling out cups while the water heated.

"Did our agreement stipulate that I had to get this done as quickly as possible?" I asked tersely.

"No," he admitted. "I wish it had."

"What happens after the campground belongs to Curtis?"

I turned and found myself face-to-face with him. He stared down at me with a hatred that I suppose I'd earned by now.

"I drag you back to my grove and devour your shadow, bit by bit. I'll rip your shadow's legs off first, so you can't escape, and then take my time with the rest of you. Perhaps if you hadn't been so difficult, I would have given you a quick death, but . . . I'm not inclined to do so anymore. It could be days, Kate," he whispered. "Weeks, even."

He half raised his hand, and I felt something brush along the back of my arm, like the touch of a moth's wings. I glanced aside and saw his hand poised so that his shadow—if it existed—would be touching my own.

The kettle began to scream on the stove. I turned to take it off and pour, and briefly thought I could just fling the boiling water right in his face.

"None of that, now," he admonished. "We have an agreement."

He returned to the dining room. I was a little slower to follow, carrying a tray of coffee. I confess that I used rat poison instead of creamer for the Man with No Shadow's cup, and he took one sip, coughed violently, and stared daggers at me while I finished initializing the rest of the pages. Pity it didn't work.

The last page. I stared at it, startled to see my own demise in such an innocuous thing. A single piece of paper. An empty line where my signature was going to go. My fingers rested on the pen.

"I know it's overwhelming," the Man with No Shadow said smugly. "But this will be a good change for you. Once you ... wrap things up with me ... you can finally rest. Maybe you'll even get to see your parents again."

It felt like a hand was tightening around my chest. I wanted to scream. Curtis was aimlessly chattering about how I could always come back and visit, of course, and how he could even keep me on as assistant manager or something since he'd probably need help in the transition period. I wasn't paying attention, my focus entirely on the single piece of paper that would put an end to all this.

I only snapped out of my daze because he'd stopped talking.

"Do you hear someone ... crying?" he asked.

"That's the little girl," I replied dully. "The one you saw at the fence. She killed my mother. Don't worry about her—she can't get inside."

Curtis stared in consternation at the window behind me. The incessant weeping came from the other side of the glass. The Man with No Shadow was silently digging his nails into the surface of the table and staring at me in outright hatred.

I picked up the pen.

And as the little girl wept behind me, I had a sharp moment of clarity.

I stood. I turned, ostensibly to untie the drapes and let them cover the blinds with another layer to block the noise, but instead I grabbed the cord and yanked the blinds up. Then, as the Man with No Shadow began to call my name and demand I stop, I opened the window.

I wondered if this was how my father had felt, when he went to throw himself at the beast, hopeless but resolute, knowing that death was the only way it could end.

And the little girl started to climb in, her shoulders heaving with her sobs as she stretched out her hands to clutch at either side of the wall. She was coming for me.

"No!" the Man with No Shadow shouted, standing and lunging for me. His fingers closed around my wrist, and he began dragging me away from the window. "I haven't worked this hard to let you win!"

He wasn't speaking to me. I realized this, distantly, as he pulled me through the house and toward the front door while the crying of the little girl drifted after us. He was speaking to her. I tried to dig in my heels, but he was too strong.

"Move, Kate. Damn you!" he swore.

Behind us, Curtis began to scream. A long, uninterrupted shriek. I know it well. It is the scream of someone who is in the process of dying, horribly and painfully, and cannot do anything to save themselves.

The Man with No Shadow ripped open the front door and switched his grip to the front of my shirt before dragging me behind him across the yard. Getting me over the property line. Only once we were past the road and in the field that led to the forest did he pause and spin to face me, his hand still tight in the fabric of my shirt.

"Curtis is family," I laughed. "The little girl kills my family line, remember?"

"Then you're now *useless*!" he snarled. "I'll rip you apart right here! You get a fast—albeit agonizing—death after all. Then I start this all over with your fucking brother."

I laughed, hearing the touch of hysteria in my own voice.

"Your buyer is dead," I said mockingly. "She's probably spreading his intestines across the walls. Where are you going to find another gullible cousin?"

Pain shot through my abdomen. Frantically I glanced at the ground, where in the bright moonlight I saw his hand intersecting my shadow, against my stomach. I doubled over but did not fall; some terrible pressure held me up. I curled up around it, like a spike in my gut, the pain lancing all the way through to my back. I coughed and tasted blood.

"I'll figure it out," the Man with No Shadow said evenly. "You might want to save your breath for screaming. It might help with the pain."

Another burst of agony, higher up, just below my ribs. I did scream. Just like Curtis had.

"Or perhaps it won't," the Man with No Shadow said thoughtfully.

And then he pitched backward with a cry of his own, a gunshot echoing through the night sky.

"Run, Kate," yelled the Old Sheriff.

I guess I hadn't sounded as calm on the phone as I thought I had. I had never been so happy to see him.

I struggled to stand. My fingers clutched at my abdomen. It felt like glass had been shoved through my body, and my lungs seized up in reflex. I felt nothing but unbroken skin under my shirt. My shadow was what he'd attacked, I told myself firmly. Just my shadow. I could survive it—but only if I kept moving.

I took a second while the Man with No Shadow was reeling to take stock of my surroundings. He'd dragged me out the front and down toward the woods. The tree line was only a few yards away.

The sensible choice would have been the road. The path to it was free of trees, hopefully giving the sheriff another shot. Following it would get me off the property and out of the Man with No Shadow's reach. But he was between me and the road, and he was getting to his feet, panting hard with pain, but eyes bright and focused on me.

I chose the woods.

Perhaps it was instinct telling me where to go. The woods are where we fight our monsters, after all, and emerge from them changed—or not at all.

Or perhaps I was blinded by pain and fear and merely got lucky.

I stumbled through the trees, catching myself on their trunks to keep my balance. The Man with No Shadow followed in a dash, but he was not directly chasing me—he was trying to get under cover. Another gunshot broke the silence, and I used the noise to move quickly, just enough distance to break the line of sight between us.

Then the hunt was on. The Man with No Shadow pursued, but quietly, as a hunter stalks their prey. I, too, tried to stifle my breathing and step carefully so as not to give away my position with an errant branch. I can be quiet when I need to be. I grew up in these woods, after all; they were where my brother and I played our games of chase and hide-and-seek. When I was older, I hunted monsters through these woods. I'd learned my lessons well.

Still, despite that, I could not quite shake the Man with No Shadow. His pursuit was not entirely by human means, and I could do nothing for his preternatural senses.

Then, as my strength waned and the toll of my injuries threatened to drag me to my knees, I put my hand out for support, and while my fingers touched the cool bark before me, I could no longer see them. I could no longer see anything at all.

All light had gone out.

Instinctively I squeezed my eyes shut. Somewhere behind me and to the right, I heard the Man with No Shadow stop as well.

I felt the Thing in the Dark close by. I could wait for it to pass. And then what? Resume the chase, one that I was losing by inches as the minutes slid by? It was only a matter of time until he found me.

Or . . .

I turned. The Man with No Shadow's ragged breathing

was faint, but there was no other sound in the woods under the Thing in the Dark's influence. I homed in on his breath, breaking into as fast of a run as I dared, my hands stretched out before me as I ran tree to tree, pulling myself forward by touch alone. All around me the forest began to shake. It was like a strong wind, rattling the leaves and snapping the branches. I heard the Man with No Shadow cry out—just enough sound to push me forward those last few feet—and then my hand closed on his shirt.

"Here!" I cried. "We're here!"

And I opened my eyes.

The wind intensified. I saw the dirt and leaves of the forest floor rise up around me in the gale, but there was still no light, it was like they were outlined on top of the darkness, and there was something alive in that wind. Small pieces of debris struck my exposed skin like the sting of a wasp. The Man with No Shadow grabbed my wrists, trying to pry himself free of me, but I did not relent. We would die together.

A massive presence loomed over and around us, and then we were falling. All time seemed to stop, and I tensed, waiting for that final impact, and then I landed hard on dry leaves and brittle branches. But I was alive. The wind was gone. The air around us was cool and tasted damp. There was no light. My eyes widened, instinctively trying to find some spark of luminescence, but there was none.

"What have you done?" the Man with No Shadow hissed. I heard him stand.

"I kind of expected us to die," I said, also standing. The

effort left me breathless, and I clutched at my stomach and waited for the pain to pass.

"No. This is much worse."

I raised a hand and walked forward until my fingers touched something. I traced its contour gently, feeling the seam of wood stripped clean of bark, felt it curve upward and downward like the rib of a ship. Then I felt it move away from my hand, and I froze, and then after a few minutes, it drifted back, and my fingers were once again touching its cool surface.

Like a heartbeat.

I knew where we were.

A Place Without Shadows

We were inside the Thing in the Dark. For a moment, I was at a loss on what to do. I hadn't thought this through, because, well, I hadn't thought I'd need to, on account of being dead and all. Nearly dying twice in less than an hour was trauma I could deal with later, though.

"How about a truce for today?" the Man with No Shadow said from behind me. "We'll both get out of here, and then tomorrow we can go back to trying to kill each other. I hurt you; your friend shot me; I think we're even."

"You're helpless here, aren't you? There are no shadows."

A long pause and then he admitted that yes, he was. But neither could I hurt him. In fact, he said reluctantly, without shadows, he couldn't influence the corporeal world at all. He existed and I could interact with him—and he touched my hand, the lightest touch, to illustrate his point—but he couldn't exert his will. No matter how he tried, he couldn't, say, force me to budge with a shove. Like how a shadow could be altered by someone moving the object casting it, but the shadow had no ability to move the object itself. His tone was flat as he told me this, but I felt this was humiliating for him, to be forced to admit his weaknesses. I asked why he was telling me this.

"Because I need you to realize I'm harmless here," he replied in frustration, "so that you don't waste time trying to get rid of me. I might need someone that can interact with the physical world to get me out."

"And why would I need you?"

"Do you think you can find the way out?"

I was about to answer that yes, I could, but then I hesitated. My initial thought had been to simply follow the right-hand rule until I found the exit, but this was not a maze. This was the body of the Thing in the Dark. I could hardly hope to navigate the veins of my own body and find a way out, after all. The Man with No Shadow told me, with a calm I certainly did not share, that while he couldn't guarantee we'd escape, he could at least lead us to the creature's mouth. He sensed it. The head and the heart—the domains of thought and life. They were things that creatures like him knew on instinct, homing in on them much like a cat homes in on the scent of a mouse.

So I agreed. We had an uneasy truce. I might have been willing to die in the woods, but now I wasn't so convinced that I wanted to spend what time was left to me wandering the corridors of some unspeakable creature with my worst enemy.

I wouldn't make a good martyr.

He directed me forward, and we walked along in relative quiet. I kept one hand against the side of the creature's body, my fingers sliding from rib to rib. The flesh was woven branches and dry leaves. Debris cracked under my feet as I walked. Not all of it was wood. Small bones, mostly, from rabbits or squirrels. Sometimes my feet slipped on something larger, perhaps a deer, and there were a handful that felt like they could have been human.

"I don't suppose you'd tell me what your end goal is here," I said, "seeing as I still have a shot at killing you. But now that he's dead... was Curtis under your control too?"

"He was not," the Man with No Shadow laughed. "His mother was. She kept him hidden from your uncle and told him lovely stories to make him fall in love with Goat Valley, so that he'd come back someday. Leaving his mind alone was a gamble, but once I met Curtis, I saw he was so desperate to help and so *naive* that I felt I could take the risk."

"I can't believe he was that gullible," I muttered.

"You're used to that, though, considering the people that visit your campground."

I mean... he's not wrong.

We walked a bit farther. I had to pause and catch my breath, pressing a hand to the spot just below my ribs where the creature had stabbed through my shadow. He remarked that perhaps I wasn't as resilient as he'd thought, and he'd have to take care not to kill me prematurely, when he had me in his grove. Not until he was satisfied that I'd suffered enough.

"Shut up," I hissed.

He started to speak, some other petty, cutting comment, and then he obligingly did as I asked.

He'd heard the noise too. The crack of branches from ahead of us. I shrank into the recess between the Thing's ribs, my back against the matted debris. I felt the Man with No Shadow crouch at my back, and he quietly whispered in my ear that it was a human approaching, but that perhaps it'd be best to let them continue on past us.

I held still, scarcely daring to breathe. Their footsteps drew closer and then they stopped entirely, and for a moment all I could hear was labored, halting breathing. Then bony fingers latched onto my wrist.

I shrieked and jerked away, thrashing and twisting in an attempt to throw them off. But the person's grip was unrelenting, and as they drew closer, I could smell the stink of them—stale sweat and rot—and then their fingertips caressed my face, feeling the flesh of my cheek and the line of my jaw.

"Please," a female voice croaked, raspy with disuse. "Help me. I've been here for so long."

I couldn't breathe. April. It was April. She was alive. I could bring her back with us; I could save her; I could unravel some of that grief and suffering I'd been carrying for so long.

"She's not begging you to save her," the Man with No Shadow said coldly from a safe distance away. The asshole had abandoned me the moment she grabbed my wrist. "She wants to die."

"Shut up!" I hissed. I wouldn't let him take that thin sliver of hope from me.

I reached up and seized April by the shoulders. She finally let go of my wrist and fell silent, reduced to a trembling, shaking wretch before me in the darkness. Her skin was stretched tight across her bones, like even her very muscles had wasted away.

I didn't want to do the math on how many days she'd been here. Too many. This was what I faced, I realized with horror. This is what would happen if we didn't escape. Condemned to wander the body of the Thing in the Dark for eternity as my body shriveled for want of water and food and light.

"Okay." I exhaled. "April. It's me, Kate. Your cousin."

"Y-yeah," she breathed, finally focusing on me. "Kate."

"Right. You're going to be okay. Come with us. We're going to get out of here."

"This is a mistake," the Man with No Shadow muttered from behind us as we started walking again. "Sentiment only gets you hurt. Haven't you realized that by now?"

I coaxed more information from April as we walked. There were others, she said, wandering in the dark. Some had given up and lain down and stopped moving, and in time, the wood and the leaves covered them up. They weren't dead, she said. She'd found one, cocooned into the floor, and she put her hand through the branches and felt their breathing and the beat of their heart. This wasn't what she wanted to become, so she kept moving. Constantly. Always moving, always searching for a way out. And her breathing grew quicker, and I went silent for a little while so that her panic could subside enough for her to remain coherent. The Man with No Shadow gave us directions when we came to forks in the corridors, and sometimes he hesitated or even told us to turn around and take the other passage.

One of them had tried to kill her, April said. He hadn't been here long and was mindless in his terror. He wasn't himself and he'd lunged at her and she'd sidestepped, knowing how to navigate this darkness better than he. And then she'd shoved him into the wall and wrenched a sharp length of wood from the debris and stabbed him through the stomach with it. He'd remained there, pinned to the interlaced branches, and then they grew to cover him up and muffled his screams. Sometimes she found herself in that corridor again, by accident. She knew it because she could still hear him screaming from his tomb.

Sometimes, she said in a small voice, she would sit and listen to his cries just to hear another human voice for a little while.

Just as he couldn't die, neither could she. She was trapped in a body that should have died a thousand times over from deprivation, and some horrific power kept her bound inside her bones.

I dropped back a few paces so that I could talk to the Man with No Shadow.

"Do you think she'll die as soon as we escape this thing?" I whispered.

"Probably. This place is the only thing sustaining her. But that's what she wants."

I was quiet. I wanted to argue, to accuse the Man with No Shadow of lying. I wanted to save her, like I'd failed to when she'd called me for help. Yet after so long in the darkness . . . perhaps there is no way to come back from this. Perhaps if I were trapped for so long, I would feel the same.

We kept going for a bit longer before he stopped and asked me to put my hands against the wall and tell him what I felt. I swept my palms along it, to the left and right, then up and down, and when I reached up—I felt a ledge. My heart sank. This maze was in three dimensions. But the Man with No Shadow sounded more confident now, saying that this was why he kept getting turned around. I boosted April up first, and then she turned and helped pull me up into the tunnel. Then I reached down for the Man with No Shadow. He was as light as a feather, and it took almost no effort at all to pull him up after us.

Then we resumed walking. Onward and up along the slope until it opened into a new passageway. Our progress was quicker now that the Man with No Shadow understood more of what we were looking for. I hate to say it, but I don't think we would have found our way out without him. We had a few more passageways leading up, one so steep we had to half climb, pulling ourselves from rib to rib. Then the Man with No Shadow warned us that we were going to pass by the heart of the creature.

"What's in the heart?" I asked.

"I have no idea and no desire to find out," he replied tersely. "Those places aren't meant for . . . lesser . . . creatures like myself, and certainly not for mortals."

It was tense going after that. I was on edge, every part of me straining to hear some sort of sound other than the snap of branches and bones beneath our feet, and fearing that I would. Then my hand slipped off the rib and found only empty air beyond. The Man with No Shadow said to keep going, and I stepped out into open space, expecting to find another rib just a few paces beyond. Nothing. This passageway was wider than the others. I opened my mouth in warning when a whispering raced up out of that gulf, and I froze. Like the rustle of leaves.

The floor beneath me shifted. I let out a cry of surprise, and then everything was sliding, the leaves and the bones and the branches rolling and tumbling under my feet, and I fell and slid with them, in a river of debris. It pulled me down into the artery, and then everything stopped. I tumbled a few more feet and hastily picked myself up, listening intently, hearing only the startled cries of April and the swearing of the Man with No Shadow as they came after me. For a moment, everything was still.

Then the floor began to slide again. I lunged this time, and my hands closed on a rib. I put one arm over it, locking my body in place as the floor rushed past me, anything loose drawn inexorably farther down the tunnel toward what I now realized was a vast, empty chamber.

The heart was beating. And though the Thing in the Dark was made of wood and plants and had no blood, it had a heart, and everything in the artery was rushing to fill the empty chamber as it pumped air through the creature's body.

And then I realized that I could see. There was light coming from the heart. Pale gray, diffuse, but light nonetheless and more than enough for my sun-starved eyes.

I turned to look once the floor settled in the lull between heartbeats.

The beast waited for me.

The one that will someday kill me.

I saw the glow of its white eyes in the darkness. I felt its presence, felt its patient desire.

Whenever someone goes missing, I know if the Thing in the Dark swallowed them up because I dream of the beast. I dream of my death.

April reached me first. She slammed into the wall, having kept her feet despite the shifting terrain. Her fingers clawed at the rib, she couldn't find purchase, and then she slid back toward the heart, and I reached out and her hand closed on mine. My arm trembled to hold on to the rib, keeping us both anchored there; then the floor's flow slowed and stopped.

I saw her face. White like bone, impossibly hollow with hunger, lips cracked and peeling, her eyes narrowed against the light. Her hair was almost gone, just a few tattered patches clinging to her scalp.

"Grab hold of the wall," I urged her, panting with exertion. "That heart is going to beat again."

April looked back at the archway and the chamber beyond. The beast waited for me, its double set of eyes opening and closing as it blinked patiently, knowing it was only a matter of time before I died under its claws. My heart pounded painfully in my chest.

"There's nothing there," she said.

She resisted my hold, stepping toward the heart. I tightened my grip around her hand, crushing it between my fingers in desperation. The heart would beat again soon, and she'd fall away and I'd lose her like I lost her months before. I yelled at her to please, grab hold, don't do this to me again. Not again. I was so, so tired of losing people. I couldn't watch her die.

And she looked up at me, and I saw that this was what she was yearning for, it was exactly as the Man with No Shadow had said, and she saw nothing inside the heart because there was no death that she feared.

A heartbeat.

And I let her go.

She half fell, half ran into the heart, and it swallowed her up and there was a burst of light, like the birth of a star, and I shut my eyes tight against the brilliance.

A hand closed on my arm. The Man with No Shadow, given strength by the presence of light, and he pulled at me, yelling that we had to move before it dragged us in as well. So we did. We fought our way up. There was a cadence now. I flattened my body to the wall against a wooden rib and waited for the river of debris to pass and for the floor to grow calm, and then I ran forward until I heard that whispering approaching from the chamber behind me, telling me to seek an anchor once more. And the entire time the Man with No Shadow didn't let go of me, refusing to lose me to the beast that waited inside the heart, just as he refused to lose me to the little girl.

We emerged into a T-intersection and threw ourselves to the side, huddling against the wall. The heart whispered and the debris beneath us shifted, but faintly, and only a few pieces rattled their way into the passageway. I watched them dance and roll. I was too numb to even weep for my cousin's death.

"Twice," the Man with No Shadow snarled. "This makes

twice I saved you. The pleasure of killing you with my own hands had better make up for this."

I had no indication of what he was going to do, not until there was a wrenching sensation in my side and then blinding pain. I remember screaming, and then I remember nothing, and then I was flat on my back, waking to pain, disoriented and feeling like I would slip away back into the darkness at the slightest movement. It hurt to breathe. Like one of my lungs was filled with fire. I took shallow, halting breaths, and my eyes filled with tears.

"You should still be able to walk," the Man with No Shadow said calmly, standing over me. "I can be precise when I want to."

"Why . . . ?" I moaned.

"I only need you alive to get out of here," he replied. "I don't need you whole, and you are far less of a threat with a maimed shadow. Now get up. I've dragged you as far as I can. The light is gone again."

I didn't. Not right away. The Man with No Shadow sighed and crouched nearby. I heard the rustle of his clothing. He told me that certainly, I could lie there and wish for death, but that wasn't in my nature. His biggest mistake had been underestimating my capacity to keep fighting even when I should have given up long ago.

As he spoke, my fingers curled on a piece of bone. It'd broken in two, leaving behind a jagged end. I slipped this into my belt as I got up, letting the noise of my struggles to stand mask the sound of me concealing it.

Yes. I was still willing to fight.

I struggled onward, guided by the Man with No Shadow's directions. I needed light in order to kill him, after all, and for that I needed to escape. That was the mantra that kept me going. I needed light to kill him. I called myself prey before, but prey can still fight back, even to its last breath. Weakened by pain, I drove myself forward, fighting that urge to sink back to the ground, because I knew that if I rested even for a moment, I might not get back up again. The bone stake I carried with me was my source of strength. It and the hope it represented. One last chance to fight back.

The passageway sloped upward. A long, gradual climb, but one that left me drained nonetheless. I stumbled the last few steps through the widening tunnel and into an open space that echoed with my ragged breathing. The head of the Thing in the Dark, the Man with No Shadow whispered to me. Just as he'd promised.

"Now," he murmured, and made no effort to disguise his malice, "it's your turn. Beg it to let us go."

"That's your plan?" I gasped, shaking with exhaustion.

"It's all I have. You're the campground manager. It might actually listen to you."

I didn't ask what we'd do if this failed. I knew the answer. We'd wander the corridors, desperately seeking a way out, until our will broke and we sought the heart and the death that waited for us within. I wondered what was waiting for the Man with No Shadow. What kind of death he feared.

"Hello?" I called into that vast emptiness. "It's Kate. I'm here. You swallowed me up."

I held my breath and waited. Silence.

"I've never looked at you before," I continued, my voice trembling in desperation. "I've tried to get others to do the same. But we make mistakes, and all I can offer is a plea for you to release me, so that I can keep trying."

The floor beneath us lurched. I stumbled and fell. The Man with No Shadow cursed under his breath.

The Thing in the Dark was waking up.

Its voice came from all around us.

"You gave me a home," it rumbled. "You gave the land near me to people who are kind. They leave me offerings in the summer, of food and drink, of which I cannot partake, but it is an offering nonetheless."

The senior camp. Of course.

"I forgive this transgression," it continued. "Just this once."

The blackness in front of me split open and light poured in—sunlight, and after the hours of darkness, it brought tears of pain and relief to my eyes. An opening yawned in front of me like the mouth of a cave, jagged with branches and roots like teeth. I saw the blurry outlines of trees beyond. We were inside the Thing in the Dark's mouth. I stumbled forward, and a hand seized my arm. The Man with No Shadow was by my side, his fingers digging into my flesh, his face tight with fear. He stayed close, and I realized this was why he wanted me alive, so that he could slip out unnoticed with me. But the Thing in the Dark was not naive.

"You I do not forgive," the Thing rumbled, and I felt liquid trickle out of my right ear as I lost all hearing in it.

Behind us, the branches and leaves whispered and converged, rolling into a ridge, and then they engulfed the Man with No Shadow's feet. He jerked, like a fish on a line, and toppled as the Thing in the Dark began to drag him back into its maw. He screamed in incandescent rage and threw out his hands, and even though I tried to step away, I was weak and slow, and his grip closed on my leg. I began to slide, being pulled back into the darkness, and the opening before us began to close. I knew the Thing in the Dark was not a patient creature, and it would only afford me one chance to claim my freedom.

The weak perish. There is no mercy here in Goat Valley.

I twisted. I seized the bone from where it rested in my belt. And the Man with No Shadow's eyes widened with horror, but it was too late; he was holding on with both hands while the carpet of branches and leaves continued to engulf him, already covering his body up to his knees.

I drove the sharp end of the bone through where the shadow of his wrists would land.

He screamed, and I jerked hard on my leg and was free. Then I was half running, half crawling toward the narrowing gap, and I grabbed hold of the broken limb of a tree and pulled myself through, squeezing between its teeth, and then I rolled down the mound and came to a rest on the damp soil of the forest.

Beside me sat the mound that housed the Thing in the Dark. It was silent and still, but for a moment, I thought I could hear the Man with No Shadow. Screaming.

I think it was only my imagination.

I believe I fainted after that.

I next remember being carried. There were arms under my shoulders and under my knees, and when I looked down at them, there were plain metal rings around the fingers that clutched at the lip of a skull cup.

Maybe I Can Finally Take a Nap

Today I saw the doctor. I have a few scrapes from my falls, but otherwise my only serious injury is my shadow, and they can't do anything about that. If I stand in front of a wall, I can see clearly how much the Man with No Shadow tore away. An entire lung would be gone, had he attacked my corporeal body. I don't like looking at it. I'm weak and I'm winded easily, but I'll recover in time. I still can't hear out of my right ear, either. My eardrum ruptured from the Thing in the Dark's voice, but it will heal.

I made some calls to the people in town who were in that grove. They remember what happened. They heard the Man with No Shadow call them and tell them to come to the campground, so they did. Some were told to come with a gun, and they did. I told them the Man with No Shadow was gone, to assure them they were safe, and they said that they knew. Somehow they knew. Like a weight was off their shoulders.

I keep thinking about how the Thing in the Dark refused to let him go. It's been bothering me as to why. I've never had any indication that the Thing in the Dark was anything other than indifferent toward the creatures it shared the campground with. Then, after I got done calling the people in town . . . I realized why it had been angry.

I'd recognized one of the campers who'd been in that grove with a gun held to their head. I don't know a lot of campers, unless they consistently help organize events or return year after year. Otherwise, they all tend to blur together over time. But this was Erin. She's part of the senior camp, the one that I put next to the Thing in the Dark because I know they'll be careful not to disturb it.

Erin is one of the people who leave offerings. And the Man with No Shadow would have killed her. He knew what he'd done. That's why he needed me alive.

On one hand, I am intensely grateful there was one of the senior camp among those the Man with No Shadow was going to kill. I'm not sure if the Thing in the Dark would have dragged him back into the darkness unprovoked. On the other hand . . . out of everyone who camps here, they should really have known better than to talk to him.

We all make mistakes, I guess.

I called a family meeting today to update everyone on the situation. Tyler was there. I asked him how things were with Danielle before the meeting began, and he said they were figuring things out. Then he cut the conversation off by going to find his seat. He avoided making eye contact with me.

I started the meeting by apologizing for keeping everyone ignorant as to the full scope of the situation but explained that we'd been dealing with something that could manipulate minds, and it had been hard to tell whom to trust. My brother looked put out at that, but I suppose that's understandable. I think him being at the meeting at all was his way of saying I was forgiven, even if he's salty with me for a while.

Then Great-Aunt Lorna spoke up with something that would have been really nice to know years ago.

She did a genetics ancestry service a while back and found a relative we didn't know about. Yes. Curtis. She thought it would be wonderful to connect with him and arranged for him to come out to the campground. Great-Aunt Lorna admitted that she'd been remiss in not telling him the rules before he came. She thought it would be safe if he was only here for a few hours, but she didn't think about how my entire family, no matter how distantly related, are targets. But he never showed. And he never answered any of her messages, and she assumed he'd chickened out and was now ghosting her.

I think we can fill in the blanks from there. He'd reached the campsite, and the New Sheriff had been waiting to have a conversation with him. He was looking for someone to buy the campground and would broker the sale, if Curtis was interested.

There's a new rule for the family. No more genetic ancestry ANYTHING. We don't need to be bringing more surprise relatives in who don't know what they're getting into.

I'm a campground manager. I've still got a lot of work to do. I'm not convinced that getting rid of the Man with No

Shadow is going to keep this from being a bad year. I'm going to be wary. I'm going to keep watching and doing whatever I can to keep my town and my campers safe. I'm going to keep telling you about my land and my rules and why they exist. It's spring, after all, and it's time to open my campground.

You should come visit.

ACKNOWLEDGEMENTS

First off, thank you to my agent, Maria Brannan, for her support, encouragement, and enthusiasm. I will always be glad that you saw the potential in *How to Survive Camping* and created the opportunity for it to grow.

Thank you to my editors Charlotte Trumble at Simon & Schuster UK and Tim O'Connell at Saga Press. Their insight and guidance was invaluable in turning this book into what it is now.

I admit when I started this process, I didn't have much idea of all the work that went into making a book. I'm deeply grateful to everyone who has contributed.

At Simon & Schuster UK, thank you to Sarah Jeffcoate, Kate Kaur, Laurie McShea, Katie Forrest, Karin Seifried, and Isabelle Gray.

And at Saga Press, thank you to Caroline Tew, Savannah Breckenridge, Christine Calella, Ella Laytham, Emma Shaw, Alex Su, Chloe Gray, Lewelin Polanco, Meryll Preposi, Amanda Mulholland, Lauren Gomez, and Olivia Perrault.

And thanks to James Fenner for his excellent covers that bring so much vibrancy and life to this book.

I'm grateful to my friends for their support, especially

Helewyse, Chris, and Katherine. Thank you for being a solid support I could turn to when things felt overwhelming. And Sherri, Bob, and Crystal; for their excitement about the book and their understanding when I had to cancel D&D for two months solid.

Special thanks to my family, who believed this could be a book before I did. And in particular to my brother for his excitement and the bubble tea drop-offs.

And finally... when I wrote the first post of "How to Survive Camping," I had no idea how far it would go. It was just a fun idea I had, but people connected to Kate, then I connected to the story, and for two years I was posting another chapter every five days. I'm very grateful to the community that grew up around Goat Valley, as you have been the best part of this journey. It's been a lot of fun, it's been exciting, and I can't wait to see where we go next.

So, to all of you that have been here since the start, I have one final very special thing to say to you.

ಠ_ಠ